Enjoy!

Hunter Carocite

Nantucket Island

2016

:)

The Wauwinet Caper

PENNED BY
Hunter Laroche

A NANTUCKET MURDER MYSTERY SERIES
AUTHOR OF MURDER ON THE 'SCONSET EXPRESS

authorHOUSE®

AuthorHouse™
1663 Liberty Drive
Bloomington, IN 47403
www.authorhouse.com
Phone: 1 (800) 839-8640

Published by AuthorHouse 05/04/2016

ISBN: 978-1-5246-0381-6 (sc)
ISBN: 978-1-5246-0379-3 (hc)
ISBN: 978-1-5246-0380-9 (e)

Library of Congress Control Number: 2016906123

This book is dedicated to one of the few remaining gentlemen in this world, Dr. Thomas Sollas.

I was fortunate enough to meet Tom and his wife Ann in the late 70's on Nantucket. Tom was always very supportive in my ventures and also loved to hear of my travels around the globe. Tom was one who enjoyed pushing my buttons. A few examples follow.

One day I received a call from Tom telling me that he had just rented a house in Hopetown, Abaco Islands. He told me there was a hotel a block away and that I was expected for dinner in two days' time. I located the information on the hotel and made it to Fort Lauderdale. I booked a small six seater plane and made it on time for dinner and enjoyed Rum Tingles every afternoon made from the juice of a fresh local oranges, soda water and vodka.

This little jaunt to the island lasted almost a month.

Another call was, "Hey Hunter, I am headed to Havana, Cuba in tomorrow and I'm staying at the Sol Melia Hotel. See you for dinner on Friday at the National Hotel 9 p.m. Don't be late."

Well accepting the challenge, I called my friend the Barron von Bokelman, who managed to travel to Havana numerous times, and said, "We are taking a trip. My treat." Since I had never been to Cuba, I figured an experienced friend could manage to get me in under the radar.

We flew out of Nassau in an Old DC 3, the wonderful Cubano Airlines, that was an event all within itself. I had also contacted Baby "Doc" Duvalier the dictator of Haiti and asked him to join us.

We arrived and checked into Myer Lansky's hotel, The National, and did a quick change of clothes. I requested, with the help of the hotel manager and some crisp American bills, for two lovely ladies to escort us to dinner. When we arrived at the table Dr. and Mrs. Sollas, Jean-Claude Duvalier were already seated.

I, the Baron and our companions, who looked like Cuban runway models with the shortest dresses we had ever seen, approached the table. Everyone's eyes opened wide. The night continued into the wee hours of the morning. At one point Ann Sollas asked, "So what do you girls do for work?"

Tom leaned over and said, "Well Ann they are not School teachers!" which brought a huge round of laughter to the table.

One other time I received a call from Tom around 9 a.m. "Hey Hunter, let's meet for lunch tomorrow. One O'Clock."

I was in Boston at the time so I figured not a problem. I'll hop on the train in the morning, arrive at Penn Station, grab a cab and arrive on time.

Tom very casually says, "Grab a pen. I will give you the address. It's the Brasserie de I'Isle St. Louis."

I think to myself, "Sounds nice," knowing that Tom enjoys many of the great restaurants in New York.

He then says, "Here's the address. Brasserie de I'Isle St. Louis, Paris France." He then adds, "Don't be late or your buying." and hangs up.

I run out to Liberty Travel, passport in hand, and I book a very expensive first class ticket, landing late morning the next day in Paris.

I manage a quick clean up on the plane, grab my carry on, make it through a long line at customs, jump in a taxi with a good hour to spare and then we hit traffic.

Now I am checking my watch thinking I am not going to make it on time. I pull up and enter the restaurant at 12:55, stroll up to the table like it's nothing and promptly say, "Your buying."

I peruse the Carte de Vin and order a very expensive white Burgundy. The Paris trip lasted for a good two weeks with meetings for lunch and dinner daily.

Those were the good old days Tom!!

I would like to thank Nick and JoAnn Casselli for listening to all of my weekly updates on this story; Michael Clary for his time and effort in helping with the editing process, and most of all KGR for her numerous hours and painstaking efforts in correcting all the mistakes that were involved almost daily with my typing skills.

WAUWINET

Nantucket Island 1974

"Nantucket Police Department. What is your emergency?"

"There's blood-blood everywhere!"

"Excuse me?"

"I think he's dead!" screamed Steve.

"Who's dead?"

"My carpenter! He's been working on my house doing repairs. I have blood on my hands! My shirt! It's awful! Send help!"

"OK sir, slow down. Whom am I speaking with?"

"Germain-Steve Germain."

"And what is your location sir?"

"Umm-I am-I'm at my house here in Wauwinet."

"What's the address?"

"It's ah-it's-Oh God! I can't remember. I just bought the place a few months ago. I know how to drive here but the house address? I can't remember."

"Okay sir. Who did you purchase the house from? What road are you located on?"

"I bought it from, let's see-um, Oh, I can't remember. Only thing I remember is signing the papers in the lawyer's office. We are on Wauwinet Road about a mile and a half down on the right. There's a big rock out front with a red mailbox. Wait, now I remember. His name was Cate, the last owner."

"Okay Mr. Germain. Sit tight. Don't touch anything. Help is on the way..."

Wauwinet 1973

Winship was staring out the kitchen window. He was watching the two deer that appeared almost nightly in the field out back of the house as he washed his lonely dish and coffee cup after his dinner. It was dusk with an overcast sky. The weather forecast was talking about a light morning frost for the upcoming day. His cat, Marshmallow, was rubbing up against the outer leg of his dark green corduroy pants. Just as he was placing his silverware into the drying rack the phone rang. Winship walked over to the yellow wall phone and picked it up. It was Sunday evening at 7p.m. He knew it was his son Leonard. He always called at almost 7p.m. on the dot every Sunday even if he was traveling.

"Hi Dad. How's everything on the island?"

"Fine Leonard, just fine. Not much has changed this week, the weather is good. It's a little cooler at night but the days are still warm. It's just about time to start lighting the fireplace in the evenings. There is a slight chill most nights after the sun sets but it's relaxing reading in front of the fireplace with Marshmallow."

"You know Dad, it's been almost six months since Moms passing and Sam and I are hoping you're keeping yourself occupied."

"Oh I am, today I was at the Wharf Club with the guys and we played some cards. Yesterday morning, I took the skiff out from the Madaket Marina and spent the early hours fishing. Not much luck, just a few bluefish here and there. I spotted a few seals swimming around near the Jetties. I went to the Dreamland Theater on Friday and saw '*Chinatown*' with Jack Nicholson."

"How was the movie?" Leonard inquired.

"It was pretty good. I found it quite entertaining. I also have dinner with a few friends once or twice a week and we still enjoy going to Cioppinos often. I've also been going to lunch every Saturday at the Opera House with Robbie Egan and there's plenty of yard work. So, I am staying pretty busy."

"Glad to hear that Dad but there's something I want to run by you."

"OK, what's that?" replied Winship.

"Well after Mom died, when we were all there for the funeral, Sam and I, along with Cousin Sandal and Louise, started talking among ourselves about helping you organize and getting rid of some of the junk that has been collecting in the house for so many years. I spoke to you about it briefly the next day after the funeral. Remember? It was Cousin Sandal, Louise Hourihan, Sam and myself. We all discussed going through the house starting in the basement and working our way up to the attic including the back storage shed and your fishing bungalow. We also discussed the garage as well as the room above it. I mean, we have never been up there. It's been locked ever since you and Mom bought the house.

The people who you bought the house from wanted to store some furniture for a few weeks until they got settled in their new home. Remember? They never came back and picked up all the stuff they stored up there did they? It's been like, what twenty years?"

"Yes, it's been well over twenty years I would say," replied Winship.

"I had written the Oberg family. They were the people who we purchased the house from about coming to remove all the furniture. After the second letter they wrote us back and said no one really wanted it or had any need for the stuff. They said that they would pay to have it removed or we could keep it and do what we wanted with it. I just put it on the back burner and never really paid it much mind. Now it's just been sitting there all these years. I have always meant to go up and clear it all out but it just never happened. I actually have no idea what has been stored up there for all these years."

"Well Dad, Sandal, the General that she is, and Louise made a quite detailed list on how to attack the removal of so many years of clutter. Sandal and Louise met the next day at the Downy Flake to put together a to-do list after we went through the house with them. They have lined up all the people needed to complete the task and wanted to wait about six months before broaching the subject with you. Well guess what, I have been elected the spokesperson. Dad, the house needs a good if not a major cleaning. There is so much junk and knick-knacks you have gathered over the years. It really is time to clear a lot of it out," Leonard sighed and said wearily.

"Okay," Winship replied after a short pause pondering over what he just heard his son say to him. "You might be right Leonard. Now that you mention it, there is quite a lot of stuff all over this house. What did you come up with? Or should I say, what did Sandal and Louise figure out?"

"I'm glad you agree Dad. Here's what we came up with. It's going to take quite a bit of time. We are talking weeks if not longer. Louise thought that she and Cousin Sandal, if she wanted to come to the island

3

and help out, could start in the basement and work their way slowly but surely upstairs, including the outside shed, your fishing bungalow, all of the cupboards, broom closets, bedrooms, bathroom cabinets and they will even tackle the attic. They were thinking that they could finish with the garage as well as the locked room above it. You know you always wanted to make that your fishing and chart room. Well it's never too late to utilize that space. You know Dad, ever since we lived there, no one that I know of has ever entered that room above the garage."

"Yes," replied Winship. "We bought the house way back in 1952. It's been just about twenty years now since we first set our sights on purchasing the house. I wrote the Oberg family, who were the previous owners, two letters a few months after we moved in. They were slow in responding. I finally received a reply and Mr. Oberg said that they were just going to let us have all of the furniture because their kids had no interest in renting a truck, bringing it over to the island and collecting everything. I never had any notion to go up, though your mother had brought up the subject numerous times. I never got around to the task. And as we know, it has been just sitting above the garage collecting dust. I have no idea what they left behind except Mr. Oberg told me it was some large pieces of furniture along with some lamps and other household things. As time slipped away I paid it very little thought."

"My idea was when we purchased the house, that the room above the garage with all the windows surrounding it, would have made such a great room for me to lay out all my fishing charts and be able to tie fishing flies, but it never happened so I just used the bungalow out back. I still have the key to the room hanging inside the kitchen closet with their name on it. Oberg was their name. Mr. Curtis Oberg. They were from West Hartford, fairly close to our home in Farmington. I used to think it was funny how such close neighbors in Connecticut would ever end up here on Nantucket. I wonder if the old key will even work anymore. I might need to put some graphite or something into the old lock. I figure, so I don't break the key off in it just in case it's rusted shut."

The next morning Winship was greeted by a brisk but clear day. He sat on his porch inhaling the fresh Nantucket air and enjoying his morning coffee when the phone rang. He looked at his watch. It was 8:00a.m. sharp. "Who could be calling me this early?" he thought to himself as he walked inside to the phone. "Good morning Winship. What a beautiful day it's going to be. This is Louise here. I hope I didn't wake you." Louise had been such a close friend of Winship and his wife Mary ever since they moved to Nantucket in the early 1950's.

"Leonard called me last night and said he had spoken to you about plans to arrange some clearing and cleaning of your house. I'm sure there is lots of dust, dirt and other collectables that have been laying around for such a long time. It might be a good time to de-clutter. So, if you are up to the task, just tell me when and I will arrange everything. We can tackle the job whenever it's convenient for you."

"Well Louise I guess there's no time like the present," Winship said with a chuckle. "Any time works for me."

"How about tomorrow 9:00a.m.?" Louise replied. "We could enjoy a cup of coffee and make our plan of attack and go from there?"

"Perfect," Winship replied. He said good-bye and gently replaced the receiver back into its cradle.

Later on in the afternoon Winship took a good look around the living room. He never really noticed just how much stuff there really was piled around the house. There were stacks of magazines he had read quite a while ago, with the intention to pursue an article in several of them again, but the pile just seemed to grow larger and all sorts of knick-knacks all over the house. Why did they ever save so many things? Clutter is actually what it amounted to. Some of the furniture had been there since they bought the place and moved in. The kids were right. The house needs some T.L.C.

Winship went to his desk in the study to grab a pad and a pen and started making some notes on what to get rid of. Thinking to himself, "This is the time to move forward."

Winship stopped for a moment to reflect. Had he actually ever taken the time to look around the house? Not only recently but all the years he was married to his wife Mary. Did it just become a daily ritual to walk through a room and not pay it any mind? He thought back to when they first moved in. His wife loved all the old wood, beautiful mahogany paneled walls and cherry floors, the beamed ceilings and the Spanish tile in the large kitchen. The old stone fireplaces; one in the living room, another in Winship's office and den area. The house was made with such fine craftsmanship and mason work that you don't seem to find any more in the newer homes. Almost like old hand crafted boats are becoming a thing of the past.

At that moment Marshmallow came running through the kitchen and jumped up on one of the window ledge letting out a loud meow.

"Yes Marshmallow. I know a storm front is moving in, even though it's clear outside. As of now they are predicting a nor'easter. It should move at a quick pace across Rhode Island. Supposed to hit here a little later this afternoon, stall over the island, kick up some big surf and be gone by early morning. They say it's going to blow around 50-60 MPH. I better pull my rain gear out of the closet and a nice fleece pull over. As we know well, the temperature will no doubt drop a good ten to fifteen degrees. I tell ya Marsh, you sure seem to sense the change in weather. I think you must have what they say about cats, a sixth sense. You are always curled up and sleeping a good hour before the storms set in. I can't ever recall you getting stuck in a down pour." Marshmallow let out another loud meow almost in agreeance.

While Winship rummaged through the hall closet, he started to reflect back to the first time he saw Marshmallow. She was a beautiful small kitten. It must have been four years prior when he first spotted her. She had a tuxedo style of fur of black and white. Her twinkling eyes were looking in through the back kitchen window above the sink. Winship figured that the kitten was just a feral cat from the fields and did not pay much mind to her.

It was a blustery afternoon that day and Nantucket was on the verge of another nor'easter that was predicted to hit the island in the early evening. Winship had gone into the kitchen to get a glass of water from the tap and there she was sitting outside the window. Winship spotted her and tapped his fingers on the window pane. The kitten gently lifted her paw like a wave back to him. A short time later, his wife, Mary entered the living room with the kitten in her arms. "Oh no!" thought Winship because he knew the soft spot his wife had for animals. Mary had a twinkle in her eyes as she nuzzled the kitten close to her. Mary took the little kitten into the kitchen and placed a small saucer of milk on the floor which was lapped up in no time. Mary placed the kitten back outside the kitchen door but the kitten did not budge from the outside screen door. She just sat there on the stoop looking inside. The wind at that very moment gave a huge gust. Mary's heart shuddered as she looked back at the kitten. "You are just too tiny to weather out a storm all alone out in the elements. Come on little one," she said. "You're in for the night. After the storm passes I will let you back outside and hopefully you can rejoin your mother."

Winship could hear Mary talking in the kitchen and went to investigate. Of course he wasn't surprised to see the kitten back in the house enjoying a small plate of tuna that Mary had laid out for her. It didn't take Marshmallow long to lick the plate clean. "Now Mary," Winship said with a giggle, "why is she back inside? You know she is probably a feral cat from the fields. I realize that she is pretty young but they know their way around."

Mary scooped up the kitten and walked into the living room telling Winship that she wouldn't be able to sleep if she left this tiny kitten to fend for itself in this storm. "I will put her back outside after the weather clears." Winship knew better than to try and change her mind. The storm hit with a vengeance and Mary was so relieved that she had made that judgment call. Winship was trying not show any emotion toward the kitten but deep down he was also glad that the kitten was safe.

Mary placed an old towel on the floor in the den near the fireplace so the kitten could make a bed for the night. A fire was lit and Mary and Winship read their books. They were very grateful that they did not lose power during the storm. The kitten curled up on the old towel and slept away like she did not have a care in the world.

The next morning, Mary set a saucer of milk out and a small morsel of chicken from their dinner the evening before. After the kitten had finished enjoying her breakfast, Mary placed her outside. At first the kitten did not move off the stoop but when a few light winds kicked up some leaves, the kitten started chasing them around the yard. Around noon time Mary was back in the kitchen clearing the lunch dishes and up on the same window ledge was the kitten. She again raised her little paw in a wave like motion. Next thing you know she was adopted. They expected that the mother would come looking for her but to no avail. The kitten, after only a few days had moved right in, slowly starting to inspect every inch and cranny of the house. Every cabinet and door had to be opened for her to inspect. She was named Marshmallow a couple days after. Winship and Mary were enjoying an old fashioned hot chocolate a few afternoons later. Mary had added a few small sized marshmallows to the hot chocolate and one had dropped on the kitchen floor. The kitten had a field day batting it around for hours and that was how she was named so many years ago.

Winship, many months after Mary had passed away, was in the kitchen when he said to Marshmallow, "The wind is starting to pick up out there. I'd better go around in a while and make sure that all the outer doors of the house, shed, the bungalow and garage are not ajar. If a good gust gets ahold of one, it could rip it right off its hinges." Again, Winship said to himself, as so many times before, "What am I doing having a conversation with a cat?" Winship chuckled to himself and said out loud, "You're the best company one could have these days Marshmallow."

Marshmallow was enjoying the warmth of the sun through the kitchen window when she jumped off the ledge and followed Winship into the den, looked at the fireplace, then to Winship, then over to the leather chairs, and back to Winship. He also looked over at the two matching deep brown broken in soft leather chairs that sat facing the fireplace. Between them was a lamp, which had an attached round glass shelf that you could set your book, magazines or a drink upon. "I know you little rascal. You want the fireplace laid and ready to be lit. When it's all toasty you are going to curl up in your favorite chair on top of your old towel." Winship always kept her towel clean and folded on her chair just for Marshmallow's comfort. "Just about time the storm hits, you're going to doze off with the warmth of the fireplace crackling away. I think I will join you. Let's plan it for right after dinner. I have a book I want to finish up." Marshmallow let out a loud meow as Winship rubbed the top of her head.

"It sounds like a good excuse to enjoy a glass of red wine and finish up reading 'One Flew over the Cuckoo's Nest'. I am three quarters of the way through it so tonight would be a perfect night to finish. Great idea Marsh!"

Winship spent the next hour going from room to room looking at things he took for granted daily. He was quite surprised at how much they had gathered over the years. Why had they kept adding to it? A table here, an odd chair there, a chest, a bookshelf. It really was clutter and best to be rid of much of it. He then went room to room on the second floor. He finished making his list but was sure it was only part of what they would discover that needed to be tossed out and he had not even descended into the basement. After an hour and a half and pages of notes, he placed the list on the kitchen table and laid the fireplace.

Around six in the evening the storm had come ashore. The winds had been slowly kicking up since late afternoon. By this time Marshmallow had jumped up on her chair and was sleeping away. Her head cocked to one side like she had not one care in the world. The rains hit with a furry and the winds were rattling the windows. Very typical of the island storms that time of the year.

Winship added a couple of logs to the fire, poured himself a glass of Chianti and settled into his chair. Marshmallow looked up gave a loud meow and a look as if to say, "It's about time you joined me," she quickly drifted back to sleep.

By the following morning the storm had passed. There were a few limbs that had fallen here and there around the property but no visible damage was apparent.

Promptly at nine that morning Louise arrived along with Donna Affeldt and Shelia Egan. Winship had the coffee in the peculator ready to go. The ladies had, what Winship thought to be, a lot of cleaning items; three buckets, two mops, cleaning fluids, rags, and two vacuum cleaners with long extension hoses, a large box of floor soap, pot scrubbers, sponges, feather dusters, several brooms and who knows what else.

Louise mentioned to Winship, "That was one quick moving storm last night. We're lucky. Otherwise the weather would have most likely put this job off for a couple of days but we are good to go now!"

Louise explained to Winship, "Sandal was a big help putting this all together. Did you know that she made a detailed list after the funeral and then reworked it a few times? She made several notes on what to remove, what to send off to Rob Coles, the antiques dealer, what to put out for a garage sale and what to offer to the auction house. The rest is for Isky Santos to haul away to the dump and, mind you, there will be plenty!

"Sandal also made a time frame and figured we were thinking it will take almost a month to get this project finished at two long days a week. Sadly, Sandal won't be coming to the island though we love it when she visits. So what two days a week are good for you Winship? I know you enjoy lunch every Monday at the Opera House and you also play cards on Thursdays down at the Wharf Club with your friends. As for your fishing trips, they can be put on hold. You will just have to work that leisure time around our cleaning schedule."

SHAWKEMO

They all sat down for coffee. Winship added more water to the percolator as he did not expect Shelia and Donna to be joining him and Louise. He also took two more coffee mugs out of the cupboard and a few spoons out of the drawer as they all waited for the coffee to finish brewing. Louise went over the plan of attack. She said that they will start at one end of the basement and go methodically from one side to the other. Winship nervously poured everyone a cup of coffee and offered some Danish he had previously laid out. He was a little worried that the girls had no idea how much work laid ahead of them.

They finished their coffee and headed downstairs to the basement. As the day wore on, Winship was quite amazed at the amount of useless things that they had uncovered. He was taken back at the amount of space it freed up once much of it had been removed. They barely stopped to take a lunch break. Shelia brought tuna fish sandwiches, potato chips and some dill pickles. The main topic of conversation was the storm from the night prior. "Who ever built this house did a great job on the basement. Even with all that rain we had last night its dry as a bone down there." Donna stated.

It seemed to Winship like they had just sat down to eat when the girls were up and back at the task at hand.

It was close to three-thirty when the girls decided to call it quits for the day. Attacking the basement was quite a chore. It took the four of them almost five hours with only a short break for lunch.

The ladies put one of the mops upside down to dry, emptied two of the three wash buckets, rinsed the rags and placed them on the edge of the sink next to the washer to dry but Louise held onto her mop.

Just as Winship thought the work for today was done, Donna turned on the vacuum cleaner, attached the hose and was collecting all the cobwebs that remained. Louise and Shelia were filling up one last mop bucket and following behind Donna's footsteps. Louise mopping every nook and cranny of the basement floor while Shelia was moving anything that was in the way of Louise's mop. When they finished and were heading upstairs for the day Louise said, "I will give this a final re-mop tomorrow." "Really?" Winship inquired. "Oh yes. One more going over with a clean mop is the way to go!"

They all stopped at the base of the stairs and took another quick look around the basement to admire the work they had accomplished. Grinning from ear to ear they headed up the stairs very satisfied with the task completed. Before departing everyone stopped to give Winship a hug. Shelia said in his ear, "We all know this is a huge step for you to clear out so many memories but in the long run I think you will agree that it was time. Mary was very close to all of us and we are sure this is what she would have wanted you to do as well."

Winship followed the trio out the back door expressing his gratefulness and watched them drive off. He headed downstairs to shut off some lights and took a moment to look around. All he could think was, *wow,* what an improvement. The room now looked twice its size.

On Friday, two days later, the ladies showed up again at nine in the morning sharp. This time Winship was ready with the coffee mugs and doughnuts from the Downy Flake. "Today," Louise said over their coffees, "we are tackling the main floor. We are cleaning from one side of this house to the other." After about fifteen minutes of enjoying their coffee and doughnuts Louise said, "Let's go girls! First let's hit the basement floor for the final mopping." Louise sounded off. It was like being in the Army Winship thought but he was ready and also kind of eager. He had gone down to the basement several times since they had cleaned it and was so pleased at the transformation that he was excited to continue the adventure.

Again, at the end of the day, the piles had increased outside. The dump pile, the antiques pile, and the yard sale pile. Winship and Donna had it all covered with a large tarp weighed down by several bricks. Marshmallow very cautiously circled the covered piles. It seemed as soon as the cleaning started she was nowhere to be found and only showed up after the tasks were completed. After the girls had left Winship was amazed. So much clutter gone in a few hours. The house was becoming quite a relaxing but changing site and he was starting to notice old pictures that needed to go, furniture that was out dated and worn, lighting fixtures that were actually rusted. How had he not even noticed these things, which now stood out like an eyesore?

After a total of two weeks of the cleaning at two days a week, Winship was enjoying his little get together with the ladies. He started to bond with each of them. He now had no doubt why his wife thought of them as such great friends. Winship was quite taken by the amount of time they spent helping him on this project and not asking for anything in return. They offered decorating ideas, what to remove, what to re-finish, and what to just get rid of. Winship was just down right enjoying their company not to mention how efficient they were. It was nice to have a woman's touch around the house. At times, it really made him miss his wife Mary.

The third week, after a few odd tasks here and there, one final chore remained. It was the garage. For this job the ladies recruited their husbands to help. They all met at Winship's house around ten o'clock on Saturday. The men could only attend on the weekend, otherwise it conflicted with their work schedules.

All of them, including Winship, enjoyed their coffee, Danish, some small talk about the weather, past storms, the latest local gossip and the men had a conversation about fishing. When they finished with their coffee they all headed out to the large two car garage. Actually the garage was close to a three car sized building. One large area off the ground floor was built for tools. The ladies had discussed prior that there would be quite a bit of oil cans, lawn equipment, old bikes and more items that the girls had no idea what to do with. It would probably be better to have Winship talk it over with Randy, Robbie, and Bill. The men could decide what to keep, toss away or try for the yard sale pile.

In a few hours, just around noon, after moving the large work table, an old oil drum and numerous old boxes of junk, tools, piles of newspapers, and magazines, the garage looked so immaculate and orderly that you could hardly tell there were glass panes in the window frames. Donna finished washing the windows a third time and was making funny faces at Shelia through the glass pane on the other side.

When they seemed to be finished with the ground floor of the garage, the girls filled the three buckets with a mixture of cleaning fluids and water and proceeded to mop away, almost like a scene of swabbies mopping the deck of a Naval ship. Again they said it was going to take a good two solid mopping's to get most of the years and years of the outside elements and car drippings washed away.

They took a lunch break and Randy asked Winship what was above the garage. Winship related the story of how when they bought the house the sellers asked if they could store some items up in the attic of the garage. After about six months they sent a response to Winship's letters saying that he could just keep it or have it hauled away. The door has been locked since the day they had purchased the house. Winship got up from the kitchen table and removed the key off the back of the pantry door. "You never went up there?" asked Bill.

"No, never. It just kind of slipped my mind. Never gave it much thought."

"Well this ought to be fun." Randy said turning the key over in his hand. "Oberg?" reading the faded writing on the key chain. "Was that the last owner's name?"

"Yes it was."

"Well let's give it a go," Robbie chimed in. "Do you have any graphite or any type of rust lubricant?"

"I don't think so. I don't remember seeing any since we started cleaning."

"I've got the answer," Louise said. "There's a can of Crisco lard in the pantry. That might work!"

With that thought in mind, Louise retrieved the can of Crisco and they all headed for the garage stairs which would lead them to the mysterious locked room above the garage.

Randy offered the key to Winship but he said, "I would hate to break the key in the lock. You give it a try," he said to Randy.

"Not me pal, not me. I don't want it to snap off either. Here Robbie, you're the mechanic, you give it a whirl." Robbie took the key and ever so gently dipped it in the lard, smeared some on the outside of the lock and wiped his hands on his jeans.

Shelia started rolling her eyes. "Robbie use a rag! That's cooking grease you're smearing all over your pants."

Robbie, not paying any attention to what Shelia said, gently slipped the old key into the lock opening. He gave the key a gentle twist movement but it would not move. He tried again and nothing. "Are you sure this is the right key Winship and not one to another door?"

"Nope, that's the key. I hung it there the day we moved in and it's never been off the hook for as long as I can remember."

"Okay, I believe you." This time, Robbie still being gentle but with a little more force, was jiggling the key around and sliding it in and out of the door lock saying, "It might take a few times to get the Crisco into all the lock's cylinders. It will hopefully loosen up the lock's innards." Again nothing. The lock would not budge.

Robbie did not dare to twist the key too hard and break the only key. He slowly turned the key from side to side, as much as it would allow, trying to spread the Crisco around the locks inner workings. It was quite dark on the top of the stairs. There weren't any windows in the hall leading to the room. Robbie looked up and noticed a light fixture above the doors landing. "Hey Randy, can you hit switch for this light?"

"Sure bud." Randy flipped the switch back and forth but the bulb was evidently burnt out. Randy made a noise like a ghost, "Whoo-whoo." Everyone started laughing. Donna said, "Quit messing around Randal!"

"Hey Shelia, give me the Crisco." Robbie said. He rubbed the key in the lard again. Just as he was going to wipe his hands on his jeans, Shelia produced a rag and said, "Don't even think about wiping your hands on your jeans."

There seemed like a lot of rust particles had formed on the silver skeleton key from the old rusted lock. After Robbie had removed it, yet again, he used the rag to wipe off the key and tried again. After a moment or two of more jiggling, the key started to ever so slowly turn. At first it only moved about an eighth of a turn so Robbie slowly brought the key back to the starting position, waited a few seconds and slowly turned it again. After second or two later the lock clicked open. Randy started his ghost noises again and everyone started laughing. The door opened with a slight push of Robbie's shoulder and gave off a low squeak. They all entered and saw mounds and mounds of sheets all worn and faded covering the contents of the room.

Louise said, "First thing is those curtains are going right into the trash." They all entered slowly as a group not knowing what to expect. "Could be a nest of mice nestled somewhere. BATS!!" Randy yelled out. "Everyone duck!" As the ladies screamed and the guys ducked Randy started laughing so hard saying, "You should have seen all your faces!"

"Cut it out Randy!" Donna said. "You wonder why I have nightmares with all your teasing. You're lucky the kids don't wake up in the middle of the night screaming!"

"Well if there are mice up here they won't last long with Marshmallow on the case," Winship stated, still holding his sides from laughing. The men slowly started removing the sheets covering all the furniture and placing them gently on the floor, so not to kick up a lot of dust. Louise, Sheila and Donna tackled the curtains. The light that shone in the windows was almost blinding. If it wasn't for the caked on dirt that had accumulated over the last twenty years, they all would have needed sunglasses. As they removed more and more of the coverings, Louise's husband Bill said, "Wow, there's quite a bit of stuff piled up here. When did you say this stuff was moved up here? Over twenty years ago?"

"Oh My God, a rat!" Shelia screamed seeing a tail under a sheet.

"Watch out!" Robbie yelled. "They will run right up your pant leg!" Randy lost it on that one. He burst out laughing as the girls once more let out a scream. Randy knew it was only Marshmallow who sauntered into the room a few moments after they had opened the door. Bill Hourihan was rolling with laughter as he quickly saw it was Marshmallow's tail. Marshmallow somehow knew they were talking about her let out a big meow. They all started laughing. Shelia said, "You and Randy belong to the same band of clowns, don't you!" They all calmed down and had a chuckle about this episode. Marshmallow just kept going under the maze of furniture like it was a newfound adventure. All of them started to scratch their chins, a bit overwhelmed by the amount of furniture that was stored in the gigantic attic space above the garage. Seeing all this stuff, Winship thought to himself and then mentioned, "It's going to cost me a bundle to get this place cleared out."

Louise told him, "If people had a tenth of your wealth they would never have to work again."

Bill, who was Winship's banker, just gave him a wink and said, "I am sure you will be just fine," and patted him on the back.

"I know," Winship replied to Bill. "It's just a thought that popped into my head. I was thinking that I should have taken the Obergs up on their offer to have it all hauled away. I guess now the cost just rolled onto me."

Bill mentioned, "Some of these dressers and bed frames are beautiful Mahogany pieces. Pretty much antique status, I think. Some of these pieces might fetch a good penny. Actually for most of this stuff. It looks like it is all in great condition. These two highboy dressers have some very nice inlaid wood in them. What I am saying is - there's some nice stuff here," Bill continued. "I think the best thing you can do is get an appraiser here after we sort most of it out. You should probably toss the junk. Then you can have him give you a fair value price for each piece. We use a person that's accredited through the bank on some of our estate sales of homes that need to be auctioned off. Some pieces could go to Rob Coles, the antiques guy, but the really nice pieces need to be looked at first by our guy, Mr. Jube - Steven Jube. I could give him a call on Monday and see what he has available for appointments this week?"

"That would be great," Winship replied. "Well ladies, I think the best course of action would be to wait until we can get this room cleaned out before attempting to clean this up. But let's at least get rid of the moth eaten curtains."

"I would like to Murphy's oil soap some pieces or wax them so that after twenty years of dust they will look in pristine condition again before anyone comes to look at them," Louise explained to Winship.

Louise asked Winship, "If this end table is not included in the antiques pile or collectables could I purchase it? It would be for my new friend Kathy Rodgers. She is one of Bill's secretaries at the bank. She started about two months ago and she's from the Seattle area. Kathy's a very lovely person and just purchased a home. I think I know the perfect spot where she could place this."

"It's yours Louise, no need to wait. Take it with you when you leave and tell the lady I hope to meet her someday."

"Well let's hold off until midweek after the appointments," Bill stated. "Tomorrow we can bring in some of the neighborhood kids to help us toss the junk and make an inventory of what will go to whom."

CHILDREN'S BEACH

Later on that week Mr. Jube arrived and went through each piece, with the help of Winship moving some of the remaining headboards; dressers couches, chairs and side tables along with some lamps. Mr. Jube was finished in just under two hours. He told Winship that there were some very nice pieces. A few of them were very fine. Within two days he would make his suggestions on what to offer Mr. Coles. Mr. Jube also said he would include a pricing guideline. Noting to Winship that he knew Mr. Coles. "He has very good knowledge in his field of expertise and is a very honest and fair man to deal with," Steve stated. Mr. Jube said he would also assist Winship in separating some of the stuff for yard sale items and what to take to the dump. Mr. Jube then continued, "You know Winship, the majority of what's up in this room holds some or if not more than a good amount value."

The following Monday morning Mr. Coles showed up promptly at eight. Winship told him and his workers that he was joining friends at the Opera House for lunch at noon. "If you get caught up and it takes longer than we anticipate, don't worry. I will be in town most of the afternoon. I trust you will do the right thing while I'm away. Here is the list of what goes where. Mr. Jube has compiled a very detailed list of all the items and prices."

Mr. Coles, with his team of six helpers, said they would have the job finished within a couple of hours. Winship had spoken to Mr. Coles a few days' prior about clearing out some of the furniture for his antiques shop. He explained that Mr. Jube was going to take some of the pieces for an upcoming auction which was about thirty-five percent of things in the room. Mr. Coles agreed to help move all of the pieces out of the attic for

Winship. They also offered to help remove the other pieces, which included placing the items for the yard sale and the dump out in the yard.

Mr. Coles and his crew went to work removing the furniture. They slowly packed the pieces that were set aside for Mr. Coles to take to his antiques store and warehouse into his van. They also gently packed the ones for Mr. Jube's men to pick up onto the lower level of the garage. He would move those pieces to his temperature controlled storage area until he could review all of his notes and final inventory. Next week he planned on sending out letters that included some photos of the very fine pieces to collectors. Mr. Coles agreed to make a detailed inventory of the items he was taking and he, as well, would send out a few inquiries to some of his customers.

Winship asked if they could clear the room of everything. The pieces that were not going with Mr. Coles could be taken out to the yard where he could direct them to which pile to place the items in. He also wanted to keep the deep leather chair, matching ottoman, the floor lamp and the side table.

The following morning Louise Hourihan and Donna arrived promptly at nine. Shelia planned to arrive about thirty minutes later, as she had a client booking a forty-five-day cruise and she needed to go over the final preparations for the contract. Louise and Donna enjoyed their morning coffee ritual and told Winship that there was no need for him to help them today. "The room has been cleared, so we are fine," and off the ladies went. They came down to the kitchen right at noon and Winship had lunch prepared and sitting on the table, roast beef sandwiches and a pot of cream of chicken soup.

"Well Winship, we are finished with the room," Louise said. "Donna has the windows on the inside clean and Shelia has vacuumed every inch twice! After three washings on the inside of the windows, you would think they are new but they will really sparkle when we get Donna's sons over here this Saturday to wash the outside of the windows. We noticed you have several ladders in the garage. A little elbow grease and they should be looking great."

After they left, Winship walked up to the garage attic and could not believe his eyes. They had dusted, vacuumed, moped, and waxed the wooden wide pine floor boards. In the corner, between the bay windows that surrounded the exterior walls on all four sides, they had set his leather chair. They must have waxed or oiled it as well along with the matching ottoman. There was a side table and lamp. The lamp was plugged in but Donna said that she thought it only needed a new bulb and not to forget to replace the one above the entry door that was also out.

Winship sat in the chair for a moment and put his feet upon the ottoman. He took in a deep breath enjoying the breeze flowing across the room from the open windows. He felt ashamed of himself for not clearing out this room many years ago.

Marshmallow had entered the room and quickly joined him, settling upon his lap all set for an afternoon snooze. "Sorry little one. I am only sitting here for a few moments."

After several minutes Winship retreated back into the main house where Marshmallow, who had been full of spunk for the last month managing to get into every area where they were attempting to clean, had followed him back into the kitchen, jumped up and settled into a chair near the phone and fell fast asleep.

Marshmallow had made her sweep of the room above the garage right when they opened the door for the first time; getting under the sheets, into the corner eaves, up on the couches, anything she thought was worth investigating, she managed to inspect or lay on.

After the room was cleared, except for the items that Winship had asked to remain behind, she quickly lost interest. She seemed to find the basement her latest area to play around in.

Later on that day nearing dusk, Winship went to the pantry and searched the shelves for spare light bulbs. He had replaced several all over the house while they were cleaning in the last month after trying several switches that he hardly ever touched and finding several bulbs had burnt out. He was hoping he had not used up his last ones. He was in luck. There was a two pack of sixty watt bulbs still on the shelf.

After he found what he was looking for, he headed back up to the room above the garage. He rubbed Vaseline on the bottom part of the new bulbs, where it screwed into the socket, so they would not rust in place. He took the small step ladder from the kitchen closet with him and replaced the bulb above the entry door which was very tightly screwed in and hoped it would not snap off in his fingers. After a moment or two it unscrewed out of the socket. He placed the burnt out bulb on the shelf of the ladder and left the ladder sitting it in front of the door, tried the switch and there was light.

Then Winship went into the large room and over to the corner with the lamp. He had tried the switch on the lamp earlier in the day which Donna told him did not turn on. The bulb in the lamp was also slightly rusted in place but ever so gently he managed to get it unscrewed without breaking it. He set the used bulb on the floor and it rolled right into the corner eave. Paying it no mind, he put the new bulb in, turned the switch and viola it worked.

Winship sat down in the beautiful leather chair placing his legs on the ottoman and shut his eyes. The breeze and the sunlight fading slowly, put him in a very restful state. After a while he realized he was almost asleep when he roused himself from the chair. He looked down for the light bulb he had placed on the floor but it had seemed to roll pretty far into the eave's cubbyhole. He shut off the lamp and started to head back down the stairs with the ladder and old light bulb from the hall to the house. As he made his way down a few steps, he felt guilty thinking what a beautiful job Louise and the girls had done in the room. He should not leave the light bulb around, like a discarded piece of trash, but then again he did not want to stick his hand into a dark cubbyhole and risk a spider bite. He continued to the kitchen, grabbed a long pair of tongs and went back up to retrieve the bulb. He got down on his knees and spotted it. Even with the lamp on it was very dark in the cavern and he could not clearly make it out as it had rolled pretty far back. He trudged back to the house to find a flashlight.

Marshmallow, wondering what all the fuss was about, followed him out to the garage and headed upstairs. Winship got down on his knees, for a second time, and shinned the flashlight into the cubbyhole and saw that the bulb was within reach if he used the tongs. It took him two or three tries to grab the bulb without it popping out of the tongs grasp. At last he succeeded only to have it pop out and roll a little farther back into the eave.

Marshmallow, thinking their might be a mouse in there, kept nudging Winship's arm trying to get in as well.

"Marshmallow!" Winship said. "Knock it off you silly goose. I am trying to get a light bulb out of here." Marshmallow took this as a signal that maybe this is a fun game and nudged Winship even harder.

After another try, Winship shinned the flashlight again aiming the beam for the light bulb but he thought he saw something that looked like a box in the farthest area of the hole but he could not make it out. Whatever it was faded right into the darkened aged wood of the eave. He was thinking it was just part of the construction. Right then he succeeded to snag the bulb.

Winship slightly pivoted to place the bulb on the table. He was quite uncomfortable and getting a leg cramp while kneeling down and turning his neck to get a better look into the eave's corner. He shone the flashlight inside again out of curiosity and said, "Come on Marshmallow." The cat had sauntered into the cavern. "It's time to go!" He could see that she was sniffing around what he originally thought might be a box. On the second look with the flashlight, it did look like a box. Definitely not part of the construction. It also looked like it might be covered in a ragged dark cloth. "What's back there Marshmallow? What did you find?" Marshmallow turned around and sauntered back out covered in a few cobwebs. Winship looked again and as his eyes adjusted to the darkened room and the even darker cubbyhole. He said to himself, "There is something back there." He stretched his arm out with the tongs as far as he could into the hole and managed, after a couple of tries, to get a grip the mysterious box. On the first try just the ragged cloth came off in the tongs grasp. The box wasn't so easily moved. He tried to get the tongs securely around the edges of the box but it took a couple of tries. Once he got a good vice grip on it the box slid out easily.

CODFISH PARK

Winship picked up the box and sat in the leather chair. He set it in his lap and slid the remaining shreds of the cloth off and wiped the film of mold and dust that it was covered in. He placed the original cloth on the floor and took a quick study of the beautiful inlaid wood which had two small brass hinges on the back and a larger brass latch on the front. He slid the front hooked brass latch aside and opened up the box. Inside was a small well aged and worn bible and a few non-descript letters that were well faded and yellowed that were not dated. All of them were hand addressed to a

> *Ms. Nola Regan*
> *Wauwinet Rd.*
> *Nantucket Island, Massachusetts*

Both of the letters were from the same sender with the return address badly faded and barely legible but read:

> *Caroline Cook*
> *Oceanside Avenue*
> *New Castle, New Hampshire*

There were no legible postmark dates. The letters were not much about anything. A comment on the weather and on the New Hampshire coast. A mention of her mother and brothers but nothing about her father. One letter also stated that her cousins were coming to visit in a few weeks and how she hoped that she would find time to get down to Nantucket for a visit before the gales of November set in.

There were also a few keys, four to be exact, a couple pencils, a silver but tarnished heart locket with tarnished neck chain and a small gold ring that resembled a man's wedding band fairly plain and non-descript. There were also a few old coins from different parts of the word. Possibly brought back from an uncle or aunt who had traveled on a voyage to Europe.

Nothing of any real value but Winship tried to figure out why this box would be hidden way back into a corner attic's eave where it could not be seen or even possibly ever be discovered. As its contents were surely not valuable and he did not think that this had anything to do with the Oberg's furniture collection that was left behind so many years ago. What did it mean hidden in such an obscure place?

At this point Marshmallow had grown weary and was laying on the arm of the leather chair dozing away. Winship noticed the wood on the box had such an intricate and beautiful inlaid design and thought to himself, "Was it made of cherry?" Then he said, "Okay Marshmallow. It's time to go down and prepare some supper." Marshmallow just gave a slight yawn and remained in place. Winship went to set the empty box down on the floor and he turned it over to see if there were any markings on the bottom when something moved inside of the box. The movement was ever so slight that he almost did not notice it. He looked at the box again and thought it might have been the brass latch. As he turned it back over the same sound was quietly heard. Again, it seemed to be coming from inside the box. Winship turned the box upright and opened it up once more but there was nothing inside. He gave the box a little shake and again the sound was there. He examined the box closer, tapped the inside bottom and said aloud to Marshmallow, "What do we have here? It looks like this possibly has a trick base. A secret compartment? Well let's just see to that Marshmallow." Winship took the box, leaving the light on with Marshmallow still resting on the arm of the chair. He headed downstairs to the house and into the kitchen. Winship turned on a few lights as the sun had already set but there was still a glow faintly shining through the trees. Winship placed the box upon the kitchen table and went to outside to his fishing bungalow to retrieve one of his fish filleting knives along with his magnifying glass that he used to tie his fishing flies. He returned to the kitchen table. With the help of the magnifying glass, he studied the bottom of the box from the outside then from the inside. There seemed to be a very fine line running around the edge of the inside bottom of the box he thought quietly to himself. He took his fillet knife and carefully

23

placed the tip of the knife into the back edge of the antique box, breaking what seemed to be a type of glue sealant. After a few twists of the knife and edging it carefully all around the interior of the box he felt it give way. Winship slowly started to break the rest of the seal around the edge. Right then Marshmallow jumped right onto the kitchen table and gave Winship quite a startle. Marshmallow had to stick her nose right into the box and Winship said, "Knock it off." He picked her up and placed her on the floor. With a loud meow she sauntered away and headed down the basement stairs. Winship again started to gently pry the loose piece of wood away from the edges of the interior of the box. It took a minute or two but he wanted to be extra careful. If there was something to be found, he did not want to possibly damage it. Finally, the piece of wood was totally freed from the interior of the box. He gently pulled it off. Winship then placed it on the kitchen table just as Marshmallow hopped back up and decided to investigate what was going on. "Careful there little one," he said to her. "Let's find out what we have uncovered."

As Winship looked at the silk bag inside the newly opened space, he figured it measured just about the same as interior of the box about 16" by 12". He slowly and carefully picked up the deep purple colored silk bag that encased something that felt like a hard thin newspaper. Whatever was inside was very light and made the sound of a dry paper crackle as he removed it from the box. Winship ever so gently slid it out from the confines of the wrapping. As Winship slid the heavy grade paper out of the silk enclosure, he was extremely careful as he did not want it to crack or tear apart. It appeared to be a larger paper, folded over four times to reduce its size. He deduced was to fit snugly inside of the box's interior in the best possible way.

Winship placed Marshmallow, who kept poking her nose at the newly discovered paper, on one of the chairs. He then cleared everything off the table, took a dry kitchen towel and wiped the table clean. He did not want any moisture, crumbs or spillage to effect the paper that he was about to lay on the table. He began to unfold the paper very carefully, slowly and cautiously. It was a well-worn yellowed paper. Winship placed it directly under the hanging lamp over the table's center. It looked to be quite old, possibly a hundred years or so, just randomly guessing in his mind. It had a sketch on it with some faded writing. The first thing he noticed was Foul Cay, Exumas in the center top of the paper. Below that was a sketch of the island with a slight hill on it looking easterly onto the shore which he believed if he was reading the faded hand written legend, or notes of N-S-E-W correctly. The letters HT/LT were also written in the lower right hand corner, quite faded but still legible. And near the coastline he could see what looked to be the marking of a large "X". It looked as though at one point the X had been circled. It was quite faded but Winship could barely see that it had been circled.

"What do we have here Marshmallow?" Winship quietly said. "What do we have here?" He took his magnifying glass and studied each part of the map inch by inch. He held it up to the light. Not much more to be seen there but just then, as he was putting the map down, he saw some backwards writing. Trying to decipher it he flipped the map over. Ana Sofia Barcelona was all it read. "Okay Marshmallow. This is what we have. A hidden box, a secret compartment, some old family letters, a silver tarnished necklace, an old small bible, a man's gold wedding band and a hand sketched, old faded and dated map which looks like it reads 1875 but it's pretty faded. What do you think this all means?" Winship studied it all again for a while, grabbed a piece of paper and made some notes. First thing tomorrow was a trip to the Athenaeum. But for now where could he hide this box? Someplace out of sight where Louise will not come across it if she comes around to do more cleaning. Then he decided in the trunk of his car, she certainly will never go anywhere near there!

MADAKET

That night Winship had a very restless sleep. It took him a good long while to fall completely asleep, then when he finally did he had wild vivid dreams. When he awoke in the morning his pajamas were damp with sweat. He was still tired from such a restless sleep. Winship remembered tossing and turning a lot during the night. Marshmallow, who was curled up at the end of the bed, kept meowing every time Winship interrupted her slumber.

When he finally shook off the numbness that he felt from such a terrible night's rest, he laid in the bed trying to recollect his dreams. He could remember small bits and pieces; a boat, snakes, a cave with bats, the hot Caribbean sun, a dry thirst, his pale skin burnt by the sun, palm trees, coconuts, cracking them to get at their liquid, and scenes from the movie Robinson Crusoe. His night clothes were still soaked with sweat.

He rose from the bed and took a long hot shower, noticing it was only 6:30a.m., started a pot of coffee and went out to the car and removed the box from the trunk and again went over it inch by inch seeing if he might have missed something, anything but that was not the case.

He turned the box over and over examining each side of the of the box in and out. Nothing else looked different, not even the false bottom area that he had removed the covering from the night before.

He went into his study and looked at the books on his shelves but did not have anything that might have helped in his search for information on the Exuma islands. Winship selected an old atlas and he searched the index for a section on the Caribbean and located a page where the Exumas were listed. He learned that they are a part of the Bahamas Cays. The capital is Georgetown. Very thinly populated. There was a listing of Great Exuma, Little Exuma, along with Sandy Cay and a few other cays but no mention

26

of Foul Cay was given. He knew the Athenaeum would not be open until 9:00a.m. So he placed the box with the map back into the trunk of the car. Winship drove into town early, headed up the cobble stone streets and parked in front of Congdon's Pharmacy. He entered the drug store and settled on a muffin and a coffee.

Every few minutes he glanced at his watch while sitting at the soda fountain. Winship pulled out his pen and paper that he had written his notes on to review when David McCoy entered the Pharmacy, walked right up and sat next to him. Winship quickly folded up his piece of paper and put it in his top jacket pocket and buttoned it tight. "What ya got there Winship? Some secret love note?"

"No, nothing really. It's just my grocery and hardware list. If I don't put it securely away I will leave it someplace." He thought to himself, "Old nosy McCoy has to sit right next to me and start asking questions."

Then McCoy started to ramble on, "You going to sell your house and get something smaller? You going to keep both of your cars? My grandson is looking for a car. He doesn't have much money though. If you're looking to get rid of the Ford give me a call, let me remind you, he doesn't have much money!"

All Winship could do was glance at the clock on the wall and think 9:00a.m. can't come quick enough!

His knew McCoy was just looking for a cheap deal. Most likely he wanted the car for himself. Finally, after about fifteen minutes of McCoy rambling on about nothing, Winship paid his bill and started to leave. "Wait a minute. If you're headed to the grocery store, I'll join you. I have got to grab a few things myself."

"Sorry David, but I am going to hit the hardware store."

"That's okay, I'll go with you," McCoy said.

Winship thought to himself, "This can't be happening right now!"

"Sorry but prior to that I have a meeting with All Kovalencik, my attorney. We have a few things to go over with Mary's trust and he has some papers for me to sign."

"You selling? That's what it is. I knew you were going to sell. I've been telling everyone that and you see I was right!!"

"Catch you later David," Winship said, walking off.

Winship was the first person in the Athenaeum. This was a bright sunny morning. Not a cloud in the sky and the birds were chirping away as he entered. He quickly found the section about ships and history of the seas. Winship searched several books. There were several on Europe and Spain. A few had sections on Barcelona, Valencia and a few with sections on Spanish boats, but to no avail. He looked for the history of ship wrecked boats but again nothing showed any information on the Ana Sofia boat. The only real references were to Columbus and his sailing voyage.

As he drove back to Wauwinet, it came to him. "My God, I need to get in touch with Simon!"

Simon Gilmore was old friend whom ironically he met at the Whaling Museum on Nantucket. They had remained close friends for many years. Simon loved boating and is a registered captain, often traveling to San Sebastian, Barcelona, and other ports on the coast of Spain and Portugal. Simon loved boats and their history, especially Spanish history. He was going to draft him a letter and send it first class postage to his home in Dartmouth England. Winship returned home and immediately started to compose what would be the first of many communications between him and Simon.

September 18, 1972

Dear Simon,

I hope this letter finds you well. I am still enjoying life here on Nantucket. Things are about as good as can be expected. Life is a little lonely at times with Mary being gone but I manage to keep myself fairly busy. I wanted to know if you could do some research for me?

What I am seeking is information on a ship that might have sailed around seventy-five or more years ago. The name is Ana Sofia. I believe it was from Spain. It's possible that it was built and christened in Barcelona. I'm not 100% sure but that's what I believe.

If I am correct, it might have run into problems while sailing to or near the Exuma Islands. Possibly it was wrecked off the coast there. I do not know the size of the vessel or anything else about it but if you could spend some time on this I would greatly appreciate it!

It's a long story but might turn out to be a good one. If it does pan out, we might be taking a trip, my treat!

All the best,

Winship

September 29th 1972
Dear Winship,

What a wonderful surprise it was to get your letter, I am hoping your adventure you're referring to is a trip to lovely Nantucket in the spring.

I made a few calls to some mates in the Barcelona maritime sector. They have sent me this information and I also visited the Maritime Museum here in Dartmouth. Not much information on the Ana Sofia here, sorry to say but the following is what my friends from Spain could find out. Ana Sofia was launched in 1885 from Barcelona. It is 48 meters with six masts. It will crew 12 when fully staffed. Records show that it was shipwrecked somewhere in the Bahama Cays around 1889. No crew reported surviving and no manifest of any cargo was listed.

I hope this might help you with what you are seeking. It's the best I can do.
Sincerely,
Simon

October 12th 1972 (Via Telegraph)
Dear Simon(stop) Could you please telephone me at your convenience(Stop) Please reverse the charges(Stop) Winship(Stop) (617) 228-6213 USA code is 001(Stop)

It was October 13th, 10:00a.m. Nantucket time when the phone rang.

Winship picked up the phone to a crackling voice. "Winship? Simon here."

"Hello you old dog you!" Winship spoke into the phone.

"Back at ya," Simon responded. "So nice to hear your voice."

"Same here," Winship replied.

"So what's up Winship? Why the need for a call?"

"Well Simon, I will fill you in with more details later on. My question to you is, if I sponsored the whole trip and then some, would you consider chartering a boat out of Miami or Fort Lauderdale and taking us over to the Exuma Islands? A good solid boat. One that we could comfortably stay on for a let's say, about week or two? I will cover all your expenses. Your trip up to London, your flights and any other costs that might arise.

We could combine this together as a fun adventure and an old reunion expedition trip!"

"I can do that but what is the reason? Getting island fever there on Nantucket? Is the cold, damp, foggy weather getting to your bones along with the shorter fall days?"

"Well I will explain it all to you when we arrive in Florida. Get the information on what we need for supplies. We can also get other items prior to casting off. Get me the information where to wire any money that's needed. I will pack my passport and travel gear and meet you in the warmth of Florida. I will also have my travel agent get you some flight options. One thing Simon, I would like to do this sooner than later. I think I would prefer it if you called me on any updates as getting a telegraph here is like publishing it in the newspaper. Everyone will know and start asking nosy unnecessary questions. You know this town is small and full of useless gossip."

"Totally understood," Simon replied. "Mysterious dealings sound fun!"

"How many days are we talking to get to the Exumas via a nice sea worthy boat?"

"I will have to pull some charts and see but my best estimate is it will take about two possibly three days from Fort Lauderdale. That is with the weather permitting and just doing day time voyages. So what's this about Winship?"

"All in good time, Simon. All in good time! Let's figure on the following; we meet the day prior in Miami when you arrive. We spend the next day getting provisions, stock the boat so we are ready, and sail off. Book the boat for two weeks with an option for one more just to cover our bases in case this little expedition takes longer than we have planned."

Right after Winship hung up, he looked up the number for Swains Travel. He dialed it and on the first ring the voice on the other end answered, "Shelia Egan. How can I help you?"

"Hello Shelia, Winship here."

"Well hello Winship. How's the house looking?"

"Oh, it's really great Shelia. I can't thank all of you enough. I am going to take everyone out to The Harbor House for dinner soon or maybe a fun lunch at Cioppinos or the Opera House."

"What can I do for you Winship?"

"Well a good friend of mine has offered to take me on a trip from Florida to the Bahamas on a boat he has chartered."

"Wow that sounds great!" Shelia added.

"So what I need is to start getting information on flights to Miami for him out of London. We could try to coordinate them to see if I could arrive close to my friend's flight time from London in Miami. That way we could meet up, spend the night and head to the boat. It would be best to take a hotel for the first evening so he can adjust to the jet lag and we can make some fun plans, not too rushed."

"I will work on it straight away and get back to you with options. I can see what time flights depart and arrive from London to Miami."

"Oh Shelia, do you think your niece Macy could stay at the house and watch over Marshmallow while I am gone?"

"I'm sure she would love it. You know she's a big fan of Marshmallow but then again who isn't?"

The next day Winship stopped into Swains Travel to see if Shelia had found any flight options. She gave him a print out of several different dates and options for Simon's flight out of London to Miami. Winship telephoned Simon with the available flights and they selected a day and a flight time. Winship gave all the information to Shelia. She booked Winship on a direct flight from Boston to Miami on October 20th.

In the late afternoon, before heading out to dinner on October 18th, the phone rang. "Hello Mr. Cate. This is Macy Collins, Shelia's niece."

"Hello Macy. So nice to hear your voice. I was just getting ready to head out and catch an early dinner. I have left some written instructions for you on the counter top in the kitchen and in the cupboard where the dinner plates are. I have left you some spending money in an envelope there. Please feel free to enjoy yourself here or in town."

"That is very kind of you Mr. Cate. How long do you think you will be gone?"

"Well that's kind of hard to say at this point. My good friend Simon has charted a boat down in Florida and we are going to sail around the islands for a week or two so my best guess is at least ten days if not more. I will leave you plenty of spending money in the envelope at the house so you can go out and enjoy a lunch or two, possibly a dinner and a movie as well. If you would like, feel free to invite Robbie and Shelia to join you. My treat." Macy replied, "Well I plan to come over around 11: 00a.m tomorrow. I assume I will stay in the same guest bedroom as the last time?"

"Yes, that's correct," replied Winship.

"How's Marshmallow doing?" she asked.

"Just fine. She's going to love having you visit."

"Well," Macy said, "don't worry about a thing. I'll have it under control. If anything happens I will call Shelia and Robbie." Winship told her that Bill Hourihan was coming over to drive him to the ferry around seven-fifteen in the morning and that he was all packed and ready to go.

"One more thing," Winship explained, "I have arranged for Randy Alfeldt to stop over every afternoon and clean and restock the fireplace for you as needed. The nights here in Wauwinet are getting pretty chilly with the breezes blowing in off the ocean. The heat works really well but if you'd like to enjoy a crisp warming fire, feel free to light it nightly. I have enough firewood to last a century. Marshmallow will keep you company in the leather chair with the folded towel on it. One more thing, if you run short on money let Bill Hourihan know. He will take care of restocking the envelope." Winship said his goodbye and replaced the receiver back down, grabbed his jacket and headed out.

Winship was enjoying a nice simple dinner of roast chicken, mashed potatoes, peas, and a nice fresh chilled green salad with a glass of house red wine at the Mad Hatter, sitting at a table in the bar area. He was lost in thought most of the meal wondering exactly what he had gotten himself into. Several people had stopped by his table to say hello but he kept the conversations short. He was busy reflecting on his new travel plans. Thinking he could get up as usual tomorrow, go to the lunch counter at Congdon's Pharmacy, possibly run into McCoy again and go home to cook a lonely dinner for himself and watch the days pass by, or he could have an adventure. Throw caution to the wind, meet up with his good friend Simon and have some fun! The answer was simple. He was more than ready to start his adventure.

After he finished his dinner, declining an offer for coffee or dessert, Winship drove home under a clear sky. The temperature was slowly dipping into the low forty's. After arriving back at the house he sat in front of the fireplace with Marshmallow in the chair next to him. He considered looking over the map again but thought better of it. "Don't get your hopes too high," he thought to himself. "Think of this as a getaway. A vacation." He gave a sigh and said, "Marshmallow I am truly going to miss your company but you behave and don't give Macy any trouble." Marshmallow just rolled over onto her back, gave out a quiet meow and went right back to sleep.

Winship left the den a short while later and placed a call to Leonard to inform him of his upcoming trip, not disclosing any information about the discovery of the mysterious box and map. Leonard was slightly taken back at his father's quick decision on a boat trip to the Bahamas like this but at the end said, "Go for it Dad. You and Simon have a ball. Enjoy yourself. You need to get out more."

On the morning of October 19th, Winship took the 9:00a.m. ferry to Hyannis and the bus to downtown Boston. He hailed a taxi and checked into The Lenox Hotel. That night he felt restless while he enjoyed a fine dinner at the Union Oyster House. After he finished his meal, he strolled around the Back Bay area before heading back to the Lenox but again sleep evaded him. At first, he tossed and turned thinking about the map and what it meant. Was there treasure? Finally, he fell into a very deep sleep. The last thought on his mind was, "Is this all going to be a waste of time? No, no one hides a map like that without a reason." Thinking that he, himself being the only person in possession of the map, was sure no one had ventured down to the Exumas to search it out. Was it possible that someone had already found what the **X** represented?

LOW BEACH

Winship arose early the next morning, took a hot shower and went down into the lobby where there was had an assortment of pastries, coffee and teas. He sat in one of the large winged back chairs enjoying a blueberry Danish and a steaming hot cup of coffee and began reading one of the complimentary Boston Globe newspapers, not finding much of interest. He finished his morning snack, took the elevator back up to his room on the sixth floor, packed his suitcase and had the doorman summon him a taxi. The next thing he knew; he was on the plane en route to Miami. The flight was very smooth and he hardly even felt the plane touch down on the tarmac when they landed. He anxiously walked to Simon's gate to await his dear friend's arrival from London. Winship did not even have a chance to ask the person at the counter what time Simon's plane was scheduled to land when the door opened up and people started entering the terminal. The fifth person to enter the terminal was Simon, all smiles. Giving each other a big hug and slap on the back as they made small talk while walking over to the luggage arrival belt. Simon grabbed his sea worthy duffel bag off the conveyor belt and explained to Winship that he had been in contact with a guy named Barefoot Davis about the boat charter.

They hailed a taxi and directed the driver to take them to their hotel in Ft. Lauderdale. Effortlessly, they checked into the Marriott Marina Resort Hotel under the reservations that Shelia had made for them, both agreeing to meet in the hotel lounge around 6:00p.m. That would allow Simon to get some rest. Simon mentioned to Winship that he was not in the least bit hungry but could use a nice long hot shower and a few hours rest.

They both entered the lobby almost at the same time. Winship mentioned to Simon, "I will give you all the particulars of what this trip is about. Let's first get settled at a table."

34

After selecting a table off to the side by the large paned glass sliders that looked out over the water for privacy, Winship ordered two beers from the very attractive cocktail waitress who was wearing a nametag that read Jennifer, Naples, Florida. Winship slowly and very precisely went over all the details from the very beginning with Simon, including the discovery of the box and all the contents. When he finished explaining all of this to Simon, he pulled the box out of large beach style bag he had brought with him. He showed it to Simon explaining where the concealed compartment was and how he had removed it.

"This is when I found the map which was originally folded up in a silk covering and located under the false bottom," Winship said excitedly, pointing to the hidden chamber. "I have the map with me but I am a little worried about showing it to you in public." Winship continued to explain everything in detail about the map. "I have it here in the bottom of the bag but I think we should go to your room Simon. I don't want any possibility of someone overhearing this conversation. I might sound paranoid but one never knows!"

Winship could see the excitement building in his friend's eyes. Simon was very intrigued by the details and couldn't contain his curiosity a minute longer. "Well what are we waiting for Mate? Let's pay the bill, get out of here and get down to business," Simon blurted out, bubbling over with excitement.

Arriving securely back in Simon's room, Winship pulled the round table that sat near the lanai's glass door directly under the overhead lamp. He removed the map from his bag and its covering and slowly gut gently unfolded it and placed it upon the table and gave Simon the magnifying glass he brought with him to study it with. Winship had also brought along a flashlight just in case they needed more precise light to read the weathered map.

Winship looked around nervously as Simon slowly studied the map but in the confines of Simon's hotel room, privacy was not an issue.

"Holly-Moly!" exclaimed Simon. "And your saying this was hidden deep in a garage attic eave?"

"Yes. If I didn't discover it, I don't think anyone would have. I found it by total accident. If Marshmallow had not crawled into that corner eave, it would most likely be undiscovered for another hundred years, if ever discovered."

"Well it is a mystery we have on our hands. One that we shall solve together."

"One thing," Winship said. "Simon, I am cutting you in for twenty-five percent of any value we might get out of this venture."

"That's okay," Simon replied, "there is no need for that. This is going to be a fun trip that we are going to enter upon."

"No Simon. It's my deal. I pay for this whole trip and your time, as well as a commission. I insist."

The next day they went to locate the boat Simon had chartered which was in Fort Lauderdale at Pier 66. The boat was forty-eight feet with two cabins, two heads and a full galley. It was a Grand Banks "East Bay" boat named the Karen-Marie registered in Delaware.

Simon said the boat should be perfect for their journey. Simon had called the marina from England, explained what he was searching for and where they would be taking it. Captain Davis was in charge of leasing the boats and explained his background. Working in the industry many years, he was well seasoned at matching a boat to ones needs. He gave Simon three options. Simon knew a lot about this style of boat the man was suggesting, a Grand Banks. He confidently secured the charter and had given the leasing agent a detailed list of supplies they needed for their upcoming trip.

Simon and Winship took a taxi to a few stores for some last minute provisions. A camping and a hardware store, a grocery, and a place called 'The Bait Stops Here' for some extra fishing gear that they thought they might need. Last but not least, a quick stop at an ABC Liquor store for some beer, vodka, mixers, and six bottles each of red and white wine for their trip to Foul Cay.

SHIMMO

They casted off the next morning at 6:00a.m. It was a cool sixty-four degrees according to the deck hand that was helping them load everything onto the Karen-Marie, telling them there was a light chop and winds of 5-7 MPH from the south west.

The first day was fairly uneventful and smooth. It was more or less a straight, short trip out to Bimini. Winship was the galley cook and made a good first mate. Always ready with a cold beer or water for Simon as he mastered the boat and sailed it to Bimini late in the afternoon without a hitch and docked for the night.

They decided to take two rooms at the Sea Crest Hotel that was located right in the marina instead of staying on the boat. Before going to dinner, they again pulled out the map in the privacy of Winship's room. They took turns both going over it again with the magnifying glass still trying to see if there was anything they could have missed.

During dinner at the Bimini Fish House and Bar, while enjoying a fried grouper dinner with a couple of cold beers, Simon and Winship kept trying to figure out what the initials LT/HT represented on the map. Neither of them could come up with a solid answer except the possibility it was the initials of two people who had sketched out the map, marking it as theirs.

Winship explained to Simon that he had tried, after the discovery of the box and the letters, to find any information out about the person Caroline Cook of New Castle, New Hampshire by calling the local librarian on Nantucket and also the Visitor Information Bureau without much luck. He did track down the New Castle town historian and their local library without any success. That direction seemed to be a dead end.

Winship had no idea that a letter had arrived in his mailbox a few days after he had departed for his trip. The return address simply read:

Edward Jurgelas, Town Historian
New Castle, New Hampshire

The next day they casted off from the docks of the Bimini Marina sharply at 4:30a.m. The eastern skyline was still dark but within the hour the skies started to lighten up. Warm breezes and smooth seas made for a nice voyage. They arrived under the last light of darkness into Georgetown, Exumas.

Upon docking, the harbormaster greeted them. "Hello gentleman. My name is Mr. Hayes - John Hayes. I am the local customs and harbormaster here for the Exuma Islands."

"Nice to meet you. I am Simon Gilmore and this here is Winship Cate."

"Where are you guys from?" asked Mr. Hayes.

"I am from the South of England, Dartmouth, along the coast. Mr. Cate is from Nantucket Island, Massachusetts."

He requested their passports, without much of a formality, and then asked where they were arriving from and where they were headed. Simon explained that they wanted to spend a week or two just cruising in and out of the many cays that the Exumas offered. He asked the harbormaster about the best places to catch grouper, snapper and wahoo, and if possible, some tuna. Simon was also inquiring about the best place to grab a couple of rooms for the night and where they could pick up some local nautical maps as well if there were any tricky or dangerous reefs to watch out for, handing the harbormaster a vague mapping of their intended route.

Winship booked two rooms at Phillipe's Guest Cottages, which offered a comfortable bed and a nice hot shower. Complete with a packet of coffee and a percolator. Phillipe's wife, Danielle, recommended the Cracked Conch for a cold beer and, of course, the cracked conch for dinner.

The Crack Conch offered what Simon described as the most tender, sweet, succulent fried conch and very cold beer. They finished off with a whole roasted five-pound snapper dinner served by Kenny, the happiest Jamaican Simon had ever encountered.

Simon said to Winship, "Whatever happens, remember we are the outsiders here. This is a small territory. Everybody knows everybody and most likely they are all related. Let me do the talking. You just say you're here to fish. Nothing more, nothing less. Tell them we are longtime friends and this was a dream that we both had talked about and saved our hard earned dollars for over the years."

"Done," Winship said, as they chinked their bottles together. "Oh and one more thing, "Simon mentioned, "island folk can be a little strange so don't let them spook you."

Simon told Winship that if his calculations were correct and they cast off by 7:00a.m. - they should be able to make Foul Cay in three to four hours depending on the tides. "Let's just be cautious," he told Winship. "Just act like we are out to enjoy the deserted beaches. Maybe manage some snorkeling off the reefs and do some fishing. If anyone starts asking questions, refer them to me. You can tell them that you're just the galley guy! You never know, there might be rumors floating around the Exumas about some lost treasures. Mainly the one we are seeking. Stories of lost gold, sunken ships, and pirates never fade away. They just become more intense even if nothing is ever found!"

As they were finishing their dinner Simon kept looking around trying to see if there might be someone who looked like they were native to the area, maybe an older sailor type of person. He wanted to inconspicuously see if he could land his eyes on one. He was hoping to gently stir up a casual conversation toward lost treasures or ships that have sunk in the area.

Usually the local islanders loved to share the old folklore of pirates, sunken treasures and ghosts. Sometimes bits and pieces of the stories are true. Nothing seemed to come of his searching, at least not until very early the next morning. Simon had risen at 5:00a.m., showered and was enjoying a coffee on his small porch. A bad storm had brewed in the middle of the night making it almost impossible for them to cast off. He looked out at the end of the pier where there was an older, tanned man wearing ragged clothes and hat. "A real local," Simon thought to himself as he watched him cast a line into the water off the dock into the choppy bay. "Bingo!" he said to himself.

Simon slowly he made his way to the end of the dock. Once he was standing near the man, he started a conversation with the old timer who, as it turned out, had been born in Georgetown. His family owned the only dry goods store in the capital. Simon and the old timer, who never gave his name, made idle chat for about ten minutes. In a very monotone voice Simon said, "There must be a lot of fun pirate stories with ship wrecks and lost treasure in the area. Huh?" The old timer just nodded his head and said, "Lots and lots of them. "Do they sell any treasure maps?" Simon inquired. "My friend and I are going to cruise around for three or four days. We plan on doing some snorkeling and fishing. Maybe collect driftwood and shells for the family. It might be fun to take some photos of a pirate's map for the grand kids. Maybe pick up a seashell or two from the area that the lost treasure is supposedly from. You know, the grand-kids will love that stuff. They will eat it right up!"

"My brother in law, God rest his soul, passed away at the ripe age of 92. Said he knew lots of stories and told us about many of them over time. He told me of one many years ago about a wreck off of Foul Cay. A ship that crashed on the rocks back a hundred or so years. Rumor has it that there was pirates gold in the wreckage but many divers who have searched the wreckage never found any." The old timer looked at Simon squinting his eyes from the bright morning light even though there was grey cloud covering and said, "Yup. It was called something like Sofia. The only reason I remember the name of the boat is that I fell in love with a girl named Sofia. She was Italian. Her family docked here on a smaller boat fifty or so odd years ago. Stayed in Georgetown three days. She was the most beautiful girl I ever laid eyes on. She didn't speak much English and I don't know a lick of Italian but her eyes told me the story of her heart and how she felt about me. They soon left and I never saw her again. I still look out to the sea hoping she will return someday."

"Well that's a beautiful story. Thanks for sharing. I'm sorry, so what about the ship wreck?"

"Yup the wreck. It was a Spanish boat. It's rumored to have gold and diamonds aboard it. She was a relatively small ship from what I remember being told. It's been many, many years since anyone has brought that story up. No one ever found any treasure. The boat sunk after running aground on one of the reefs off of Foul Cay. Yup, the western shore of Foul Cay. If there were any treasure, it must have been swept out to sea. It's a rough current on the western point of that little cay. It runs between two other smaller cays which forces a strong rip current. Of course it's just mainly folklore that's been handed down like so many of the island stories. No one has ever found any treasure since I've been around. A doubloon here and there, some old sea glass, a piece of silverware, broken parts of plates and cups in the surf but that's about it, I reckon. Been plenty of people diving and fishing off of the Cay's around here but never heard of anyone having any luck!"

"Thanks again. I'm sure the grand kids will love the story." Simon wished the old-timer good luck with his fishing and walked back down the dock to his cottage. The sun was rising through the grey clouds and it looked as though it was going to be a beautiful day. The storm had passed but with the choppy seas, they were not going to be able to cast off today.

Winship appeared with a mug of coffee on his deck as Simon strolled off the pier. He was anxious to tell him about his conversation with the old man at the end of the dock and about the storm that kicked up at sea in the middle of the night. In a hushed tone, Simon told Winship that the ship was real. "It's rumored to have crashed off of Foul Cay and possibly had gold and diamonds aboard it," he said. "I got the story from the old man out on the dock fishing."

"Really? I mean, really?" Winship said excitedly.

"Calm down, quiet Winship!" Simon grabbed him gently by the arm. Winship realized how he had reacted and immediately lowered his voice and said, "Fill me in." Simon went over the whole scenario. How he handled it, his approach, his reaction and his story of them wanting to get driftwood, seashells and enjoy some snorkeling and fishing. He told Winship, "I was very vague in my conversation with the old timer and left it at that."

They spent the rest of the morning chatting with others who had docked in the harbor. They made an attempt to cover their story by enjoying some fishing off the dock. They stopped into the ships chandlery to look around. Not purchasing much except each of them picked out a hat with good covering for the back of their necks and the top of their foreheads. They also bought three tubes of mosquito repellant.

Winship looked out at the grey clouds that were just standing idle in the sky. There was a very light breeze coming off shore. He looked at the Karen-Marie and noticed there was a lonely seagull perched on top. It made him think of the book he saw at Mitchell's Book Corner a few weeks back. The cover was of a very impressive seagull. 'The Adventures of Mr. Hawkins' was the title. He was going to have to purchase it after his return to Nantucket.

Later on in the day they strolled up to Cynthia's, a local restaurant with a deck overlooking the marina. As they climbed onto the outside deck, a friendly voice came from the bar area, "Sit anyplace you'd like. I will be over in a minute with menus."

They selected a table along the water's edge. Simon mentioned, "This is the life. A nice little joint on the bay, warm weather all year long and great fishing. Lots of islands to discover." Simon looked up as a very pretty blonde approached their table and offered them both a menu placing two wrapped silverware settings down on the table. "Hi-ya. I'm Cynthia. Can I get you guys something to drink?"

"If you have two cold beers we are up for the task of making them disappear," Simon told her.

"Two Kaliks coming your way. You guys staying on a boat here?"

"Well we are docked here but we are staying at Phillipe's.

Cynthia said, "Danielle runs a tight ship over there. Keeps a tight leash on her husband Phillipe. Otherwise you would find him here or at the Cracked Conch with the locals playing cards most of the time."

When she returned with the beers, both men took two long swallows. "Wow that' really cold. Got to love it!"

"Today I have a few additions to the menu. Freshly made conch fritters. Just made a new batch this morning. They come six to an order. A great way to start off. They are served with a spicy mango dipping sauce, which I must say, when we offer them, the customer's love'um! For main dishes, I have a crab and coconut callaloo and last but not least, we are known for our jerk chicken, Jamaican style, served with a black beans and rice. We use Kenny's recipe. He works at the Cracked Conch and is from Jamaica. Both of the main dishes are served with corn bread which I also just baked about an hour ago."

"We met Kenny last night. Is he always that friendly?"

"Ha - Yes he is. All the time - like a natural high, but I don't think it's all natural," she said with a laugh.

"Can you start us off with an order of the fritters and bring us two more of these beers?"

When Cynthia returned Simon asked, "You're evidently not from around here. Where do you hail from?"

"Well I came here six years ago from Florida on a trip with friends. It just felt so special and a great pace of life. I returned four months later, stayed two weeks at Phillipe's Guest Cottages. I became friends with Danielle and Phillipe. I cooked them a few meals at their home and they told me that this old broken down shack of a place was available. It needed a lot of T.L.C. I said it was a nice idea but I don't think so. The next morning Danielle took me out horseback riding and started to quiz me.

Did I own my home? I told her I rented. Did I like my job? I truthfully gave her all the answers.

"Then when we returned Phillipe was sitting on the rotted steps here of this rundown beach shack. He called me over and said he had gotten up at 5:00a.m. and started measuring out this place. He had made several sketches of a new deck, a kitchen layout, an upstairs apartment, the bar and a storage area. He has even sketched a sign to go above the entry 'Bennett's'. That was his first choice after my last name but then we decided on the name as it stands now, 'Cynthia's Harbor Side Restaurant.' He is something else. He had even figured out the costs to redo this place and said he could get the workers we needed to do the build out. Next thing you know, here I am and I have never looked back. All of my friends are so envious of me. It's surprising how many come to visit. I truly love it here! I went back to Naples, sold my Corvette, put everything worth keeping in storage and packed a suitcase. The rest is history!"

After a lazy afternoon of conch fritters, jerk chicken and some ribs. Simon and Winship went back to Phillipe's and their dreams of hidden treasure.

The rest of the afternoon was quiet. Winship started one of the three books he brought with him. Simon fished off the dock catching a six-pound snapper.

That night they went back to have dinner at the Cracked Conch. Starting off with coconut bean soup, both of them using the crusty bread to get every drop out of the bowls. They followed that up with two remarkable grilled fillets of black grouper that had been speared in a grouper hole earlier that afternoon by a friend of Kenny's, who described himself as the bartender/server and chief bottle washer. The meal was accompanied with some fried plantains and warm hush puppies. Winship and Simon were the only two having dinner that evening. A few people had been at the bar when they entered but otherwise they were all alone. They both were wondering to themselves, what the upcoming trip might unveil, while finishing their nice quiet meal. Both of them enjoyed a quick nightcap of an aged Haitian Rhum at the bar with Kenny who was sporting a tee shirt that read "Rhum Bhum". By then it was time to say their good nights and headed off to their rooms by 8:00p.m.

The next morning, they were up having a simple breakfast, which consisted of doughnuts and coffee. Danielle explained the night prior where to find breakfast just in case they awoke before she was available.

They headed off to the boat by 7:00a.m. and within twenty minutes of loading the boat were casting off. Mr. Hayes, the harbormaster, was watching them depart. Winship had a feeling that he knew they were up to something. While making their way out of the harbor very casually, trying not to draw attention to themselves, Mr. Hayes was making them feel uneasy as he eyed them sailing away. Simon was anxious to see if they might possibly have a real treasure map in their possession. The Karen-Marie was stocked with enough provisions to stay on the boat for several days.

Winship looked up as they were sailing out and there was the same seagull hovering overhead almost following their charted course. An hour later the gull landed on the top of the highest mast of the boat. He knew it was the same one because of his remarkable spotted wings. The majestic bird looked as if he was guiding them almost like a lucky charm for their voyage.

It was close to 11:00a.m. when they arrived off the western tip of Foul Cay. Studying their rough sketched, antiquated faded map and looking over their compass and coordinates, Simon figured they were in direct line sight of the X on the map. It was too rough to anchor the Karen-Marie for very long in this spot. The coral reef underneath would tear the boat's hull to shreds if it drifted towards the rocky shoreline. Winship looked up to see that the sea gull was still with them and made a mental note to feed it some bread at one point. They moved the boat about half a mile to the north along the shoreline to calmer waters. The gull, which now had a name given to him by Winship as Mr. Hawkins, was still following their every move. They dropped anchor and climbed into the rubber dinghy and Simon paddled them to the shore, Winship keeping the map totally dry and protected in a satchel hung over his shoulder. It was wrapped in a water tight sack Winship had picked up at the Sunken Ship Store prior to leaving Nantucket.

Climbing out of the dinghy on the smoothest part of the beach, they began to scour the rough shore and scrub brush area searching up, down and all around finding nothing but driftwood and numerous discarded plastic bottles and cans that had washed upon the shoreline. They searched for a cave or an opening for three hours. It took the better part of an hour just to walk the rough shoreline around the entire Cay. Then they choose to head back to the boat. Coming up with nothing, not even anything close to an opening, it seemed like it was a fruitless effort.

Simon again pulled out the binoculars searching the shoreline from the boat, which they had moved back to their original anchoring position in the rough choppy waters earlier. He rechecked the map and said, "The X should be right there," pointing towards the rocky shore. "Next venture out to the cay we are going to place a stick standing straight up where we presume the X should be on the hillside. Just to make sure from this vantage point that we are not off by a good twenty feet or so."

"It should be right there," Winship agreed.

"I know we are looking in the right place," Simon replied. "But I tell you, nothing, nothing at all that even resembles a cave. Damn! What are we missing? I mean, who would create a map, go to such pains to hide it and create a false bottom in a box? No one would do that unless it was for a good reason. The box itself was so well hidden - no one was ever supposed to find it. Tomorrow I say we do a morning and an afternoon search. We will find a large stick to place where we think the X should be on the land. We should start at 8:00a.m. and go until noon, break back to the boat for lunch, move the boat directly in front of where we believe the X should be and see if we have placed the stick in the correct area. We can head back to the cay around 1:00p.m. if we need to relocate the stick to another position."

"Unless we find something," Winship chimed in.

"But for now, we have to move this boat to a safer place to anchor for the night. If another boat spots us here they're going to wonder what we are up to and we have to mind the rough coral. Let's get it a good half mile from our search area."

After anchoring the boat for the evening, they headed to shore in the dinghy. Winship quickly built a fire. Above them Mr. Hawkins was soaring around keeping watch over them.

Winship placed some sliced potatoes, onions, garlic and butter directly on the coals. He had them wrapped in three layers of foil paper he had prepared earlier in the galley of the boat. Once the potatoes had time to precook, he placed their small metal grate over the fire pit, balancing it on a couple of rocks. He placed the fillets of snapper that Simon had caught while in Georgetown on the grill. Each fillet was pre-coated with dried herbs, salt, pepper, butter, and very thin lemon slices and were wrapped parchment style inside of tin foil. Both of them enjoyed a couple of cold beers, relaxing on the beach, while the fish and potatoes were cooking. The sun started its decent in the sky from the west as their dinner finished cooking. The aroma was mouthwatering when Winship released the potatoes and snapper from its foil holders onto their plastic plates. Simon pulled out a bottle of Italian Verdicchio, popped the cork and poured it into their plastic cups. Toasting each other Simon said, "To the lost treasure of the Ana Sofia!" He then added, "Even if we don't find any treasure, I will never forget this dinner!"

After nearly licking their plates clean and the watching the sun set, it was time to breakdown their camp and take the dinghy back to the boat with heavy thoughts of what they hoped to discover weighing on their minds as they turned in for the night.

As the sun started to rise in the early morning, it was time to start their quest again in search for the mysterious hidden cave even if there was no such thing that it existed. The two of them were back on the cay scouring every square foot, slowly and methodically turning over loose stones and placed the stick, held up by some rocks, where they believed the X should be on the island. Around noon, it was time to take a break.

Paddling the dinghy back to the boat, Simon and Winship had again managed to cover, what they believed was, every inch of the surrounding landscape. According to Simon's calculations they were very close, if not right on the spot marked X. Anchoring the Karen-Marie directly in front of the western tip of the cay again, it looked like the upright stick was placed directly where the X should be, or so they thought. Returning back on to the cay after lunch, the sun and the dry salt air was beginning to take its toll on them. Especially Simon who never encountered hot sun or humid air like this back in Dartmouth. Simon brought the cooler ashore with them along with several plastic containers of water and the iced tea that Winship had made the evening prior. At one point, figuring something had to be calculated incorrectly, Simon asked, "Could the map be deliberately miss-mapped and we are on the wrong side of the island?"

"Good question. What if it was to fall into the wrong hands? Now we have a dilemma. Is this a deceptive map?"

"Are the N-S-E-W transfigured to different coordinates?" Now that brought in a whole new set of objectives for Simon. "This could take another week or two if we need to switch our thinking around. Do we even have the right cay? We might have to go back to Georgetown, regroup, gather more supplies and review our options and the map, yet again, from top to bottom left to right. Hell, we might as well turn the darn thing upside down to get another perspective," Simon continued very frustrated and overheated.

"I have heard that sometimes you can take a secret map, like the ones kids get in mystery games, turn it over and read it from the backside. The kids put a bright light in front of it to see if the map will reveal some hidden clues. The trip back to Georgetown is going to raise some questions with the harbormaster."

"You think?" Winship asked.

"Oh you bet! Why would two guys like us be hanging around a scruffy old island area like this for two weeks?"

"But you do have to admit, the snapper you caught were absolutely fantastic that we enjoyed last night for dinner. That's worth the time staying here in itself."

"Not in a million years would we hang around here and they know it. I am sure we are the talk of the island or islands right about now. We will have to come up with some type of explanation."

"Let's just tell them we are loving the weather and the fishing and there's no real need to go back to the cold northern weather."

"Well let's finish today's task. We can talk about it tonight on the boat over a bottle of red wine. The great thing is the marina is almost empty and I can get us into a slip with no other boats next to us. At least this will allow us some peace and quiet. No nosy neighbors, so to speak." They managed to explore the whole day, north, south, east and west by 5:00p.m. A total of two days' time with no luck at all.

Sitting back on the Karen-Marie enjoying a few cold beers and starting to laugh together about the adventure, Simon said, "We can't even find the X on the map." "Well tomorrow let's head back to Georgetown, check into Phillipe's again. We can have another great dinner at the Cracked Conch and have a laugh or two with Kenny!"

"We can regroup. We have two options; either give it up and head back to Florida, which I think is foolish as we have the time and we have the financial resources. Or, we can hang around for a while and enjoy this great weather," Winship stated.

That night Winship kept saying over and over, "Why would someone make a map like this and hide it? Maybe it was some kind of farce?" Someone thinking that if anyone ever found the map, they would do what we just did?"

"That's highly unlikely," Simon concurred.

"The person or persons who made this map are probably rolling over in their grave laughing at us!"

Right then, Mr. Hawkins, their new best friend, landed atop the wheelhouse and looked directly at Winship and gave him a wink. Almost saying, you're close now. You just don't know how close." It gave Winship an eerie but good feeling inside.

The next morning, they pulled the anchor up and agreed to head back to Georgetown, get some supplies and give the search three or four more days. Possibly expanding and changing their search venue.

As Simon prepared the Karen-Marie for sail, Mr. Hawkins left his perch on the mast and started to fly away from the boat. They were rounding the tip off the western edge where the boat was first anchored two days prior when Winship spotted Mr. Hawkins circling around the area where the stick was standing upright. The spot where they thought the X was on the map. Mr. Hawkins then swooped down and perched on a rock right at the crest of where the ocean's waves were breaking along the very rough coastline in front of the stick. He was watching him while scanning the coastline through the binoculars when he yelled, "SIMON. Stop! Stop!!!"

"What is it Winship?"

"I think I just saw something. Hold on. Give me a second. I swear it looked like an opening to a cave, or a cavern of sort."

Simon cut the engine to idle and Winship kept his focus on the spot just below Mr. Hawkins. He gave Simon the binoculars. "Look directly between the waves. Look straight ahead, right where Mr. Hawkins is perched and then scan directly below that spot to where the waves are crashing onto the rocks. Is that an opening?"

"Where?" asked Simon as he was looking up on the hill above the sea level. Simon looked again into the binoculars and studied the shoreline where the waves were crashing upon the hilly rocks.

"I don't see anything."

"Keep looking. It might take a second. You have to look in between the timing of the waves crashing along the shore at sea level. Where the crashing waves meet the coral directly below where Mr. Hawkins is perched." Mr. Hawkins then flew up into the air and did a dive bomb into the water.

"I think I got it! I think. I mean, I think I see it! It looks like an arch. Possibly the top of a cave? It's tough to spot with this boat bobbing and rocking and the waves crashing on the coral but I think I can make it out. It looks like a slight curved top of an opening. I think I now know what HT/LT stands for," Simon said pulling the binoculars away from his eyes.

"What?" asked Winship.

"It's High-Tide, Low-Tide. You can't see the opening unless you're positioned exactly off the western tip like we are right now and at a lower tide! It's not quite 100% low tide yet but even so, I don't think the sea level will drop much lower. If and when it does it will be for such a short time period that if you're not at the right place at the right time, you would never spot it. No one in their right mind would ever snorkel or scuba dive that close to such a jagged shore. They would be torn to shreds."

"I swear," Winship told Simon, "Mr. Hawkins was trying to guide us to that very spot!"

"You think so? You know, so far this is our best shot. I hope that's what we are looking for." Both men were extremely excited about their latest and only real clue to the mysterious X on the map.

"So it's a very distinct possibility that it is not a cave on the upper part of the hill side but a cavern that cuts into the side from the ocean's edge. Right into the coral almost completely hidden from sight under the water level."

"Yes, my good man. It's a sea cave!"

"You really think that's the X on the map?"

"It's got to be old man! It's got to be! We have plenty of time. Let's turn this tub around and get to a safe spot to drop anchor, hop in the dinghy and see what we might have found."

POCOMO HEAD

Simon and Winship motored in along the coat, anchoring almost directly in the same spot they had left along the shoreline earlier. Both eager with anticipation about what the prospect of their new discovery might possibly hold for them.

"That part of the terrain is all very sharp coral. We will need our tennis shoes and some gloves to carefully maneuver over it. One slip can slice you pretty good; knees, ankles, hands, forearms. It could get a little tricky so let's take it slow and steady. We don't want to head back to Georgetown all bandaged up. Let's make a short list of everything we need so we don't have to come back to the Karen-Marie if we forget something. Snorkel – mask – flashlight – rope – fins - water satchel – gloves - and shoes. Let's take the water protective satchel that we had the map stored in as well as the beach bag just in case we find something to bring back to the boat."

The men climbed into the dinghy and Simon rowed them ashore. They were like two school kids on Christmas morning. "Now let's not get our hopes up too high but it's sure fun to imagine."

Above them, almost keeping watch on the two men, was the sea gull Mr. Hawkins, soaring overhead. Simon grounded the dinghy securing it, always careful not to let the tide come in and sweep their only transport back to the Karen-Marie away. The two of them made way along the rocky coral shoreline. "Careful," Simon mentioned, "these rocks are sharp and can become very slick when wet. We will need to put on the gloves and keep our shoes on for sure footing, as we are going to have to scale along the rocks, and when we get a few feet before the opening we can to get into the water."

"It looks like the tide just drops about a foot if that much at all depending on the swell below the top. That's why we never saw the caverns opening. Even in the lowest tide, it only shows the curvature of the cave and only if you were in the right place at the right time looking directly at it. Even then you would most likely not be able to spot it. The chances are extremely slim because the arch is only visible for a very short time period. It's only about a twelve inch opening at the maximum above the water line. The cavern is almost impossible to spot one hundred feet out from the shore and it's been quite choppy ever since we started looking in this area. Any passing boat, if they were not looking at the exact spot at the correct time, would never see it. The chances are pretty slim that the cave would be noticed and if so, it's most likely that no one has paid much attention to it.

"We have about two hours before the tide comes back in at a pretty good clip. I don't know how long we have until the water line raises back up blocking the light from the outside. Due to the small opening the water, we will be forced to go through the narrow passage into the cave. There might be a pretty strong current so let's not let the waves crash us into the sharp coral. Okay?"

They were close to the cave's opening and lowered themselves into the clear aqua blue water. Not being able to touch the bottom, maneuvering was slow along the water's edge. It was still at least another fifty feet to reach the caves opening. It was very slow moving carrying the satchel, the beach bag, flashlights, snorkel equipment, and the crashing waves to deal with. Once reaching the cave's opening, Simon pulled out the two water proof flashlights and tied them onto a good three foot of rope each, to link them together, then tied the rope around their belts. He told Winship, "This way, if you drop it, you won't lose it."

Both men were wearing life preservers and were bobbing along trying not to let the waves crash them into the sharp coral rocks as they easily glided into the cave's opening. Simon guessed it was about ten feet deep in this tide to the bottom. They peered towards the back of the dark cavern with their flashlights. The water swelled and splashed against the far back wall. Simon estimated the size of the cave might possibly be maybe a hundred yards deep. It was tough to judge even with both of their flashlights beamed inside towards the back of the darkened walls. They clung to the side of the rocks stopping every few feet to shine their lights around the sides of the cave, not spotting anything. Then Winship asked, "What if the treasure or whatever it is that we are after is submerged below the water's surface?"

"Well let's start above the water line for now. If we have no luck, then we might have to go round up some scuba gear. The snorkel idea seems a little tough. The swells coming through that narrow opening could just smash us against the cave's walls."

"I can dive it without a problem. The water is not very deep at all. It looks like ten to fifteen feet maximum," Winship said as he slipped the mask over his eyes and looked into the water. "But then again, I think that if I were the one hiding something, to possibly come back for, I would put it above water in a drier and more secure area. Under water, the force of the tide is way too strong, plus it would rust or rot any container that you use. I would think it might sweep the container, or whatever remained of it, back out to sea. The sea is a very forceful animal."

They tried to make their way to the back of the cave ever so slowly. The water current was trying to push them forward and then backwards farther and faster than they were comfortable with. They were bobbing up and down in the salt water while the waves crashed into the small opening of the sea cave making it hard to keep their heads above water. They both had managed a gulp or two of the warm salt water making them cough it up. "God, I hate the taste of sea water," Winship said, choking some of it out through his mouth and his nostrils.

Simon guessed that the maximum height above the water line was only about fifteen feet. He wondered, "When the tide was high did it reach the top of the cave? That would not seem possible," he thought.

Nothing stood out as they made their way along the sharp coral walls lining the dark cavern. As they went in deeper light from the caves entrance became less vibrant. A few times when the waves crashed at the entrance it blocked out all the light. Slowly they moved to the back of the cave their hopes were not fading but actually increasing almost like at the end of a race.

With anticipation on both of their minds, the tension and excitement mounted. Every few feet they stopped and shone their flashlights together to make a more powerful beam up and down both sides of the rough walls of the cave and still nothing stood out.

About two thirds of the way to the end of the dark cave, Winship, who was behind Simon, tapped him on his shoulder. "Look over there where I have my beam focused. See that darkened area? It looks like there might be a ledge up there. I can't make it out. It's too dark. Let's hit it with both our lights. It's about ten feet ahead up on your right side. It is the only thing I can see that even resembles a ledge. If you were going to hide something maybe that's where you would place it?"

"I can barely make it out Winship. Hold still. Let's try to get a good light beam on it. Hold your light from that angle. Let's try to get a little closer. Yeah, right there. That does look like a ledge but from this angle I can only see the bottom of it. It's not really protruding out much, maybe six to eight inches and I can't really see how far back it goes from down here."

"It does seem to resemble a ledge doesn't it?" Winship asked.

Simon chuckled, "Well my good friend, this looks like the only place we have seen so far that would even resemble an area to hide something. Well, the only way to know if it is a ledge would be for me to climb up higher. I should be able to manage that easily enough. It will take me a few minutes. I am going to try to scale up there." Slowly Simon maneuvered his way upward, relying on the beam from Winship's light. Simon took his time. Carefully making sure he didn't slip. One wrong move and the slick, sharp coral would shred his skin. Making his way up seemed to actually be much harder than he had anticipated. He inched his way, finding the footing difficult but not impossible. He never knew going up a mere ten feet could be so such an exhausting task. When he finally was able to secure a grip on the top part of the ledge, he stabilized his footing and pulled himself up to peer over the flattened surface. It was quite dark so he pulled out his flashlight and shinned it over the ledge. He was just hoping that nothing would jump out at him and make him slide back down the wall of the cave. He finally managed to get in a position to get a better look and now he could see that the ledge was about three feet deep and possibly about four feet wide. He shined the flashlights beam into the small alcove and was stunned and surprised that there was something there. At first he just looked at the object, not saying a word. His mind was racing, holding the sight into his mind marking it into memory.

"Anything?" Winship asked with baited hope? Anything at all?"

"Winship you're not going to believe this!"

"What? What?" excitedly exclaimed Winship.

"Winship! It's a chest. An old sea trunk that looks like it's been here for a long time."

MONOMOY

As Winship floated in the water below clinging onto the sharp rocks he echoed, "A chest? How big? Is it locked?"

He shined his beam on Simon and watched as he managed to climb upon the ledge. Simon extended his legs off the ledge and began examining the chest from top to bottom side to side with his flashlight. He tried to shift it around on the rough ledge as he told Winship, "Man it's heavy. I am trying to move it but I can't. I think the coral rock underneath is too rough to let me. I'll see if I can slide it around using my legs as there is no way I can lift it."

"How heavy?" replied Winship.

"I don't know exactly, but heavy. Maybe a hundred pounds or more. I mean, I can't really even move it." Simon slid his body in right next to it and was able to actually sit (uncomfortably) on the ledge right beside the chest.

"Can you open it? Is it locked?"

"Let me see if I can slide it around using my legs. I want to see the whole thing. It's got a good amount of sea slime and built up salt on it from the air but it looks to have always remained above the water line. I can't really slide it around and I can't see the back of it either, but I guess it doesn't matter.

"Yes Winship, it's locked but it's an old style padlock. Looks like it's pretty ancient. I would guess well over a hundred years old. It's pretty well rusted. I'm going try to clear off some this corrosion that's formed around the lock itself and see if I can snap it open with my knife. The knife is the satchel. Can you to get it up to me?"

"What do you think is inside of it?"

"Well we are soon going to find out. I mean remember what the old timer said gold and diamonds and with the weight of this box it feels like gold. I really don't know but it's got to be something. Why else would anyone take the time to hide it in this cave? Of course with the whole mystery of the hidden map, it's got to be something valuable. This could either be a bust or a gold mine. Knowing how you found the map, I would bet on the latter! Well hopefully we will know soon. Focus Winship, I am going to need that knife we brought along in the sea bag to pry this lock open. I'm undoing my flashlight rope from my belt and I'll send it down to you. If I roll over on to my front and stretch my arm down towards you, hopefully you will be able to reach it. Just be careful and steady. Don't drop the knife! Make sure you tie the knife securely onto the rope and I will pull it back up and see if I can jimmy this lock open then we can see what we might have here. This is the most exciting thing I can ever remember happening. It makes me feel like I am a kid back in England when we used to do scavenger hunts," Simon added in his excitement.

Winship fished the knife out of the sea bag, tied it onto the rope Simon had lowered down to him. Winship said, "It's ready! Haul it up!" Winship thought to himself, if only his wife Mary were alive so he could share this wonderful story with her of finding hidden treasure in the Caribbean!

Winship was waiting impatiently and kept asking, "Any luck?" Simon who was also filled with anticipation told him, "In a second. Almost there." Simon placed the strong knife blade in between the corroded latch and the lock. He gave it a twist and shouted, "Houston we have lift off! It's open!" Simon methodically cleared off the many years of crusted salt and slime that had adhered to the top of the chest and slowly opened the lid. He sat there for a few moments without saying a word as Winship watched through the beam of his flashlight. After what seemed to be a very long time to Winship, but was really a matter of seconds, Simon shouted out. "WINSHIP - WE ARE RICH! - I Tell ya, - RICH!"

"What's in there Simon?" Winship yelled up.

"Ha ha. You're not going to believe this. It looks like gold bars and coins. Possibly gemstones and I mean there are thousands of the stones like rubies and emeralds. I can't get a good read on them in this poor lighting but it looks like they might be rubies and sapphires. I think after we get this stuff cleaned off and under some good lighting we will be able to access our findings more accurately! I am not really sure of how much stuff is actually in this chest but it's going to take several trips to haul all this out of the cave. I swear it must weigh a couple hundred pounds!"

"Really! You've got to be kidding," Winship howled back. "Okay-okay. Let me think. Okay," said Winship, trying to pull all of his excitement and emotions together. "Alright, I have the water proof sack tied to my waist. I can get it up to you and we can take a small amount to the boat and examine it. How much weight do you think we can manage per trip out of this cave?"

Simon replied in an out of breath and husky voice, "Well as the sack hits the water the buoyancy of the salt water might help us. I'm thinking we can take around twenty pounds a haul. I figure about ten pounds each or so. We have the water proof bag and the canvas beach bag correct?"

"Yes – Yes, I have them both right here." Winship managed to say."

"Alright. Let's calculate this." Simon replied while rubbing his head in disbelief. "If the contents weigh two-hundred plus pounds - it will take around ten to fifteen trips if both of us carry around ten pounds each. I think the best way will be for us to take a small amount in the sea sack and beach bag we have with us now. We will come back in the next low tide around the same time tomorrow and will need to work fast to fight the tide change. Well I don't think this treasure is going anywhere. It's secure so let me take one gold bar, some of the coins and a few of the stones. Tomorrow we will return and make as many hauls that we can in the morning and maybe a few more in the late afternoon. With the both of us and some ingenious thinking of a way to float some of it out, we should be able to empty the whole chest by late tomorrow. We just don't want to be spotted so let's stay cautious and focused, as it will take us a good fifteen minutes to get out of the cave. Then we have to get from the cave's opening to where we can climb out of the water and back onto the shore. It is still another short walk to the dinghy. I mean if by chance anyone spots us on this rough shore line, which I doubt will happen, it's going to seem awfully strange to them."

SURFSIDE

By early evening, after returning to the Karen-Marie, Simon had repositioned the boat a good half mile away from the cave's entrance in another small secluded bay just in case any other boats came in the area. Why rouse any suspicion?

They had laid everything out below deck on the table and polished the stones and coins as best they could with what they had to use on the boat.

Simon and Winship starred at the gold bar and started to dream. "How much do you think we are looking at?" Winship finally said, coming out of his clouded mind.

"Well after we get everything on board we can try and make some sort of guess at an estimate of the value but it will be a pretty rough estimate."

Winship pulled the cork on a bottle of Pouilly Fuisse to celebrate their findings. "I think the best idea would be to make an inventory of what we find as we unload our haul as we go along," Winship announced. Simon went below and grabbed his note book. They decided to make certain categories of the treasure; stones- coins - gold - quartz pieces. After they had finished with the inventory, Simon casted off the back of the Karen-Marie in hopes of catching another fish. In what seemed like minutes, Winship was filleting their catch, a beautiful yellow tail snapper. Winship prepped and prepared it the same way as the night before along with some whole baking potatoes wrapped in foil. They took the dinghy to shore, laid a fire, and kept giggling between themselves. They finished up what Simon declared was another masterpiece of a meal and headed back to the boat where they resurveyed their findings, put them in a satchel underneath the bench in the galley and headed off for bed.

The next day, as planned, they made their haul slowly but surely out of the cave onto the dry sand of the beach. They did not want to leave any of the treasure on the beach while they made another haul just in case, while they happened to be inside the cave, a passing boat might see their dinghy and come ashore to say hello. They had not run into any other boats since mooring off Foul Cay but they wanted to be cautious.

Their plan was when they left the boat each of them would carry three sacks with them ashore. Two smaller ones for hauling the goods out of the sea cave. Then they could transfer into the larger one. Each time they would then head back to the Karen-Marie and place them underneath the bench in the galley.

They took a total of ten satchels out of the cave by noon - two per trip. It was slow going but they were full of energy. Each satchel from the cave weighed between ten to fifteen pounds.

Simon placed the larger satchels on the floor of the dinghy and covered it with a couple of towels and some netting.

In the cave Simon sat on the ledge lowering each of the filled smaller satchels, one at a time, down to Winship via a secured tied rope. God forbid if one broke off and scattered its contents into the ocean.

Then Simon climbed down and they made their way out of the cavern, headed to the shore and transferred the jewels onto the dinghy, then paddled out to the Karen-Marie putting everything below deck. They managed to get twelve total, of the larger satchels, out in the afternoon for a total of twenty-four small repacked satchels. The estimated guess was a total weight of what they figured was close to three hundred pounds, or possibly more, of precious stones, gold and coin.

They had a few difficult moments as the tide flowed in and out but their decision was to just go as long as they could, low tide or not. They agreed not to take any serious life threatening risks.

They completed their task by 4:30 in the afternoon. Back on board they reviewed their huge piles of jewels, gold and the doubloons and did an inventory. Both agreeing, at that point, their best bet was to clean it all before pulling anchor, which would take them through the better part of the next morning.

"What do you think the value of all this is?" asked Winship.

Simon took an educated rough guess and said, "I am not really sure but if it's really precious cargo, maybe twenty-five million dollars plus or minus a couple of million. It could be higher, could be lower, but we need to re-do the inventory now that everything is on board and it's going to take a while. We will need to re-sort the piles like; coins – jewels - gold bars - miscellaneous stones, like all those large quartzes."

"There seems to be a thousand stones," Simon expressed. "We can just clean and separate them by color. When we sail back into Georgetown, we need to act casually. Like nothing is going on and I mean, very casual, no one has any clue what we have been up to."

"Got that right," Winship replied. "It's not going to be easy. As nervous as I am just thinking about docking there and trying to act normal."

"Relax old man. No one has a clue about the map, the cave, or our expedition."

"Why don't you go and catch us some dinner. By the way, snapper is my first choice!" Winship said as his mouth started to water. "I will start cleaning some of this right now. Why not get a start on the project."

"Let's go over our cover story this evening before our return tomorrow. Something plausible and easy-like two guys coming back from a fun island hopping adventure."

"Let's dock there for the night and we can check into Phillipe's again. Let's follow our old routine - dinner at the Cracked Conch and a nightcap at the bar with Kenny. We will go to the chandlery in Georgetown. Again, just act natural. Try not to raise any suspicion. We will need to purchase a few sailor's satchels to put this stuff in and then we will quietly cast off in two days, stop in Bimini, then head to Miami."

"Miami?" asked Winship. "Don't you mean Ft. Lauderdale?"

"No Miami. We want to unload this prior to returning the boat. We don't want some nosy owner or dock master at Pier 66 asking questions about what are we hauling off. When we get to Miami, we take a slip for a couple nights and plot out removal of said items. Best bet would be we take a rental car up to our hotel and unload it. No one will think anything of hauling stuff into a hotel room."

"I can drive back to Miami with the rental car the next day. Then I will cruise up to Ft. Lauderdale and return the Karen-Marie to the dock master and hop off like it was a fun trip. You can stay at the hotel and keep an eye on the loot. That way there will be no questions of what we were hauling off the boat. If they are watching me at Pier 66, I'll just be unloading the gear we boarded with. By then we will have all of treasure loaded into our rooms. We take it straight through the lobby and avoid the marina until I return to pick up the Karen-Marie. You will also want to keep the 'Do not Disturb' sign on both of our rooms. Don't need any maids accidently finding our haul."

"I am thinking we can try to cash in a gold bar or two in the Miami area, just to see the response we get from a dealer. We will have the rental car to get us around," Winship thought.

"You know Simon, even if we find a few sturdier bags to move this stuff around in, I'm not sure if it's at all feasible to possibly ship some of this back to the island. I think our best bet might be for us to take a train up to Boston and rent another car. We could ferry the car and the treasure to the island. That way it's locked safe in the trunk away from prying eyes. It would look pretty strange hopping on the ferry with all the heavy bags."

Simon agreed, "There is no way we are flying with all this. It must weight close to three-hundred pounds and we are not letting it out of our sight."

"I can also contact my travel agent Shelia when we are back on the island and have her rebook your ticket out of Boston when we figure out our dates. No muss, no fuss, no questions. What do you think Simon?"

"That sounds like a pretty good plan. I like the way you think Winship!"

They sailed into Georgetown around four in the afternoon the following day under a remarkable clear sky. Winship looked up and Mr. Hawkins was soaring around. "He's keeping watch over us," Winship thought to himself. He pointed the bird out to Simon who said, "We owe Mr. Hawkins a toast tonight over dinner."

During their trip back they rehearsed their story that they had come up with and repeated it out loud several times. "We headed out to several cays, casted off our lines early every morning, managed to trap some lobsters and grilled on the beach. We were both in bed by 8:00p.m. nightly. Falling asleep under the sweet Caribbean sky with the soft breezes."

When they pulled into the Georgetown Marina's settlement, it was very quiet. Making small chat with the harbormaster, Mr. Hayes, telling him they loved their adventure and hoped to repeat it yearly. They were going to get two cottages at Phillipe's and enjoy a long hot shower, freshen up and have dinner at the Cracked Conch.

Right then was when the old timer Simon had met on the dock approached them and said, "Find any treasure?"

Winship stiffened up and looked at Simon. Mr. Hayes gave them a very strange look and said, "You guys are here on a treasure hunt? I thought you were just here for some fishing?"

Simon gave out a nervous laugh and said, "No. I was joking the morning before we sailed out of the marina with this gentleman here. I was saying maybe we will discover some treasure while snorkeling. It didn't happen but we found some great conch shells and two lovely island girls!" The old timer let out a laugh and so did the harbormaster and they all parted ways. "Calm down Winship," Simon mentioned. "All is good, just relax."

After a nice long shower both men went into the ships store and took their time browsing at what the store offered. Looking over the different satchels, they quietly bought two along with two smaller duffel bags and tucked them underneath their arms. What they did not notice was the harbormaster watching them intently from outside the window. John Hayes thought that was odd. "Why did they need two matching satchels and duffel bags?"

That night over a dinner of jerk chicken, they toasted Mr. Hawkins with their beers at the Cracked Conch. Mr. Hayes approached their table and sat down like they were the best of friends and said, "You know, it's customary to buy the local official a drink when visitors come ashore." "Glad to," replied Simon. "Actually, let's have a whole round of drinks."

Mr. Hayes yelled over his shoulder, "Hey Kenny, grab me a tequila and a beer compliments of my new best friends!" and let out a laugh.

"Right away mon," Kenny replied.

Simon had sailed into many ports so he was used to scenes like this but Winship wasn't. A slight wink from Simon put Winship at ease.

"So I saw you two hanging around the ships store after you returned - buying a couple of satchels. Going to fill it with all the treasure you found?"

Winship started to freeze up and shot a glance over to Simon. He almost fell out of his chair when Mr. Hayes said that. Simon did not miss a beat and said, "Well John, we only wish! They're gifts. One for the Nantucket harbormaster and the other is for Winship's fishing partner back on Nantucket, Scott Whitlock. The bags are both stamped with Georgetown Exumas. Makes a great gift, don't you think? Same with the other two bags. They're for friends back home in Dartmouth."

"Did you say Nantucket? I forgot you told me that last week."

"Yes, Winship resides there. Has a beautiful old home on the island. Why have you been there?"

"No. Never but Kenny, our bartender, has. He worked up there last season in a restaurant's kitchen. Hey Kenny, get over here! One of these guys is from Nantucket!"

"Yea Mon, be over in a second."

"Kenny this is Simon and Winship."

"Hi. Kenny Houghton," he introduced himself and he reached out to give Simon and Winship a warm handshake flashing his bright smile. "I remember you guy's - you were here last week."

"Yes and Winship lives on Nantucket," Simon mentioned trying to change the subject of the satchels.

"Cool mon. I was there last June through September. Nice island. The weather was a little cold for me in September though."

"But a beautiful place. How did you ever end up on Nantucket?" Winship inquired.

"Well I met these people who came down to Jamaica. I am from Montego Bay and they were staying where I worked at Rose Hall. They were telling me about the island. Said there's a place called The Summer House Inn and they are always looking for seasonal help. I gave them my mailing address and a month later I got a letter from the manager saying they would sponsor me a round trip ticket and a place to live if I wanted to come for the season. It was a chance to travel, make and save some money so I took the job. I would have returned again this season. My mom was happy, at one point, so I took the job but she also was quite sad that I was so far away from my dad. He's not doing too well so now I am here working. Mr. Hayes has rented me a nice room about a five-minute walk from here and get I go home to Montego Bay every couple months. It's a much easier to take a plane from this island to Jamaica. So far the job here is working our pretty well!"

"Well, we're glad it worked out for you here. If you ever get back my way, I am in the phone book. Winship Cate on Wauwinet Road."

They made small talk for a while and the bead of sweat that had formed around Winship's neck, after their conversation about the satchels, seemed to slowly fade away. John rose to leave them. He said, "What time are you headed out tomorrow? It's is supposed to be fair seas all week. Where are you headed?"

"We are going back to Ft. Lauderdale. I have to be back in England in a short time."

"Well bon voyage and I hope your friends enjoy the gifts!"

NOBADEER

The next morning, after a quick coffee on Winship's porch, they went back to the Karen-Marie, boarded and went below deck and made sure their stash was undisturbed. It was just as they had left it under one of the galley's bench seats. Winship had laid all sorts of things on top of it just in case someone started to snoop around. Simon made sure he locked the entry door of the vessel before going out last night.

They loaded their new supplies on board before casting off. Winship felt a sigh of relief as he watched the island fade away, heading toward the open sea. "I will prepare breakfast in the galley as we sail out. I want to get out of here sooner than later."

"I hear ya," Simon responded.

As they headed out to sea, Mr. Hawkins landed on the bow of the Karen-Marie, staying aboard for a good twenty minutes before looking back at Simon and Winship. He let out a large squawk and flew off almost like saying, "Good-bye my friends. Safe passage." Both men waved to Mr. Hawkins as he flew away circling the boat for several minutes.

The trip to Bimini was, as they say, smooth sailing all the way. They spent the night on the island and departed early the next morning. By the early afternoon, everything was stashed into the two new satchels and duffel bags and made it to Miami without any glitches.

Simon secured the boat and reviewed their plans they had discussed the evening prior. The plan was to rent a car in the morning and take the loot to the hotel, but for tonight they would not leave the boat unattended while in Miami - too big of a city area for them to feel comfortable leaving their treasure. Once they have all of the treasure safely in the hotel, they can grab a gold bar or two and try to find a buyer. Simon went out to grab something simple at the grocery store for dinner to have on the deck. He found a local directory at a pay phone near the entrance of the grocery store and wrote down several addresses and phone numbers for local gold dealers. He bought a nice roasted chicken in the deli area of the store and picked up some baked beans and slaw before heading back to the Karen-Marie, happy with his purchases.

After dinner the two of them settled in for a quiet night perusing Simon's list together and decided on Mikes Gold and Coins. Gold was going for $139 an ounce and the bars, they figured, were roughly 100 oz. So nothing less than $12,500 was acceptable for a cash, no paperwork deal. At that point they both decided to get some sleep. Tomorrow will be a very busy day.

The two of them were up with the birds early the next day and enjoyed their coffee out on the deck before locking up the boat and heading off to pick up their rental car. The morning went smoothly. By the early afternoon they managed to move all of their stash into the safe-haven of the hotel room. The plan was going perfectly. Simon grabbed a few of the gold bars to take to Mike's shop.

When they arrived out front of the gold and coin shop, Simon said, "Let me go in alone. I am British so they will think it's a practice we do all the time. We are a mystery to them - us Brits."

He met Mike the owner himself. After small talk he asked Mike, "How much paperwork is involved in cashing gold bars in?"

Mike said, "Okay, there are two ways to handle it. One is highest price with paperwork and identification or a lower cash on the spot transaction without it."

"Well." Simon said, "I wouldn't want my ex-wife to find out about this, if you know what I mean?"

"Certainly," Mike replied. "I totally understand discretion in this matter."

"May we go somewhere more private?" Simon Inquired.

As they went into Mike's office and shut the door, Simon pulled out one gold bar. Mike let out a whistle and said, "Where did you get this baby?" pulling a gold testing kit out of the drawer. Simon replied, "No questions please. Let's just say I have been saving it for a rainy day!"

A short time later, Simon was back in the car driving away with $12,750 dollars' cash in his pocket. "Winship we are going to unload some of this while we are here but I don't want to rush it. One good thing is Mike, the owner, said he would be glad to accept more if I was willing to sell. Which is good but we need to air on the word of caution. I will call him and let him know I have two more bars, same deal, and we can unload maybe ten of these bars at a few different shops. That will bring us a total of about \$120,000- \$130,000." Winship blew out a big breath. "We have about sixty pounds total of the bars. Roughly the gold alone calculates out to a heck of a lot of cash!"

"I think I can get a good amount of this moved. Remember slowly but surely is a good motto to follow. So let's not unload too much with one dealer."

After two days they had close to \$120,000 in cash.

"Now that should lighten our suitcases for our travels," Winship said with a smile.

"Maybe it would be a good time to change hotel rooms. I think we should head up to Ft. Lauderdale tomorrow. We can stay in the Marriott Hotel that we stayed in before we started this adventure."

"You know Winship, I agree. We can drive up tomorrow and move everything into our new hotel. I'll turn around and return the car, jump on the Karen-Marie and see you back there in a day."

They headed back to the hotel and took a break for the day. Winship handed an envelope to Simon, "Here's your share of the cash."

"Winship I will accept this but it ends here. It was a great adventure but the rest of the money you can get for the stones and doubloons and gold is all yours."

"Well we will see about that," Winship replied. "I would have never been able to have done this trip or found the treasure without your help!"

The next morning Simon unloaded the last gold bar for a sum of \$13,500 without a hitch. They moved out of the hotel in Miami and drove up to Fort Lauderdale and checked in, taking two rooms. Simon and Winship loaded everything on a luggage cart and moved the bags of treasure into Winship's room. After they finished, Simon hopped back into the car and said, "See you here around noon tomorrow. Find a nice place for lunch. You're buying!"

SQUAM

Simon arrived back at the hotel a few minutes before noon the next day. He called Winship's room and said, "Where we going for lunch?"

Winship said that the front desk had recommended a place called Fishtails. It was located right on the strip across from the beach. They took a taxi to the restaurant. Before leaving the hotel, Winship placed a 'Do Not Disturb' sign on his door. He had also made Simon's bed look like it had been slept in the night before so it would not raise any suspicion of it not being used when the maids came in to clean it that morning.

After a very long leisurely lunch, on the outside terrace facing the ocean, which consisted of a bottle of Puligny Montrachet followed by a bottle of Red Burgundy with oysters on the half shell, crab cakes, and grilled chicken with wild mushrooms, Winship again brought up the fact of Simon's commission. Simon finally and reluctantly accepted his generous offer and they let it rest.

The next day they boarded the Amtrak train that would take them over a three day trip up the coast to Boston. They had arranged two private sleeper cars and stored the treasure under each of their bunks. Upon arrival into Boston, they checked into the Lenox Hotel on Boylston Street. Simon went with Winship to a few antique dealers to see if they could unload some of the doubloons where the - no questions asked - rule was put into effect by Simon.

Together they managed to sell a total of thirty-five of the old coins for a total of seven thousand dollars. The dealer was thrilled with the purchase and agreed to the - no questions asked - rule. The dealer whose name was Robert Romanos, was quite knowledgeable on the subject of old coins. He knew the doubloons were of Spanish decent and said, "If you have more I would be happy to purchase them." Mr. Romanos mentioned that the items were in near perfect condition even remarking that he had never seen coins in such fine condition.

The next day, Winship drove with Simon in the rented car to Hyannis where they drove onto the boat ferry for the three hour ride to Nantucket.

Winship was glad to be back home and no one was more pleased than Marshmallow. Simon unpacked and said he would love to spend a few days on the island, which thrilled Winship. He really enjoyed having Simon around.

Winship telephoned Louise to let her know he had arrived back safely. She told Winship, "I have kept the place spic and span. I did place some cut flowers in a vase on the table along with some groceries and lunch meats in the ice box." She also stated that Macy had kept the house in very neat order. Louise had managed to fill him in on all the latest useless gossip that he missed while gone on his trip. And she was firing off questions one after another about his trip. Winship just listened to them making small talk and told her that he would tell her and Bill all about the trip over dinner next week.

He picked up the pile of mail that had accumulated and was going through the letters and magazines sorting them in two piles when he came across a letter from a Mr. Jurgelas of Portsmouth New Hampshire. It read:

Dear Mr. Cate

In regard to your inquiry of a Ms. Caroline Cook, I searched our town records and believe I found the legal documents of a home she resided in on Oceanside Avenue. It looks like she was the daughter of Mrs. Katherine Cook of the same address. It seems her father had passed on when she was in her teens. There are some references to an uncle named Jefferson Cook, who had questionable dealings in the smuggling world, sailing the islands of the Caribbean but that's about all we can locate on Ms. Cook.

Sincerely
Mr. Edward Jurgelas, Town Historian
Portsmouth, New Hampshire

After reading that he set the rest of the mail aside and showed the letter to Simon. "Well there's our connection to the map!"

67

Winship enjoyed getting back to his routine and had hoped to plan a lunch so he could introduce his friends to Simon. He made a short list; Donna – Randy – Shelia – Robbie – Louise – Bill – Macy - Simon and himself. He would call everyone tomorrow and see if they were free and book a lunch at the Opera House.

He quickly settled in for the night and started to wonder where they could stash all the stones from Louise's prying eyes. He had to find a place that she would never think of cleaning. In the trunk of the car? Up in the attic, in his fishing bungalow? The shed? Above the garage? Then it came to him. The coal chute in the basement. He had an old lock on it for safety reasons so no child could ever climb inside of it. He mentioned this to Simon the next morning. "Let's go check it out," Simon replied.

Winship knew the key to it was still hanging next to the oil furnace. He had not ever unlocked it since the day he put the pad lock on it. They went downstairs and retrieved the key. The lock opened smoothly. He lifted the heavy black steel hatch door, slid the safety pin in place to keep it open and thought with a little cleaning they could get all the black soot from the old coal cleaned out. Winship could lock it shut and no one would be the wiser, especially Louise, who seemed to know about everything in his home. He and Simon had to make sure they did not leave a trail of the dirty coal dust as they cleaned the chute out. It will be at least a week or so before Louise will stop by to do a touch up on the house.

The next morning Winship found an old shop-vac style of vacuum that he hardly ever used anymore, unlocked the black steel cover and hoisted it up as high as it would allow and put the pin into it so it would not slam shut.

Plugging in the shop-vac, Simon proceeded to vacuum out every square inch of the small coal box. The top part of the shaft from the outside had been sealed shut many years ago and the bottom was locked for safety reasons. They then soaked several rags and washed it out about as well as they could reaching inside including the walls. The chute was left open to be sure it would dry out overnight.

The next morning Simon re-vacuumed it one more time. Winship took a mop and did the best he could by soaking it in bleach water and pushing it inside to give it the best swab of the mop that could be managed. By leaving the steel plate open, at the end of the day it was dry as a bone.

The two of them went upstairs and retrieved the satchels, one by one, from the trunk of Winship's car that was parked in the garage and brought all of it to the basement. They placed all the stones inside double lined clear gallon sized freezer storage bags, which were good for their strength. All of the stones were neatly wrapped now including the dull quartz looking pieces or what they thought were quartz to the naked eye. This also included a few large packets of manila envelopes for the gold doubloons, which they also encased in the gallon freezer bags.

Each piece still needed to be cleaned properly. Winship did research at the library and found that a light dish detergent and a cotton cloth were the way to go at it for best results. While at the grocery store purchasing the products, Winship ran into David McCoy. He mentioned to Simon, "This is all I need right now." When David spotted the items in the carry basket he quickly started asking questions. "What you buying there Winship? You doing some cleaning around the house? Where have you been? I have not seen you in a while. Someone said you went on a trip to the Caribbean and by the looks of your tan I say they were right. What happened, the insurance money kick in? Did you ever sell your car?"

"No David. The car is not for sale and my friend Simon and I are just getting a few items for the pantry in the house."

"So where did you go in the Caribbean? Meet any rich widows?"

"Nice talking to you David but we have some other errands to finish up."

"Where you headed to? I have nothing on my schedule let me just check out and put my groceries in my car I can join you."

"Hi David - I'm Simon. Nice to meet you." He put his hand out to shake it. When David grasped his hand, Simon clenched it around his and squeezed so hard David almost collapsed onto the floor. "Sorry mate but we are on a mission here and then we are off to see a friend of Winship's." The next words out of David's mouth was, "Who you going to see?" With that they just walked away saying, "Catch you at a later date!" Winship could not help but start laughing as they did.

Simon and Winship returned back to the house and brought up one satchel at a time from the coal chute and started cleaning the stones and coins. It took time but they figured the best idea was fill a bucket with hot water, add a drop or two of dish soap let them soak for a while. The gemstones came clean with minimal effort. Within six hours the task was complete and - wow - did those stones really begin to sparkle.

One by one, the satchels were placed upon a small floor rug inside the chute. All the while Marshmallow kept jumping in and out thinking this was another fun place to explore and play. Before the chute was locked, Winship placed the cash, which he had secured in bundles with rubber bands inside some clear plastic gallon zip lock bags, on a shelf above the opening of the metal chute and slipped the key back onto the hook by the furnace. Both of them looked around the area to see if there was any trace of their cleanup efforts and breathed a little easier.

That night Winship rested the best he had in a couple of weeks but again sleep came slowly. He was pondering in his mind what to do about the stones. "What were their value? How would he move them?"

The next morning, he and Simon went to the Athenaeum and researched precious stones, rubies, sapphires, emeralds, and the numerous large cut quartz which to him seemed like worthless junk.

They learned that emeralds were quite a soft stone and a good quality ruby could be quite valuable.

Winship thought that he might want take a few pieces down to Texeria's Jewelry Store but how could he explain these gems to Marty, the owner, or where he came across the stones. Marty knew Winship and his wife Mary for over twenty years and knew most of Mary's jewelry collection.

Then it came to him. He would send Simon to the store. No one knew who he was and Simon could prepare himself for any questions that might arise. What they both really wanted to know was the value of some of the precious stones they had in their possession. They had already managed to clear a lot of cash from the gold bars and another $7,000 from the coins but Simon thought that the real money was in the countless number of the gemstones. Still that idea did not pan out. Simon explained that this is a small island with lots of gossip. "Let's keep all questions for a larger market like Boston, Providence or New York."

Finally, Winship made his mind up that they should head to Boston next week and take a few stones with him there. They both could spend a few days searching out ideas for moving some of the pieces and also go back and see if Mr. Romanos was interested in acquiring more coins, then Simon could fly back home to England from there.

They made the trip back up to Boston. The same desk clerk who had checked them in the week prior was on duty at the Lenox Hotel and booked them two nights stay giving them both upgraded rooms.

Using the phone book in his desk, Winship jotted down three places all with in a close proximity to the hotel. Simon went off to meet with Mr. Romanos who was quite pleased to see him again. Winship's first appointment was with Caselli Fine Stones on Newbury Street who had been in business over thirty years and were a family run company.

Calling and making his appointment earlier that morning he put it under the name Getter as he did not feel comfortable giving out too much personal information at this time so early in the game.

He arrived at 11:00a.m. and was greeted by JoAnn who introduced herself as Mr. Caselli's wife. She had buzzed him in through the glass door and offered him some coffee. Winship declined, instead accepted a glass of water that was also offered to him. "So what can I do for you Mr. Getter?" Nick Caselli asked.

"Well it's of a delicate matter and I am going to seek out a few appraisals before deciding on any course of action."

"Smart move," Nick replied. "I can only assure you we have been in business for over thirty years and are considered top of the line with the better business bureau." Winship carefully pulled out a small paper bag that the stones were in. He had put them inside of a plastic baggie which he had wrapped in tissue paper. The first stone that Nick selected was a ruby. He looked at it through a gemologist loop and it took him by surprise. He let out a small whistle and said, "This stone is flawless. I can't remember seeing such a pretty stone. It's got to be at least twelve carats. Almost unheard of these days. May I ask where you got this stone from?"

"At this point I am not at liberty to say," replied Winship.

"Did you bring others?"

"Yes. I have what I believe is an emerald, not quite as large but still significant in size."

Again the reaction from Mr. Caselli after looking at it through his eye loop was, "Wow!"

Winship then pulled out another large stone around twelve carats of sparkling sapphire. At this point Nick was astonished. "These stones are flawless. Unprecedented I would have to say." Winship then removed the larger heavy piece of quartz out of his pocket and figured the party was over for the shiny perfect stones but he thought why not find something out about it. Mr. Caselli turned it over in his hand a few times.

His wife looked at Winship, then at Nick and back to Winship and asked Nick, "Is that what I think it is?"

Winship looked puzzled and Nick said, "We will know in a minute. Close to sixty seconds later Nick looked up asked, "Do you know what this stone is Mr. Getter?"

71

"Well not really I was hoping you could tell me."

"What you have here is an uncut diamond. It's in the rough. Hence the term, a diamond in the rough. This has got to be at least fifteen carats. In the hands of the right diamond cutter, the value of this could exceed $300,000 easily. If it is declared flawless it could be up to half a million dollars. I do have to ask you Mr. Getter, are any of these pieces stolen?"

"No way," replied Winship. "They are mine and I was just wondering what I should expect if was ever to part with them?"

"Well they are almost certainly museum quality pieces and worth quite a lot of money if put in the right hands. Whatever you decide to do with them be extremely cautious as there are many less than scrupulous dealers out there who will cheat you rather quickly. If you and I do business I am one hundred percent up front in all my dealings and can give you many upstanding references."

"Winship left the Caselli's store and went over to another - so called -diamond expert just four blocks away. He had to go up two flights of stairs to a small dingy office where he was greeted by a very sloppy looking secretary who was chewing gum and eating, what looked like, the remains of a bagel.

She said, "Wait here." He was then greeted by a man who looked like he had slept in his clothes and smelled of alcohol, dirty fingernails and unpolished shoes. "Hi. Jake's the name. Diamonds are the game," he said after slapping Winship on the back.

Winship said in a rushed voice," I am sorry I was looking for an insurance office," and quickly departed.

The third appointment, which he was early for, was on Beacon Hill. A small store front run by a Jewish lady named Maude. Again Winship introduced himself as Michael Getter. "Where you from sweetie?" Maude cried out as she pinched his cheek.

"Well...," he started to think not expecting the question. "I am from the Plymouth area."

Maude straightened her dress out as she said, "How did you hear about us?"

Winship thought for another moment and said, "I met a guy named Bernie a few weeks ago and he recommended you to me."

"Oh Berrnieee," Maude said without breaking stride in her patter. "He's such a nice boy! So what can I do for ya Hun? Need a diamond? Getting hitched? Who's the lucky girl? She will be so pleased with what I can offer you. What we talking about two or three carats? Hey! Marsha! Bring out the two and a half to three and a half carat diamond tray would ya?"

Within a minute Maude had pushed Winship into a seat and was picking up all sorts of rings. "Look at that sparkle. You know hunny, no one beats our prices. We have very low overhead with my direct diamond buying, right from the source, we cut out the middle man."

After about five minutes of Maude constantly babbling on and on Winship said, "I think it would be best if I brought the little woman in as she's going to be wearing it."

"Sure thing hunny," Maude replied. "What's the little ladies name?"

At first he almost said Mary, his deceased wife's name, but he could not bear to use her name in front of such an over bearing woman so he said Daphne.

"Oh how sweet. Bring her in and we can make you a really special deal. And I give a bigger discount to cash customers. Here's my card! See you soon hunny!"

Winship was soon realizing what Mr. Caselli was referring to by low-lifers in the jewelry trade. He went back to the Lenox Hotel, asked the concierge if they could get him the number for the Harry Winston Diamond Company in Manhattan. A few minutes later the concierge brought an envelope to Winship's room with the number neatly written on the Lenox Hotel's personal stationary.

Winship promptly dialed the number and inquired about a possible meeting to evaluate his diamond. Unfortunately, Winship was in Boston and it would take him better part of the next day to arrange travel to New York.

The lady on the other end of the line said, "We have an office in the Prudential Building on Boylston Street."

"That's a block away," Winship told the lady. She gave him the direct number and he again placed another call, this time to a Mr. Thomas Sollas. He was put through to Mr. Sollas within minutes. He explained his story about wanting to seek out the fair value of a diamond and wanted to know if a meeting was possible. Of course using the name Michael Getter, he was fortunate to book a 3:00p.m. meeting and went out in search of lunch.

After a quick snack Winship went back to the hotel, left a note for Simon with the front desk clerk reading, **'Meet me in the lobby 6:00p.m.'** He went up to his room looking at the rough diamond that was wrapped in tissue and put it back in his pocket and set off for his meeting with Mr. Sollas.

He arrived promptly at three and was shown into a large, very fancy office. Before Winship sat down he produced the rough diamond and handed it to Mr. Sollas.

"WOW," was Mr. Sollas's first reaction. "This is a pure uncut diamond. This must be at least ten or twelve carats."

Winship trying not to show too much emotion asked, "What would be the value of such a stone?"

"Well it depends on the grading and the final cut. Most likely it would be cut into three or four possibly five stones. We have our own diamond cutter that we use in New York but the value? It could range anywhere from $200,000 to $350,000." Mr. Sollas never mentioned the fact that it could possibly bring in more revenue if the stone was a VS, VVS, or VS1.

Winship did not say much but asked a few questions about their percentage if they were to resell the cut stones. Mr. Sollas quickly pointed out that they were considered one of the highest quality diamond dealers in the world and they had a higher percentage rate due to the numerous high end advertising and the outsourcing they used but their stones moved quickly and to some of the finest people in the world, kings, queens, royal families, sheiks, Hollywood stars, the list goes on and on.

Winship thanked him for his time. He enjoyed what he learned but thought to himself, "I think if I get a one or two of these diamonds spiffed up it might give me more answers on the value. I will start with Mr. Caselli and see where it leads."

That night Simon and Winship met in the lobby and continued on to the Prudential Center to a restaurant named Top of Hub. They were seated at a beautiful window table with a fantastic view of Boston Harbor. The maître'd, Mr. Carl Taylor, brought over the menus and a wine list. "May I offer you something to drink?" he asked.

"I think we would like a bottle of white and a bottle of red. We are staying right around the corner at the Lenox so we are not driving. We are not in any rush."

"Well the table is yours for the night. Any specific type of white and red?"

"Well we like white Burgundy."

"I have a nice Pouilly-Fuisse priced around twenty-five dollars."

"Do you have something a few notches above that?"

"Yes. We have a few Chablis listings."

"Okay, let me peruse the list. Don't go far. It won't take me but a few moments to select one."

Carl saw that the wine list closed so he went back to the table. "We would like the Criots-Batard-Montrachet."

Carl's face lit up at the mention of that. A two hundred twenty-five-dollar bottle sale. "Yes!" he thought to himself, as he receives a ten percent commission on all wine sales. Simon also had his eyes wide open as he knew French Burgundies quite well and the value of them. He asked, "Winship are you sure about that?"

"Quite," he mentioned. Carl returned with an ice bucket and two crystal glasses. The staff was hovering around in the background. He presented the bottle to Winship, who said, "Please have my guest try it."

"Louis Latour, 1966. A remarkable vintage. All our Burgundy wines are personally selected by the owner and Bob Rubin of Ruby Wines and we have a temperature controlled wine storage cellar."

After Simon approved the wine, Winship asked Carl, "Please bring us some bread so we don't drink it on an empty stomach and I will need a few minutes more to select the red wine."

Winship began to relay the story about his day with the jewelry shops and Mr. Caselli. He explained that the quartz pieces are not quartz. Looking around to make sure that they were not being overheard, he lowered his voice and told Simon they are raw uncut diamonds, or a diamond in the rough. The value, low end, was around two hundred fifty thousand and possibly as high as five hundred thousand. Now it was Simon's time to react. He asked loudly, "How much?"

Winship lifted his hands and said, "Calm down. I am not joking with you."

"You have got to be kidding!"

"No – No, I am not," Winship replied snidely. "I also went to Harry Winston, the high end diamond company. They have an office right here in this building and they more or less told the same thing."

"You know how many of those we have?" Simon asked. "Like fifty of them! If you meet that number on the low side, that's around twenty million dollars plus or minus a few million here or there! That's unbelievable."

"So you see, my good man. We can afford the wine and then some. And one more thing Simon, no if's and's or but's, you're getting your share of the money."

Carl retuned to the table and asked if they had made a selection for the red wine.

"Yes. We will have the 1961 Chateau Petrus." Carl almost fainted at the table and replied, "Right away sir."

Simon chuckled, "You made his day. We could probably buy the Chateau after we cash all the stones in!"

Now the whole restaurant was buzzing as the word leaked out about the expensive wines they had ordered. Their server, Elizabeth Kochor, approached the table all flustered and nervous. She recited the specials without a hitch. They ordered a caesar salad made tableside and chateaubriand for two, which when it arrived, the chef and his assistant from the kitchen, carved it personally. They decided on bananas flambé for dessert.

The next day Winship telephoned Mr. Caselli's office. His wife JoAnn answered in such a cheerful voice it brought a smile to Winship's face.

"Hello Mrs. Caselli. It's Michael Getter - I was in yesterday?"

"Oh yes Mr. Getter. It was a sincere pleasure meeting you yesterday. What can I do for you?"

"Well I thought about your offer. I am in town for one more day before I head out and I think I would like to do some business with you and your husband. Do you think we could get together and draw up some sort of a contract? I don't feel like carrying these stones all over Timbuktu!"

"Let's see, - today is actually kind of quiet so you give us the time frame and we will be here."

"Well I am staying at the Lenox so I can come by anytime"

"No time like the preset," JoAnn replied.

"Okay, see you in fifteen minutes!"

Simon wanted to join Winship on the trip to meet the Caselli's. Nick had a standard contract all laid out and explained everything to Winship. He then told Nick and JoAnn his real name and that he resided on Nantucket.

Nick explained that if he wanted to keep the account under a different name it was not a problem as many people use a corporation or fictitious name for dealing in large cash amounts. Nick also told him that they used a Jewish diamond cutter that had been employed in the past with Harry Winston but he was now semi-retired and deals on a smaller work schedule. Nick also took Winship and Simon through his security features and showed them his double steel safe called, a safe within a safe, and said that they have never encountered a problem with any type of theft or armed robbery. They kept a pretty low profile.

Right after Winship and Simon left, JoAnn took the signed contract, which she had given a copy to Winship, and the inventory sheet and locked it away. Her inventory was done in such a hand written code that if anyone ever discovered it, it would be undecipherable. Then she took the colored stones and locked them away as well. Nick took the rough diamond, triple bagged it, and placed it inside an old half-filled coffee pot that was not on. A place he always told JoAnn was the best security system.

Winship had breached the subject of gold before they had departed. Nick mentioned that it's about as solid of an investment as one can have these days or in any financial market. Winship produced one of the 100-ounce gold bars and placed it in front of Nick. He picked it up, examined it closely, scratched the outer edge of three different points and again looked at it turning it over in his hands. He did not say anything for a moment or two. JoAnn watched silently off to the side. "Okay," Nick asked, "can you tell me where you got this from?"

"Sorry but that's all confidential," Winship replied, "except for the fact it's not stolen."

"Well it is a hundred percent gold," Nick replied. "It's well - how do I say it? This is a style of rustic, older, type of gold not from a mint. Actually I don't know how to phrase it but it's quality gold. Do you have more of these bars?"

"Yes I do. About forty of them," replied Winship.

"Forty? You have got to be kidding. That's worth a small fortune and untraceable if melted and remolded."

"Let's have another meeting sooner than later," Winship said. "I have to think about this move."

"It's a good thing," Nick said.

"I know," replied Winship. "I just need to make sure we go down the correct avenue."

While they were walking back to the hotel Simon said, "I think you have found a winner with the Caselli's."

DIONIS

Winship was sitting on the train headed back to Hyannis and his mind was swirling about how much money all this started to add up to. He had been trying to figure out how much the rest of the rough cut diamonds could be worth. If one was worth approximately three hundred and fifty thousand dollars and he had around fifty of them, on the low end, the value was almost too high to count, minus the fifteen percent to the dealer of course. The numbers were a staggering amount. The rubies and other precious stones he figured had to be worth another ten million. He did not even add in all the gold bars. When he added it all up, he came to a whopping figure of thirty plus million and he did not even factor in the remaining coins. With fifty or so rough diamonds, not to mention the never ending array of precious stones and the gold doubloons, he was exhausted trying to figure out what he would do with all the money after it started to flow in. He was already wealthy way beyond his means. Possibly he could start a trust for charities. That might be the best idea yet.

As he sat in his library staring into the fireplace that was crackling away, a light cold rain had set in. The phone rang. Marshmallow let out a loud meow. Winship said, "How can you know it's Cousin Sandal?" He picked up the phone and sure enough it was Sandal.

"Hello Winship - Sandal here!"

"How nice to hear your voice Sandal."

"Boy do I have a story for you," she mentioned. "It's going to take a while so you better sit down. How's Marshmallow?"

"She's fine, you know it's the strangest thing, every time you call she knows it's you. Even before I pick up the phone she lets out a loud meow. It's only when you call. It's strange, I tell ya - strange!"

"Today I received an inheritance check from Aunt Sarah's estate. A lawyer named Wes Morris sent it to me registered mail. It's huge. The amount is staggering. I had no idea she was that wealthy." Winship chimed in, "I can explain how she accumulated so much wealth. She and I discussed it a few years ago agreeing to keep it quiet. As we all knew, Aunt Sarah's husband owned Avery's Box Spring & Mattress Company."

"FOR A-VERY RESTFUL SLEEP." Sandal rattled off their motto with a giggle.

"Your Uncle Avery had arranged to start this company after approaching the State of Maine about the eyesore of warehouse on the river banks. The state and Avery readily agreed on a sales contract. Avery purchased the warehouse for his factory and he also purchased two small cottages about a block away. He fixed them up quite nice. He placed one queen-sized bedroom set in one cottage and a king-sized one in the other. They both had small kitchens so you almost felt like you were at home.

"Avery then placed ad's stating that you could try it before you buy it. You would get a one or two nights stay in a cottage of your choice and a dinner gift certificate to one of the local restaurants. This was an unrepresented move in the industry. People were booked as much as six months in advance. It made Avery's mattress company's reputation soar in retrospect to other mattress companies and the sales never slowed down.

"After Avery passed away - ironically in a deep slumber on one of his own mattresses - Aunt Sarah inherited the whole company. She had no direct heirs except you. She did have many close friends and always wanted to gift them out a portion of her estate after her passing. She went to their family attorney and he gave her very sound advice. Who would ever think that a small town lawyer could be so brilliant at tax laws and he was also a CPA as well.

"He recommended to her that since the company was making such a good profit to take her time and not be in any rush to sell. The general manager had been with them for twenty years and had no plans of leaving. Her lawyer suggested a nice raise for the G.M. as he didn't have her husband Avery to assist him anymore. After a year they could sit down and review the business and make a decision whether to sell the company to its employee's or possibly to a competing firm, as two were already vying to get Avery's Mattress Company into their portfolio.

"So after a year they re-grouped and Aunt Sarah opted to sell the business. It was good timing in the market and she keep the real estate.

Her lawyer then gave her two very good options to look at. He had researched three of the companies trying to purchase the business, one of them was the Zablaskai Bedding Company. But the one he liked best was the Redmond Mattress Company. They were looking to expand adding factories in the Carolina's, Rochester New York and Schaumberg Illinois.

"One idea was to sell the business and offer a lease on the property with a standard fifteen-year lease option broken into three segments along with the first right of refusal to purchase the property if she ever chose to sell. Or she could take a reduced yearly lease price on the warehouse and receive a percentage of the quarterly sales. If the Redmond's company continued to grow at the current rate so would her income.

"Well she took the second option. They signed the lower lease cost with a percentage of the profits from the entire corporation and the company kept growing and expanding and Mr. Redmond was true to his word and he and Aunt Sarah were friends for many years to come.

"When Mr. Redmond was getting ready to open the new plant in Illinois, he had invited Aunt Sarah to join in at the ribbon cutting. She took the train out and visited some friends. One evening, at a small dinner party she had attended with her friends, she was seated next to a gentleman named Richard who owned RHD Investments in Chicago. They hit it off quite well and Richard kept telling your aunt that she was a very smart business woman after hearing her story.

"I was told by your aunt's friends that after everyone had finished and were departing after the evening's festivities that your aunt and Richard remained at the table for almost another hour. Their conversation turned to Richards's line of work and his savvy investment outlook. One thing led to another and your aunt opened up an account with his firm. It turned out that Richard was quite the boy-genius at his investments, studying the market daily. Your aunt's investments with Richard never stopped going up. Richard made your aunt, who was already a wealthy woman, even wealthier.

"So that's how it all played out. The leases are good for numerous years to come and everyone in the family tree will reap the benefits from the Avery's Mattress Company for years. The lease agreement and the profit sharing will never run out if it continues along the same path.

"With all my gas and oil investments and the banks I have, along with all the post office buildings I own, I have been financially set for quite a long time and I still get royalty checks from Aunt Sarah's funds. So it looks like our family has had some good stories of financial success."

SIASCONSET

As Winship got back into his daily routine on the island. He started thinking more and more about starting a charity foundation. He certainly did not need the money from the jewels. He would wire a nice amount to Simon at one point, even though he had a hard time convincing Simon that it was his fair share.

Within ten days, Mr. Caselli had called Winship to tell him some wonderful news. A friend of his, Mr. Zises, whom was one of the curators at the Smithsonian Institute was extremely interested in the ruby stone. Mr. Caselli continued the conversation stating, "The good thing is they pay promptly and do not haggle if the items(s) are top quality. They don't want to take a chance of losing the opportunity to acquire them. I sent him, via overnight express mail, several pictures I had taken by our photographer, Mr. Steven Turrentine. We use him for all our fine diamond and gemstone catalog photographs. We will have Mr. Zises' response within the next three to four days."

This brought a smile to Winship's face knowing that the lost stones found on a ledge in the sea cave would be viewable to the world. Winship thought to himself that this would be the way to go. Offer the museums the pieces so that they could be admired, not locked inside a family safe or designed into a gaudy pin or ring only brought out to wear on special occasions. He would discuss this in more detail with Nick when he called back in a few days.

The next morning, he went to see Bill Houirhan at the bank. He asked if there was a way he could arrange to have $75,000 wired to a friend's bank account in England. He told Bill that he and his friend, Simon Gilmore, were planning on investing in a rather large ocean front property in Dartmouth. He told him the property was listed well below market value and it could be a great rate of return on the investment.

Bill told him, "All you need to do is fill out everything with a yellow mark listed on this piece of paper," as he handed it over to Winship.

"I will have this information back to you by tomorrow." He went to the telegraph office and sent a wire to Simon asking him to get the following information and to call him tomorrow, if he could, at 10a.m. Nantucket time.

As he enjoyed his lunch with Marshmallow chatting away to him. Winship started to draw up ideas for his charitable trust(s). Two days later, earlier than Winship expected, Mr. Caselli called him.

Mr. Zises and Nick had made a deal. A very favorable one. Nick explained the particulars to Winship. Nick retained a ten percent broker fee and the only added costs deducted were shipping and insurance. He said, "We only insure with the Krauter Company out of New York. It's slightly more of an expensive route to go but they are a top quality insurance company and I know Mr. Krauter on a personal level." Winship agreed and the deal was finalized.

Nick told him that he and JoAnn in two weeks' time, were planning a three-day trip to Wellfleet on Cape Cod where they had a family cottage. Winship invited them to the island to spend a night. He could take them out for dinner, show them the island and he had plenty of room. Nick readily agreed and told Winship that he should have full payment by that time as well. Winship asked, "So - how will the payment be made?"

"We prefer to deal in cash. This is a large amount but it could be handled and is a pretty good tax loop," Nick mentioned quietly.

Two weeks later Nick and JoAnn arrived with cash in hand from the gemstones. No money from the rough diamond yet. Nick explained that it will take a few weeks more. Winship was given a large manila envelope with a detailed invoice from Nick. The total enclosed was $92,000.

That night they celebrated by going to Cioppinos on Broad Street. The owner, Tracy Root, had become a close friend of Winship. They met at the restaurant many years prior. Tracy told Winship, that at his request, he had selected two very fine old bottles of Bordeaux.

The next day as they were getting ready to drive down to the ferry, Winship gave Nick another six beautiful gemstones along with four 100-ounce gold bars. Nick was quite impressed but did not question Winship about where he acquired them.

Winship placed the cash from the gold bars that had sold in Florida and the $92,000 from the stones into the coal chute. But instead of laying it on the carpet with the other satchels of jewels, he placed it up on the ledge above the opening. His thoughts on this were if they ever got a heavy rain it might soak the floor of the chute and make the cash damp and moldy even wrapped in the clear gallon zip lock bags. It could not be seen from the outside of the chute looking in but that did not matter as no one was ever going to open the locked steel door covering.

The next day was beautiful. A late November clear, crisp morning. Winship went to his fishing bungalow, selected two poles, and set off for the Madaket Marina where he had his boat docked. Winship felt that this would be the last outing until the spring. It was time to pull the boat out of the water.

He filled the Boston Whaler's tanks and headed off shore about three miles facing the sun as it shone brightly. The wind started picking up. He had his back to the west and he did not notice the dark storm clouds approaching the rear at a very fast pace. The winds picked up rapidly. He reeled in his line and looked behind him to see a massive storm heading directly towards him. The storm proved too much for his little twenty foot Boston Whaler. His body was found washed up on Surfside Beach by a jogger early the next morning.

Nantucket, May 1975

Sam, Leonard, and Sandal sifted through the piles of old mail and wondered who this guy Nick Caselli was. Sandal had opened the letter over a month ago and put it in the 'get to later pile'. All it said was, **"Winship give me a call. Nick."**

The three of them were in Connecticut trying to tie up all the loose ends of Winship's estate. Sandal said, "I will give this guy Nick a call." She went into the study and about twenty minutes later she appeared in the kitchen with a startled look on her face. "You guys better remain seated. You're not going to believe this. She then retold the story of Winship's association with Nick Caselli and the whopping amount for an uncut rare diamond and the other precious stones he had left with Nick to sell.

"Where did he ever acquire them?" Leonard asked. "I never heard him talk about investing in stones but then Dad was always into something. You know he still gets around twenty checks every few months from the gas wells he bought in West Virginia and he gets monthly checks from the five post office buildings he had built. He was still involved with, what is it, six Connecticut banks? That doesn't even include all the royalties he still gets from the numerous Texas oil companies he's fully vested in."

"Well," Sam said, "when we cleaned out the house of his personal belongings we never came across any other type of jewelry or stones except for Mom's personal stuff so I guess it's going to remain a mystery."

"Another matter that we have to deal with is that note that Dad had left in his important papers box, that in the event of an untimely death, $200,000 USD was to be drafted via bank check or direct wire and was to be sent to his friend Simon Gilmore of Dartmouth England. He had added this in his most recent Will that there were to be no questions asked about it."

Meanwhile on Nantucket Island, Steve Germain was signing the papers on his new home on Wauwinet Road.

"Here are the keys and all your documents. Everything else will be sent in the mail to your Columbus, Ohio address in due time. If there are any small issues that need to be addressed, your attorney, Mr. Kovalencik can handle them such as the electric and water company arrangements."

Steve and his close friend and also his Columbus attorney, Bill Heifner, left the bank and drove out to the newly purchased home. It was a sad affair the way the past owner had died. He apparently was killed in a freak storm a few miles off the shore of Madaket while out fishing.

Bill and Steve arrived at the house. Steve did his methodical tour starting in the basement. Bill, with his pad of paper, was playing secretary to Steve. "Here are my ideas. We take this old cistern area with what looks like a coal chute and turn it into a wine cellar and we hang a nice solid door on it which will help keep the room at a cool temperature on the inside. Next we move the washer and dryer to the other side of the basement, add a workbench for tools over there and we improve the old out dated lighting and electrical plugs." They proceeded through the whole house in rapid procession. Steve firing off suggestions faster than Bill could write them down.

Bill stopped for a moment and said, "One thought, I would like to ship out some nice wines from Ohio to keep in your cellar. Not from my collection I already own but I could make the trip to Dayton. Go visit my old friend David Hulme. You've met him. He owns The Pine Club Restaurant there. He always lets me order my wine through his business that way I get it at wholesale cost. Then I can either ship it to you or drive it out when Sandy and I visit."

Steve had come out to Nantucket several months earlier in December for the Christmas Stroll with his family. While everyone went shopping one afternoon, Steve walked past Kendrick's Real Estate Office and decided to stop in and grab a brochure of homes and properties.

"Good afternoon," a man greeted him. Tom Kendrick offered his hand to Steve to shake and welcomed his new guest. Steve introduced himself. "You in the market to buy?" asked Tom.

"Well not really, I just enjoy getting ideas."

"Where you from Steve?"

"Columbus Ohio. We are in the car business and enjoy visiting the island two times a year. My family is in love with the island."

"Sorry to say, that brochure is about two months old. I've been meaning to print out a new one but time just seems to slip away. If I can be of any help don't hesitate to ask."

Steve told Mr. Kendrick, "We love the Wauwinet area and the Wauwinet Inn is always a must for dinner in the summer when it's open. They have a great lobster bake and as my son Austin would tell you, they have great clam chowder, almost as good as Cioppinos."

"Funny you should mention that. A house just came on the market two days ago. A very nice property. The owner, Mr. Winship Cate, met a tragic death out fishing off the coast of Madaket. He will truly be missed. The home is in impeccable condition on five acres of land and has an oversized two car garage along with two sheds, full basement, and four bedrooms with four and a half baths. You can see the ocean from the second story bedroom deck off the master suite."

"Really," Steve replied. "I would hate to see the price tag on that one."

"Well it's actually not priced too high. This time of year the market is pretty soft. It won't creep up until late June when the buyers are, as we say, in market."

"What is the price, if I may ask?"

"It's listed for $195,000," replied Mr. Kendrick.

"I figured it's got to be expensive," Steve said, "especially compared to Columbus prices."

"Well," Mr. Kendrick replied, "the housing and land market is quite expensive here on the island but people that invest here usually at least double their original investment if not more."

"I am sure your correct Mr. Kendrick," Steve replied. "But I think I will be getting back to the hotel. Thank you for your time. It was nice meeting you."

"Please, take one of my cards. If another idea comes your way, I am here to help."

As Steve was heading back to the hotel, he overheard a couple walking along Main Street a few feet in front of him about how beautiful Nantucket was. A few minutes later a lady was talking with two other women standing near the Post Office remarking that this Island is so special.

He stopped at the Languedoc Bar downstairs for a quick hot cider. As Steve pursued the real estate brochure, the owner, Al Cunah, made a joke to him, "Better get another job to make enough money to buy a place here," and started laughing. Steve introduced himself. Al said, "You look familiar." Steve explained that they try to book every Christmas Stroll for a lunch with Hunter Laroche.

"Ah, Hunter the International Man of Mystery. He's a piece of work that Hunter. He enjoys great food and top notch wines and he is never afraid to spend. If I had ten customers like Hunter, I could retire early. I thought you looked familiar. Those lunches with Hunter can last forever. I am pretty sure we have Hunter's usual table booked for him tomorrow at 1:00p.m. I better get the good stuff out. He only drinks the best!"

"Yes, we are joining him. My kids love to hear all his wonderful travel stories," replied Steve. Al said, "All kidding aside. This is a great place to buy. A fabulous investment."

"Really?" Steve asked.

"You'd better believe it! I currently own four investment properties," Allan told him.

Steve finished his hot mulled cider and instead of going back to his hotel, The Harbor House, he went back to Kendrick's Real Estate Office. Tom greeted him and said, "Another question?"

"Do you think it would be possible to view the property in Wauwinet?" Steve asked.

"Anytime. I have the exclusive listing for it. Keys are in my desk."

"How about now?" inquired Steve. Fifteen minutes later Steve was in the kitchen of the Wauwinet property. They took a quick tour of the house and walked the grounds. Steve not wanting to seem anxious asked, "How firm is the price?"

"Everything is negotiable. Almost everything in the house will remain and seeing as Mr. Cate's kids are selling it. They really have no more desire to own it after both their mother and their father have passed on. It doesn't hold any magic for them anymore."

June 1975

Steve arrived at the house in Wauwinet with his two sons Austin and Zach. His wife Kim and their daughter Jessica would join them in a few days' time. Steve showed his sons which bedrooms would be theirs and which one would be Jessica's.

The next day Steve had appointments lined up to meet with an electrician about lighting and new plugs in several of the rooms, and a plumber for new fittings on the sinks in the kitchen and the bathrooms and for suggestions about a new tub and shower.

A short time later he spoke on the phone with the landscaper, Emily Dutra, about ripping out some of the dead wood and scruff that needed to be removed and the driveway also needed to have new shells added. The house didn't need much, just a little T.L.C. Kim would re-do most of the bedding, curtains, and rugs, and the list went on. When Steve told Austin and Zach that he was going to make the old cistern into a wine room they thought that was the coolest idea.

He also thought about getting a carpenter for the wine room project and a few other things that needed to be done. He hoped that Mr. Kendrick might know of someone. Steve, Zach and Austin hopped into the car and headed to Marine Hardware to pick up some light bulbs and trash bags. While they were standing in line, Steve started a conversation with a young man who looked like a carpenter. After a minute or two Steve said, "I am looking to build a wine cellar. Are you a carpenter? You any good?"

"Here's my card. Names Chris Meyer. Give me a call. I have plenty of references. Been working out here for ten years." As he walked away Chris thought to himself, "Yes, please call me." He was about to be evicted from his living quarters by his roommates and he was over two months behind on his rent!

Steve was paying for his goods when the lady in line beside him turned and said, "Hi. My name is Judith. You must be new to the island."

"Yes. Steve Germain. Nice to meet you Judith."

"Welcome," she said.

"Do you know that guy Chris?"

"Chris? Everyone knows him."

"Is he any good?"

"People say he is. He did some work for our neighbors several times and they seemed pleased."

The very next morning, as his boys slept in, Steve was up at sunrise making a fresh pot of coffee. It was one of few staples they picked up while at the grocery store. He opened the refrigerator and saw the leftovers from dinner the evening before at Cioppinos and not much else. He closed the refrigerator and found a bag of English muffins on the counter and a stick of butter sitting on a coffee saucer and popped a muffin into the toaster. As it was toasting he looked out on the open field with the sunlight glistening. He saw a black and white cat hopping around. It looked like it was trying to catch a mouse. It was the funniest thing watching that cat bouncing all around in the deep grass.

Steve went to the basement with his mug of piping hot coffee after enjoying his muffin. He had a large yellow pad of paper, a pencil, and measuring tape with him. He started to measure and sketch out his idea of a wine cellar, shelves, racks, and counter top, possibly a sink, and some nice soft lights. He wondered how much this project was going to cost him but quickly brushed it aside.

Steve thought to himself, "I think I arrived in life." At this time, they had several car dealerships that were all doing a solid business and showed no signs of slowing down. Steve thought about the Don Allen Ford dealership on the island and would have to stop in and check it out along with a place near the airport called Rainbow Motors. The other one was Silva's Auto Sales. Thinking to himself, "Is there that much business to support three auto dealerships on this small island?"

As he headed upstairs, he heard a car approach the house, looking at his watch it was exactly 9:00a.m. and went out to the porch wondering who it could be.

A female in an old rusted out Jeep Wagoneer climbed out and said, "Hi-ya! I'm Diane Downing and that's my dog Luna sitting in the front seat popping her head out the window. I'm your neighbor. The good neighbor that is, not like old man Lussier. He's like an irritable bowel that one. He owns the house over there directly to the east of you. Watch out for him. He can be real troubling. Remember the name Albert Lussier. If you ever run into him go the other way! I wanted to welcome you to the neighborhood. I had heard from Mr. Kendrick that someone had purchased Mr. Cates property so I have been wanting to meet you." Diane walked over to her car, opened up the door to the back seat and pulled out a box. She brought the box over to Steve and said, "Here's a little welcome gift. I went to see Phil Bartlett at Bartlett Farms and thought I might drop off some of their wonderful freshly made jams, fresh fruits, and their killer five-grain bread that they bake right at the farm store - which is to die for. Oh and also, there is a whole blueberry pie as well in the box. One other thing, you will want to call either Phil, his wife Dorothy or their son John and reserve some of their one-pound frozen packages of Nantucket bay scallops. They sell out quickly."

"Why do I want to do that?" Steve inquired.

"Well you haven't lived until you have tried them. There considered the best in the world by several famous chefs."

"Well that was very kind of you. What store are you talking about?"

"It' Bartlett Farms out near Cisco. If you go out there you should definitely set up a house account. John Bartlett is Phil's son and he more or less runs the place. It's truly an amazing place. Phil and his wife and their family have owned it for years. It's a must on any shopping trip but a warning, the store is addicting. With all the great produce and homemade delicacies, it really becomes habit forming and just wait until their corn and tomatoes are in season. Get there early as the place becomes packed.

"Over there you can just see the peak of my house. I had heard in back January they sold this house. It was a real shame the way tragedy hit Mr. Cate. Winship was a wonderful man and so was his wife Mary but she had died about a year prior. I didn't catch your name."

"Oh sorry. I am Steve, Steve Germain. We just closed on the house a couple months ago. I've been in Ohio but we are now back for a few weeks to see what we need to do to get this place together. My wife and daughter arrive in a few days. My two boys are still under the covers sleeping away."

Right then, the cat that Steve had seen earlier chasing what he thought might be a field mouse came running up to Diane with a loud meow.

"Hello Marshmallow. How's it going?"

Steve said, "Who's Marshmallow? Your cat?"

"Well she's not my cat. In a way she is - but she's not. She's yours."

"What do you mean?" asked Steve.

"Well she was found by Winship and his wife Mary when she was just a kitten. They had her for about the last four years. First Mary passed away and then when Winship died, Marshmallow would not leave the house. She sat on the deck day in and day out. During the day she wanders the fields but at night she curls up on that chair over there like she's waiting for Winship to return. It's kind of sad. She doesn't seem to understand that Winship is not going to return. So I bring her food and water.

She stops over my house during the day and lays out in the sun on the back porch. She and Luna are close friends but at night she comes back here. When the weather starts to turn really cold I pick her up and bring her to my house. She always seems to pitch an argument about coming with me but always relinquishes the fight. She started to get used to the staying with me on colder nights. She's a beautiful loving cat with a mind of her own. Now that the weather is warming up she has started finding her way back here to the porch. Personally I think she comes with the house."

Steve said, "That's all I need is a cat."

"It's not that bad of an idea. She's great at catching mice. Better she catches them or they will invade your basement or attic!"

Steve and Diane turned as they heard a pickup truck arrive. It was the gardener. "Hello Diane," she yelled out. The cat let out yet another loud meow. "Well hello Marshmallow. Hi, you must be Mr. Germain, I'm Emily, Emily Dutra your landscape girl."

A few minutes later another automobile pulled in. "Hi. I'm Rusty Riddleberger. I'm your electric guy," he said while putting his hand out to Steve. He turned and greeted Diane. "Hey Marshmallow. What's up?" The cat let out another loud meow.

Randy was the next to arrive in his white van. "Hey, I'm Randy your plumber and heating guy all rolled into one! Hello Marshmallow!" She greeted him with another loud meow.

Steve asked, "Is there anyone Marshmallow doesn't know?" They all let out a laugh. "Everyone knows Marshmallow. She's the coolest cat ever. Oh one thing," Diane added. "She's got this thing about the telephone. It's hard to explain but if there's someone your familiar with and she's near the phone she will know it before it rings that they are going to be calling. A second later the phone will ring and it's them on the line." While everyone was standing around Steve made some small talk and then asked, "Do you guys know of a carpenter named Chris Meyer?"

Almost in unison they all said, "Yes!"

"Is he any good? I need some work done around here and I am thinking of having a wine cellar built."

"Oh he's good. Well, better than that - he's mighty fine," said Diane winking at Emily and the two of them started giggling like high school girls.

"What's so funny?" asked Steve.

"The girls are just kidding around," Rusty said. "What they are talking about is his looks."

"And he's quite a hunk!" Diane piped in. The girls wandered off laughing.

Steve turned to Rusty before he went inside to try and call Chris and asked, "Oh, and Rusty, I will need you to get me better lighting for the new wine cellar. I can take you downstairs in a bit."

Steve placed the call to Chris Meyer and, as luck would have it, Chris was at home. He told Steve he was just heading out to make a dump run but he could swing by and hit the dump after if Steve was going to be home for the next hour.

Around thirty minutes later Chris arrived. Steve showed him a few pieces of window rot, a few missing roof shingles and then they went into the basement where Steve told him his idea for the wine cellar. Chris told him he was a big fan of wine and has been studying it for years as a hobby. "I love reading about wine. I am a big fan of Bordeaux wines. I like all types of wine but there is so much history that dates back to the Chateaus of Bordeaux and the stories some of the Chateaus have attached to them."

Steve showed him his rough sketch. Chris took his tape measure and showed Steve where the best placement of the door would be. "Allow three inches from these walls for insulation and framing. I will have to cut the lock and the front latch part where the lock attaches to the old coal chute. I also need to check outside to see that the chute is well capped off for rain issues."

Steve had one more question, "Where would be the best place to get wines for the cellar?"

"You definitely want to go see Judy at Hatch's Liquor Store. She has a huge inventory and is a great lady. She will help you out big time!"

"Thanks. When can you start?"

"Next Monday would be best but I can bring you out an estimate before then. I am finishing up three small jobs. I might need a small down payment as my rents coming up along with my car insurance." Chris failed to mention that his car insurance had lapsed several months prior and was canceled. "It would also be good if you can open an account at Marine Hardware and Island Lumber Supply that I can charge on. I will turn over all the receipts every few days."

Once everyone seemed to know what Steve wanted fixed or upgraded for the house, Diane walked over to where they were standing in the driveway to say good-bye. "I will write down the type of food and cat treats that Marshmallow enjoys. I have a few cat toys as well but she's more of a chase a live mouse type."

"Wait a minute," Steve asked. "You're going to do what?"

"I am going to give you the things that Marshmallow is used to. She's not going to leave this house. It's her home. If you take off for a while she will just mosey on over to my place. She is pretty adaptable and she knows to stay away from that crotchety geezer, old man Lussier. He would most likely try and poison her if he could. He's really that mean spirited!"

"Is he that bad?" asked Steve.

"We'll let just say he's a handful," Diane replied. "He is always at the grocery store complaining to the manager trying to get something for free. He goes to most of the town meetings bitching about this or that. He can't stand development, fights with all the selectman, calls the Harbor Fuel office every time an oil truck comes to fill up someone's oil tank on our street saying the truck is making too much noise or speeding, driving recklessly. If it's not one thing it's another. Just wait until hunting season opens, then he really goes berserk! Oh and don't even get started with any type of government or local politics. You will see his blood start to boil! We think his favorite phone number is the police department. They seem to be pulling into his drive about once a week. Deputy Donato says they have to show up if he calls them but it's mainly nuisance calls. Last summer he was against the kids' skate boarding down the hill on the Wauwinet Road. Why that would even bother him as his house is a good quarter of a mile prior to the dip where they go down the hill. He never drives that way towards the beach. Or it's the day trippers trespassing on his land as they walk along the edge of the grass when a car drives past. His house is set at least a thousand yards back off the road. It goes on and on, like the bike groups hogging the road. Anyway, my advice Steve, is if you don't ever have to cross his path, don't!"

"Thanks Diane. My wife Kim and my daughter Jessica will arrive in a couple of days. We will have you over for some drinks if you'd like. It's going to take a few weeks to get this place to her liking."

"Well maybe I can take them out and do some shopping and maybe lunch at Mignosa's Market. Inside of the market is Les's Lunch Box

Counter. He offers the best BLT and his grilled cheese is to die for. I would be glad to chauffeur her and your daughter around for an afternoon."

The following morning Chris Meyer arrived around eleven. He had an estimate on the repairs for the shingles, the rotted wood around two of the lower front windows and a section of the trim above it. Also the deck needed some minor touching up. Stain and wood primer needed to be brushed on. He told Steve, "This house really is in pretty good shape. It's just the elements of winter. The salt air, strong winds and being thirty miles out at sea." Chris told him, "By tomorrow I will have the estimate for the wine cellar, also I spotted some beautiful redwood that is sitting way in the back of Island Lumber. I think it's been there all winter. The manager, Doug Wolf, is an old friend and I think if I take the whole lot off his hands we will get a great price. I could construct the door from it. I don't think there would be much waste at all. My estimate would not include any plumbing for the sink or electrical but all hardware for the doors and racking is included. One stop shopping with me."

That night Steve headed into the den. Right as he did, Marshmallow joined him. She looked at Steve, then to the fireplace, back at Steve and then to the fireplace. "You know Marshmallow; you might have the right idea. A nice fire would be perfect right about now." Marshmallow let out a loud meow and jumped into her favorite leather chair and watched as Steve built the fire. He was saying to himself, "I can't believe I am having a conversation with a cat."

As he settled into his leather chair Marshmallow jumped off her chair and went to the shelf near the telephone. She let out a loud meow. About thirty seconds later it started to ring, again a loud meow from Marshmallow. Steve looked at her and said, "Really what is it?" He picked it up and Kim was on the other end of the line.

POLPIS

Kim and Jessica arrived on a flight from Boston on the small Gull Air prop plane. Kim looked green and also very pale like she was going to faint. Jessica was not in much better shape. The winds were blowing at a good 20 MPH which made the ride bumpy to say the least and with the fog they could not see anything as they were jostled round on the small plane. It became worse as they started their decent to land.

"Oh my God Steve! Never again. I will never get on one of those small planes ever! We are lucky to be alive. You couldn't see a thing. We just kept getting tossed around like a salad! I think I am going to be sick!"

"It will pass. It's kind of like an adventure." Steve laughed and gave them both a hug. "You're going to love the house. I have all sorts of things being done, inside and out. I met one of our neighbors, Diane, she wants to take you and Jessica out shopping."

"The only place I am headed is to the house to lay on the couch with a cold beverage," stated Kim.

By the time they arrived at the house Kim and Jessica seemed to have recovered from the flight. Kim quickly hugged the boys and her and Jessica did a tour. Kim said to Steve, "Where we going for lunch?"

"I thought you were not feeling well?" Steve had already figured this was coming so he said, "I booked us at the White Elephant at 1:30 so we don't have much time." Austin asked, "Do they have clam chowder Dad?"

The next few days they were all kept busy. Kim's first stop on the shopping trip was the Eye of the Needle. Kim sat next to a lady named Karen when they were flying from Boston to Nantucket. Karen was the owner of the store on Federal Street along with her husband Manny. Kim had visited the store during their last trip to the island during Christmas Stroll weekend.

Her next stop planned that afternoon was, if she could remember what street it was on, Griggs' Quilt Shop. Kim had met the nice couple that owned it on her last visit, Molly and Jeff Griggs. They were so sweet she bought three quilts and had them shipped back to Columbus after Christmas Stoll.

Kim decided that the next few days would be a family affair, which would involve shopping for things needed at the house. Such as new pillows, sheets blankets, towels, the list never seemed to end. Austin and Zach managed to slip away and found two stools at the Pharmacy lunch counter and ordered black and whites to drink.

A few minutes later a guy sat next to them. Zach asked, "Aren't you the guy that is working on our house? My dad is Steve Germain. We bought the house on Wauwinet Road."

"That's me," he replied. "Chris Meyer. At your service."

They all let out a laugh and the counter girl, whose nametag read Taylor, was batting her eyes at Chris almost in a daze. "Hi Chris. What can I get for you today?"

"Hey Taylor, you little cutie. I will have an egg salad on white not toasted with lettuce and tomato and a large vanilla Coke please."

Taylor took his order and stood there for a moment longer just staring at Chris. "That's all of it," Chris replied. Taylor snapped out of her gaze and went to work on the sandwich.

Kathy Lee came behind the counter with a tub of coffee ice cream and as she squeezed by Taylor she whispered, "I see dream boy is having lunch." They both giggled.

When Chris finished his lunch he said, "Hey Taylor. Can you add these guys' milk shakes to my bill?" He paid his check, patted the two brothers on the back and said, "See-ya soon!" and hurried out.

"Hey Chris," Taylor said, "I am also working weekend evenings with Dexter Tutine at the Woodbox Inn. Come in for dinner?" Kathy Lee and Taylor's eyes followed him as he headed out the door.

Austin and Zach met up with their parents in front of the Hub. "Mom! Dad! The carpenter guy just bought our milkshakes at the drug store."

"Well that was nice of him. Who is he Steve?" asked Kim.

"His name is Chris. I met him at Marine Hardware last week. He has good references so I had him out to the house. Showed him some things that needed to be fixed and also the sketch I made of the wine cellar."

"The wine cellar?" Kim replied, "Really Steve, we don't even drink wine that often."

"Well Bill and I thought it would be fun. Bill wants to ship a few cases out for when he and Sandy visit," Steve said, "Look, I let you have your things for the house. All I want is a wine cellar and my fishing shed. It's almost full of reels and rods left behind from the last owner."

"Well I guess," said Kim. "That guys dead. He has no use for it now."

"Nice Mom. Great way to talk about the dead," Jessica said.

"We need a few things at the grocery store on the way home but I would like to stop and find something nice for the realtor that found the house for us. Isn't his name Tom Kendrick?"

"Yes that's correct," Steve replied.

"I have a partial list that will hold us over for a few days. What do we want for dinner kids, any ideas?"

"Meatloaf with potatoes and gravy," Zach requested.

"Anything is fine for me Mom," said Austin

Jessica said, "I just want a salad."

They went into Mignosa's Market on Main Street. Steve started to put some cat treats and a bag of Meow Mix into the cart when Kim said, "What's with the cat food?"

Steve acting like it was not a big thing, "Oh that's for Marshmallow."

"Steve what is a Marshmallow? And what does it have to do with us?"

"It's a long story. I will explain it when we get back to the house."

On the ride home Kim again inquired about the cat food. Zach said, "Dad are we going to keep that cat?"

Jessica said, "I love cats! They are so smart."

When they pulled into the driveway Marshmallow came up to the car and let out a big meow and Steve said, "That's Marshmallow."

Jessica immediately bent down and scooped the cat into her arms. "I love her. What a cutie. You can sleep in my room." Marshmallow let out another approving meow.

Kim just rolled her eyes and said, "I hope she doesn't bring us treats from the fields." Marshmallow hopped out of Jessica's arms and trotted away like she didn't have a care in the world.

As the week progressed so did the shaping up around the house. Steve looked around and every day he saw new pillows, empty shopping bags, old hangers piled up, numerous bed sheets being tossed away, dishes, silverware, and he chuckled to himself, "and Kim is complaining about a simple wine room?"

That night Kim pulled out a calendar and told Steve, "Well it's not even the end of June and our guest list is filling up. We only have the one extra bedroom which as of now is being used as a den. The boys each have their own and Jessica occupies one. What are we going to do if we overlap with guests?"

"Zach and Austin can share a room."

Kim gave a look over her reading glasses that was like, "You have got to be kidding! Steve there is no way that Austin and Zach are going to share a room. There's only one bed and we are not putting a cot in one of the rooms."

"Well then, just don't over book us!"

"It's not that easy. Uncle Zach wants to come for the month of August and the Heifners are looking for early August for ten days. My dad wants to visit and a girlfriend of Jessica's is looking for a week in July. And that's just the beginning."

"Maybe Austin and Zach can bunk in the basement?"

"No way Steven." She had that 'Oh my god! Men are impossible' look on her face.

The next day Steve had a talk with Chris Meyer. He took him to the large attic room above the garage. Chris let out a small whistle. "This is a sweet spot. It is gigantic. Great windows all around, nice breeze and what a view!"

"Chris do you think we could transform this into like an in-law's apartment? We are going to be having a lot of company and we are already running out of space."

"I am sure we could make this work. It all depends if we can get water and a sewage lines hooked into your septic system for a full bathroom. Let me get in touch with Randy. I'll see if he can meet me here tomorrow."

Steve, Chris and Randy met the next day. Steve gave them a pretty simple outlay of his ideas for the space. Randy went around the outside and thirty minutes later told Steve that it was not a problem getting a bathroom put in. The only extra thing that would be needed would be to have water power booster installed. Otherwise it would take eternity to get the hot water flowing to the shower.

Steve asked, "Here's the million-dollar question. How quick could this be done, finished, move in condition?"

"Well I think first off you can make this easily into a two-bedroom unit or a bedroom and a large den putting the bathroom in between both rooms with doors that enter from either side."

Chris said if he brought in a few other helpers for the flooring, drywall, plaster, painting, framework, tiling, and electrical, maybe three to four weeks if they moved quickly.

Steve figured that Zach and Austin could shack up in the new garage apartment if both of their bedrooms were needed for guests. That would free up a total of three bedrooms, one being the upstairs den.

"Housing crisis averted."

Things progressed along at a good pace. Emily, the landscaper, was there it seemed almost daily. Cutting the lawn, edging the walkways and along the driveway, pruning, mulching, raking and the place looked brilliant.

Chris Meyer, when not flirting with her or making a run to the hardware store or heading to town for lunch, was making headway on the new garage apartment. He brought in three other workers to help with the apartment. It seemed like he showed up, got all of his crew working and then disappeared for long stretches at a time. Chris was a big flirt constantly trying to get Emily, when she was around, to join him for lunch but she always managed to keep him and his flirtatious overtones at bay.

Several times Emily's boyfriend or actually her fiancé, Trevor O'Brien would bring her lunch and they would sit out in the field. It looked like two lovers having a picnic.

Every time Trevor showed up Chris would manage to get in his work truck and drive off. Emily's fiancé did not seem too keen with Chris Meyer.

A couple days later Steve arrived with Uncle Zach, a bruiser of a guy, who it turned out was an enforcer for the Phoenix mob. Steve did not like to announce this fact but young Zach and Austin thought this was a big deal.

Between the garage work and the wine cellar Chris kept himself occupied. Especially when Emily's fiancé was around. When Trevor wasn't there Chris spent more time talking with Emily. At one point Kim mentioned to Jessica, "He should go take a cold shower. Doesn't he know she's engaged?"

Uncle Zach took a disliking right away to Chris and he had to feel the bad vibe given off from Uncle Zach.

Kim and Steve decided to take the boys and up to New Hampshire for a few days to see Mount Washington and a few of the sights. Jessica's friend Caroline came to visit her. Uncle Zach was left in charge. Even though Kim knew leaving her brother in charge was not the best idea, the girls were probably better off under their own supervision.

Uncle Zach also kept a close eye on the carpenter Chris. He had noticed him hanging around his niece and her girlfriend while they sunbathed out back on the lawn a few times which really rubbed Uncle Zach the wrong way.

Uncle Zach went down to the new wine room area. Chris did not hear him and he stood in the shadows and watched him for a bit. Chris had gotten some bolt cutters and cut the lock off the old coal chute cover. He did not lift it up. He just tossed the lock into a pile he had been forming of scrap wood and old nails, screws, some wiring and piles of saw dust from the project.

Uncle Zach quietly went back upstairs and took a walk down the road to the Wauwinet Inn. It was his first visit to the Inn. The Inn itself was quite rustic and looked like it had been in existence for a very long time.

He stopped in the lobby and picked up a brochure not quite sure why but thought if the bar was quiet it would give him something to peruse.

He found his way into the large lounge area where a few people were seated at the long old oak counter. All the tables in the lounge were empty. The windows that looked out to the sea at a distance were caked with some salt from the sea air. The bartender approached him and said, "What can I get for you?"

"Do you have a Budweiser?"

"Sure do." The bartender placed the beer on the bar and asked, "Would you like a glass? Like to see a menu?"

"No glass needed but I will look at a menu."

The bartender brought over a menu and said, "Name's George. If you need anything just flag me down."

A few minutes later a couple walked in and started peeling off their jackets. The man took off his fishing vest and the lady removed her sweater. They sat on a couple of stools close to Zach. "How's George today?" they both asked Zach in unison.

"I guess he's okay. I don't really know him. It's my first time here. My brother in-law bought a house right down the road so I walked here."

"Well you see that rather large boat tied against the pier out there?" the man asked. "All eighty-four feet of it? That belongs to George. He's the owner of this place. My name's Brian. This is my wife Kathy. Brian and Kathy Legg. We are from the island. We were just out on our boat fishing."

"Names Zach Cisco. My sister and brother in-law are from Columbus Ohio. Steve and Kim Germain. I have a question. If this guy owns this place, why is he tending bar?"

"Oh that's the way George is. One day he will work the reception area, one day the bar, he likes to keep himself involved. His wife Mary opened up the gift shop and has her nieces run it in the summer and other staff take it over on the shoulder seasons. George Williams is a real piece of work. It seems everything he touches turns to gold."

They made small talk for a few moments when another guy walked in and sat a couple of bar stools to the left of Zach.

"Hey Brian. Hey Kathy. How's George doing today?" He looked at Zach and held out his hand and said, "Phil Bartlett."

"How you doing?" Zach introduced himself.

Brian asked, "So did your brother in-law buy the old Cate Estate?"

"I am not sure. I just arrived from Phoenix a few days ago. It's about four houses down on the left."

"Yup that's the Cate Estate. He was great guy Winship Cate. Tragic how he died. We all used to fish together," Brian mentioned.

Phil chimed in, "He was such a wonderful guy. Not a mean bone in his body! That's a great house he owned. Your brother in-law did well."

Another couple walked in taking two bar stools to the right of Kathy.

"Hey guys how's George doing?"

Phil Bartlett said, "Seems okay. You know George, he always has hands into something. I haven't heard any new gossip."

Brian said to Zach, "This is Lynn and Chad. They visit family here a few times a year. They are from New Hampshire and Florida. That is, in the winters they head south."

Things quieted down and Zach looked over the menu and ordered the 'George's Burger' topped with cheese, bacon, lettuce tomato and a creamy mix of catsup and a horseradish cream sauce.

After finishing his meal Zach said his good-byes and headed back to the house. The sun was starting to set off to the west. It was a beautiful time of the day with a slight breeze coming off the shore.

As he arrived back at the house and walked out to the back porch to see if his niece and her friend were still there. They were not but what he found was three empty but still slightly chilled glasses. He picked them up and smelled beer. Right away Uncle Zach went to find Chris. He knew his niece would not openly go and take a beer and the sight of three glasses made his mind immediately think of that sleaze ball carpenter but when he went to the garage only two guys were there plastering. He then went to the wine cellar; he was not there either. He didn't look to see if his work truck was on the property when he had arrived back at the house. He must have left for the day. Zach went back upstairs to the garage and the two workers casually said, "If you're looking for Chris, he must have gone to the hardware store." One guy said, "You can always find him at the Rose & Crown or the Tap Room this time of day, just look for a pretty girl. He will be close by. He's a real snake that one!"

Zach hopped in the family car and charged off to town. Parking right in front of the Jared Coffin Hotel, he entered the Tap Room. It took a minute for his eyes to adjust from the bright daylight to the dim surroundings. A quick scan of the room revealed that Chris wasn't in there. He headed down the street to the Rose & Crown. Just as he entered the door, he could hear Chris talking away to a couple of his friends. "Yeah that Emily, the landscaper that the people have working for them, is hot. I have never worked a job that she's been on the property before but this time I hit the jackpot!"

Zach went right up to him and said, "Hey you son of a bitch. What are you doing offering my niece and her friend beer? They are underage. Who do you think you are?"

"Chill out man," one of Chris's friends said.

Zach looked at him and said, "Pipe down punk!"

Chris Meyer stood up, "Hey what are you getting so uptight about? We only split one can."

"What am I getting up tight about? I'll knock your block off if you ever try that again."

"Well let me tell you something pal. I come from Pittsburgh and there we play for keeps."

"Well from where I come from," Zach said in an agitated voice, "I will rope you, tie you and skin you alive if you ever pull that stunt again. You stay away from my niece and her friend."

Deputy Donato, who was off duty in his regular street clothes enjoying a basket of fried clams, came over flashed his badge and said, "Let's drop this guys. Break it up and go on your way." Deputy looked up at Zach who towered over him and got a little nervous.

Uncle Zach remained for a moment staring right into Chris's eyes then said, "Sorry officer," turned around and left. As he walked away he heard Chris mutter something to his friends, "I would have pummeled him into the ground in no time at all. That's how we handle things in Pittsburgh."

Zach let it pass; he knew that punk would not last ten seconds if an altercation arose.

Across the bar and down at the other end out of Chris Meyer's line of sight sat Trevor O'Brien, Emily's fiancé. He himself not a fan of Mr. Meyer's and it was probably a good thing he didn't over hear what Chris was saying about Emily.

Deputy Donato went back to the station after he finished his basket of clams and made a small note in his daily work diary, 'Chris Meyer in slight altercation (again) at the Rose & Crown with unknown male' and noted the day, date and time.

The deputy then headed up to the Tap Room and ordered a ginger ale. June who was the hostess there, for what seemed like eternity, started small talk with the deputy. Mark, still excited about the altercation and the fact that he got to pull out his badge and show some authority, was retelling the story to June. She seemed to be excited by it but as he was getting to the main point of the story on how he broke it up she had to go and seat a party of four that walked into the pub. Mark was just getting ready to say, "No matter how big they are, once they see you're a man of authority, they back right down. You have got to nip it in the bud!"

The deputy waited for June to come back over so he could deliver the rest of story, as he started to continue telling her about what went down the phone rang and next thing you know June was babbling on about something. Poor Mark never got to relate the rest of the story to her. Again he was foiled in his attempt to impress someone.

He strolled home and he was grateful that Beth was there to listen to the events of his day.

"Oh Mark! You're fearless. I would have called for backup if I were in your place. It sounds pretty scary. How big did you say this other guy was?"

"Easily six-feet-four but he knew that I was in charge. They respect authority when it is displayed in such a manner."

"You are so brave Mark!"

"It's all in a day's work my dear, all in a day's work."

EEL POINT

The next day Chris walked on eggshells around the Germain property. He had actually had written out a list the night before and tacked it upon the wall of the upstairs garage job really early in the morning for the workers to find upon arriving there. This was an easier way for him to make himself quite scarce and not have to cross paths with Zach Cisco. When he was at the house, he was staying put in the garage apartment or was sneaking into the basement trying his best not to run into Uncle Zach.

He was working in the cistern, soon to be wine cellar, the next day as early as he could manage to sneak in unnoticed. Being quiet as a church mouse measuring the walls for the spacing of the studs. He walked over to the heavy black steel cover of the coal chute. He had already cut the lock off and had to saw off the lip where the lock slid into place to be able to make the wall straight and run smoothly across the area. He thought he might as well open it up to see if it was dry inside of the chute's landing area. He knew if he started to saw off the protruding lip it might make a lot of noise so he preferred to do this at a later time.

Chris lifted up the front steel cover and lodged the pin in place so it would remain open and not slam down. He got on his knees and looked in. It was dark inside of the chute but he could still see there were things inside. He could see the dark outline of them. He reached his hand in and felt what seemed to be some sort of satchel. What is this he's discovered?

Right as he put his hand on the satchel Marshmallow darted inside the chute. Chris almost jumped out of his skin. Startled, he had not heard the cat come up next to him. He tried to coax Marshmallow out of the dark cavern but she stood her ground almost like she was protecting what was inside the chute.

After Chris managed to shoo her away, he removed one of the satchels as he looked over his shoulder to make sure he was alone. He slowly unwrapped its contents. There were numerous medium sized plastic bags inside. He was not sure of how many in total but it seemed like a good amount of them. He pulled a few bags out and they were packed with some type of colored stones. Looking around again he knew he was alone but it was a gut instinct. "Whoa," he said to himself. "This is unbelievable." Even under the poor lighting in the cistern he could make out that they were jewels and this was just one of the several satchels inside the chute.

After looking through the first package he placed everything back inside it resealed it and removed another. Where did all of this stuff come from? There had to be at least eight satchels inside the chute. If they all are full of jewels like the first one, they have to be worth a small fortune. Do the Germain's even know it's hidden in here? Is it theirs?

His mind started racing. Chris couldn't be sure but the way the lock had looked before he cut it free, it seemed it had not been opened in quite a while and Mr. Germain would have told him just leave the coal chute as it is for now. With a stash like this you would not want anyone in a close proximity of it. Why would someone bring all these stones from a safe storage area to a basement in Nantucket? Who owns this stuff? Maybe the last owner? Who knows but the more Chris thought about it, the more he believed it did not belong to the Germain's.

He thought to himself, "Somehow I have to figure this mystery out and possibly take a small amount at first. Maybe over time, move the rest of the stuff out of here. I can leave this unlocked but what if Mr. Germain or one of the kids decided to come down and look around and just happen to lift up the unlocked coal chute door?" He thought to himself, "Here's what I'll do. I will mention to Mr. Germain that I'll soon be working on the wall with the coal chute. I will tell him about cutting off the lock and sawing off the protruding lip of the chute, open it up and make sure that it's dry inside to prevent any mold from forming just in case there might be a water leak coming from the outside before sealing it up. I will tell him that I will insulate and build the wine room wall very soon." This way he could see, if Mr. Germain has any reaction to it and if not then he had to move quickly and remove all the stones out of there. Where could he hide this stuff, if that's the way it played out?

He can't leave it in his truck as his roommates are always borrowing it. He could see it now, one of them gets pulled over and the truck gets searched. There is no place in his bedroom at the house as there's no privacy. His roommates are always stealing his spare change and his cigarettes and borrowing his clothes. They would steal him blind if they could.

Best idea he thought of was to get another lock and replace the one he had just cut off. Make it look like the chute has never been opened and keep everything status quo. It's been here this long, what are the chances of anyone discovering it now?

Chris high tailed it over to Marine Hardware where he purchased a very similar looking lock, placed it on the chute and took an early lunch break.

Chris went to the Atlantic Café. He had two of the stones, a red one and a blue one in his pocket. He overheard two girls laughing in a booth off to his left while he sat at the bar. It turned out to be Emily, the landscape girl. Oh, how she turned Chris on. After his second beer, it was still before noon, he grabbed his third beer and walked right up to the booth. Her friend Maureen said, "Hello Chris." and batted her eyes at him.

Chris said a quick hello not really paying any attention to her said, "Mind if I sit and join you?" and plopped himself right next to Emily. "Hello gorgeous," he said as he looked into her eyes.

"Hello Christopher," Emily replied back. "You know Mr. Stud Muffin; I am happily engaged to Trevor. Have been for over a month now and he's not a big fan of yours. If he caught you flirting with me, well - let's just say he's got that Irish temper."

"It's okay. I am going to win you over." At this point Maureen was so upset at not being the center of attention, said, "Emily and I were just leaving here sailor boy."

"Well," Emily said, "it would take a lot of money to woo me. And word around town is your flat broke! Your looks and flirtatious endeavors are not going to get you anywhere. I am very happy and content with my love life. Trevor is a man of dignity and honor. Something you will never find in this life time!"

"Catch ya' later ladies," Chris said as he stood up so Emily could get out of the booth and they walked away.

Chris had money problems. He had ideas now that he had found what he believed was the way to life on easy street.

But he needed to get his hands on some cash and he knew pretty fast. At this time, he figured his best option was to take the ferry to Hyannis

and see if he could pawn a piece or two of these gemstones. Hopefully they were not costume jewelry.

The next morning, he took the first boat out, which was like torture for Chris getting out of bed at 5:00a.m. to make the early boat.

Chris walked off the boat and took a taxi to Mashpee. It ended up costing him much more than he intended to spend to get to where he was going but the phone book advertisement that he had found the night prior read Graham & Clary Pawn Shop, 'Highest prices paid on the Cape.' Chris passed a lady that was leaving the shop and tipped his ball cap to her as she left. He was happy to see that he was the only person in the shop when he entered besides the clerk behind the counter.

One of the owners a Mr. Michael Clary, his wife being Jenifer Graham, stated that they had been in business for twenty-five years. Chris cautiously showed him the two stones. Mr. Clary simply stated that they were good pieces, about four carats each and he would give him a total of $800 cash for both. No questions no paperwork.

Chris thought he hit the lottery and wanted to be casual about it. Not wanting to seem a push over said he might have to think about it.

Mr. Clary, knowing they were remarkable and not wanting to be overly zealous, said, "I will go as high as $850 but not a penny higher and again no paper trail."

Chris asked, "Would that be paid in cash?"

"Always," Mr. Clary replied. "Always cash here! Private and discreet is our motto."

As Chris got back into the waiting taxi, he was laughing so hard the taxi guy though that someone must have told him a really funny joke.

"Take me to Teasers."

"Okay," said the driver. Chris gave the driver twenty bucks to wait for him out front. Chris flush with cash, entered Teasers Strip Club and sat right at the edge of the stage. He ordered a shot of Jägermeister and a cold pint of Budweiser. He then proceeded to spend about one-hundred dollars before realizing he had been in the club close to three hours.

Chris jumped into his waiting taxi and just caught the four o'clock ferry, found an empty booth and fell asleep in minutes only to be awoken by Captain Spider Andrasen saying, "Hey pal, you got to go. We have been docked for ten minutes."

Still reeling from his recent windfall, Chris headed to the Tap Room. He bought the bar a round of drinks and started thinking. If he took two

stones and was paid eight hundred and fifty dollars, then the next trip he would take four stones. Looking at seventeen-hundred, he was full of himself just dreaming away of all that cash.

Little did he know that in his absence Uncle Zach had gone into the new wine cellar and noticed the chute's steel door closed with a brand new shiny brass lock attached.

What was that all about? Zach had noticed that the old lock that had been cut off earlier was still sitting in the pile of old wood and saw dust off to the side. There was no way this clown Chris was worried that a small child was going to lift up that twenty-pound steel door and climb inside.

Zach also knew too well the look of a person in despair. Being a collector for the mob, he had a sick sense of people who had zero finances in their life. So the chances of him spending a few bucks on a lock was out of the question unless he was just charging everything to Steve. Zach pondered the situation but then just brushed it off for the time being.

Chris was back to work at the Germain's the next morning. He went and inspected the garage apartment, which was shaping up nicely along with the wine cellar. He was trying to figure out how to stall the covering of the coal chute, his hiding spot for his new discovery of gemstones.

The Germain family, including Uncle Zach, were off island for ten days. They were headed to a wedding in Rochester and also planned to visit the Finger Lakes region where Steve was thinking of maybe picking up a few cases of wine for his new cellar. They also told Chris they needed to head back to Ohio to get Jessica, their daughter, ready to go to Switzerland for a couple of months.

Chris breathed a lot easier at this point with the house empty. The garage job almost was almost complete so he had let the rest of the workers go. Why should he pay out most of his profits to the other workers?

The next day Chris filled a cooler full of ice and beer, invited a hot girl named Karen, that he was recently dating, to hang out over the Germain's house. He also brought his German Shepherd Socrates and let her run free on the property. Chris figured he could make it a relaxing day. He set up his boom box, put in a tape of his favorite mix of tunes and told Karen there were lounge chairs off the back porch. If she wanted she could lay out au natural.

Marshmallow, seeing the shepherd took off for Diane's house for some peace and security.

Chris turned up the music. The song, 'He Went to Paris', by Jimmy Buffett was playing and made Chris want to hop on a plane and head to Europe. Chris told Karen he needed to take some measurements in the wine cellar so after the song was over he headed downstairs. He found the key for the lock opened it, sat on the floor and pulled out all the satchels. Chris carefully opened each one and inspected the contents inside the bags. There were about forty bags when they were all counted.

Some of the bags weighed at least four or five pounds. There were so many stones, thousands of them he figured. So many he couldn't count them. He wondered why so many quartz pieces were also included in with all the other magnificent stones.

Chris studied the quartz pieces that were in a separate bag. He counted at least twenty or thirty of them. Strange Chris thought, "With all the beautiful stones why keep this junk?" So he placed them back in the satchel.

Karen was at the top of the stairs yelling, "Chris! Chris you better get up here! Quick!"

Chris shoved everything back into the chute, slid the lock on and placed the key back up on its hook and headed upstairs. Standing outside the front door was an old man. His car was parked cockeyed in the driveway. "Turn that music down. Who do you think you are? You're disturbing my peace and quiet. People can hear your music blaring all the way into town and another thing, I walked around to the back of this house and there was that girl!" he said pointing to Karen wrapped in a towel, stuttering saying, "And she was naked. That's against the law!"

"Calm down old man."

"Lussier is the name." he spat out. "Al Lussier. You shut that damn music off or I will call the cops." Suddenly he seemed to run out of steam, climbed back into his car and backed out almost running over the newly planted hedge.

Chris did not seem the least shaken up about the encounter with the old man. "Screw him - the old goat," Chris said.

"I am a little embarrassed," Karen said. "He saw me naked."

"Who cares, probably gave the guy a thrill," replied Chris. Chris lowered the music and a few minutes later a police car rolled up the driveway. "Now what?" Chris thought.

Deputy Donato got out of the car immediately recognizing Chris from the altercation a few days prior at the Rose & Crown. Chris said, "What can I do for you officer?"

Deputy Donato explained that someone had called in a complaint about loud music from the property. Chris said, "This has been on the same volume since I turned it on." A Rolling Stones song playing as he spoke. "And you mean by a neighbor, that old goat Lussier? He was just here bitching up a storm. Nasty guy that one. You should lock him up!"

Deputy Donato said, "Well we have had our share of complaints by him but it's our civic duty to follow up on every call. Just keep the music to an acceptable level and I am sure that's the last we will hear from him."

Chris, right before heading back to the basement, gave a loud whistle and Socrates came barreling in from the field almost knocking Chris off his feet. "Come on girl let's get you some water." Karen had returned to her lounge chair grabbing a cold beer to take with her and keeping her small bikini on.

Chris filled up one of Kim Germain's very expensive bowls with water and placed it out back of the porch for Socrates to drink out of. He retreated to the basement, removed the key off the hook and he unlocked the chute and pulled out the satchels. The one with the quartz pieces he left inside along with the stack of gold bars, which he counted at thirty-eight total.

He opened all the packages methodically and tried in his head to calculate how much all this was worth. After a while he said to himself, "There has got to be a half million dollars sitting here." He started to daydream of a penthouse suite on a beautiful island overlooking the deep clear aqua blue water with an endless pink sand beach."

Chris knew he had to move this stuff to another safe spot, sooner than later. He couldn't put off the covering of the one area of the wall forever. He figured he would go to work on the door and frame to buy him some time.

Mr. Germain was not going to question his work methods as his main concern was getting the garage project finished in time for the onslaught of arriving guests. Also he needed to steer clear of Zach. He knew that he was like a time bomb waiting to go off and wondered how long Zach would be staying on Nantucket.

FORTIETH POLE

The next day things did not go so well for Chris. Karen was once again out in back of the house sunning herself and drinking a cold beer.

Old man Lussier's car came rumbling up the driveway. He got out cussing saying that Chris needed permits for the work he was doing. The noise from his saws was disturbing his sanity. He was almost foaming at the mouth. A few minutes behind him Constable Kosmo and Deputy Donato arrived in a patrol car.

Getting out of the patrol car, Constable Kosmo tried to calm Mr. Lussier down. Deputy Donato just stood off to the side rolling his eyes. The constable finally telling Mr. Lussier sternly that if he did not calm down they were going to haul him down to the station. Constable Kosmo told Mr. Lussier, "You're the one who called in a complaint and we are here to look into the matter. Now get in your car and go home!"

After old man Lussier stopped his ranting, he headed for his car and said to Chris as he drove off, "You ain't see the last of me you young whipper snapper!"

Then Chris started in, "You got to calm that told geezer down. He's going to have a stroke getting all worked up like that. He's all full of piss and vinegar," Chris added.

"Sorry about the disturbance. Go on. Carry on with your project." Deputy Donato said.

Karen had come around from the back of the house to see what all the commotion was about off in the distance. After the Constable drove away she turned around and started to walk towards the back yard when Chris mentioned to her, "He's probably just trying to find excuses to get back over here and get a cheap thrill. He was hoping to see you laying out topless."

Karen and Socrates seemed to be enjoying a leisurely afternoon hanging around out in the sun. Chris walked around back and mentioned to Karen that the Gemain's would be back in about three or four days so this life of the rich and famous was coming to an end shortly.

Chris heard a car pull into the driveway. It was Diane arriving in her rust bucket Jeep Wagoneer.

She didn't know that Karen was sitting out in back of the main house but she found Chris who was just getting ready to walk over to his table saw and cut some trim in the shade of the garage. "How's the project coming along?" Chris knew she was eying him in his work jeans, shirtless and he liked the attention. "Where are the Germain's? Out to lunch?"

"No," Chris told her. "They are off traveling for a few days."

"I see you have your shepherd hanging around here. That's why Marshmallow has been spending so much time around my house."

"Socrates likes it here. She's free to run in the fields. I have to check her nightly though to see if she picked up any ticks. You ever have any tick problems with Luna?"

Diane said, "Well I am sure when the Germain's get back Marshmallow will abandon me and Luna and hang back here with them."

Two days later a call came into the Nantucket Police Department dispatch. "Nantucket Police how may I direct your call?"

"I am going to shoot that sum bitch!"

"Excuse me?" the dispatcher asked.

"That carpenter guy working at my neighbor's house. His dog broke into my hen house and killed four of my chickens."

"Is this Mr. Lussier?"

"Yes! Al Lussier and I am getting my shotgun and going over to shoot him and his dog!"

"Slow down Mr. Lussier. Did you see this happen?"

"No not really but I just went out to collect some eggs and they are dead. Mascaraed! Four of my prized chickens."

The dispatcher tried to keep Mr. Lussier on the line to stall him from getting his shotgun and causing a whole mess. She quickly got on the radio and contacted the constable. He and Deputy Donato were sitting at the rotary in the parking lot of the Inquirer & Mirror. "Here we go again." Deputy Donato replied. "Better hit the sirens Chief. Let old man Lussier know were on our way. Might make him think twice."

The constable just rolled his eyes sitting in the passenger seat of the patrol car. He knew that the deputy was always wanting to turn on the sirens even though they were only minutes away. "There's not really any traffic so I think we can get by with maybe just turning on the flashing lights."

"Well, you know that crazy old man Lussier and it sounds like he has a shotgun with him. There's no time to waste. Luckily we are close by," the deputy said turning on the lights and squealing the car's tires out of their parked position.

They arrived at the Germain's house ahead of Mr. Lussier but within minutes his car came barreling up the driveway. Constable Kosmo was ready for him and before Mr. Lussier could open up his door the constable leaned up against it. "Now hold on," he told Mr. Lussier. Old man Lussier had his shotgun in his arm resting out of the driver's side window.

Deputy Donato was now positioned a few feet from the opened passenger window yelling, "DROP YOUR WEAPON!" with his gun drawn, shaking.

"Chris looked up not knowing what to think. Karen came running around when she heard the commotion and started screaming, "HE'S GOT A GUN CHRIS! WATCH OUT!" when she saw the rifle.

Socrates came running in from the fields at full sprint and almost knocked Chris over in the excitement, barking and growling at the whole scene. A minute later, while everyone was yelling and screaming and it seemed like utter chaos, Diane came bolting up in a full out run through the woods slightly out of breath and tried to make heads or tails of what was going on.

Deputy Donato kept yelling, "DROP YOUR WEAPON! DROP YOUR WEAPON!"

Constable Kosmo had had it at this point and yelled out, "QUIET! Everyone shut up! Pipe it down!" he told Mr. Lussier who was babbling on about his chickens. The constable looked over at Deputy Donato and said, "Mark, holster your gun! No one is going to shoot anyone!"

"But Chief?" the deputy said. "Standard procedure is…"

"Stop it Deputy. Just holster your weapon before someone gets hurt."

Quietly and still trembling the deputy holstered his weapon. Kosmo reached through the driver's side window and took the rifle out of Mr. Lussier's hands and carried it a good twenty feet away from the car and set it down.

"Now get out," he told Mr. Lussier.

"What is all the commotion about?" Kosmo asked Mr. Lussier.

Mr. Lussier started screaming that Chris's dog broke into his hen house and killed four of his "prized" egg laying hens. "Now settle down here a moment. Did you see this happen?"

"No!" stated the old man, "But it's got to be his dog. Ain't never happened before. He brings his dog around running wild so I put two and two together."

"You are crazy old man - Nuts!" Chris yelled at him.

"Hold on everyone, remain quiet." Karen and Diane were standing next to each other. Diane introduced herself and quietly stated, "The old man is crazy!"

"Oh, I know. He's been here like three times now. Bitchin and complaining!"

"Well it does seem kind of curious that your dog and his chickens are in close proximity but with no proof it's not an open and shut case," the constable said to Chris while pulling him aside explaining the facts. He told him that Mr. Lussier could cause him all sorts of headaches if he wanted to file a complaint against Chris. He gave a suggestion to Chris to hold tight while he tried to figure out the easiest way out of this mess. The constable talked to Mr. Lussier and said he knew that the going price for the hens were about twelve dollars each, as his cousin just bought some from Lili Baker. "It's more like twenty dollars," the old man replied.

"Hold on here Mr. Lussier. Let's not get greedy. You don't even really have a case against this gentleman. But here's a suggestion. Mr. Meyer feels poorly about the noise he's made lately and the situation with your chickens so he's willing, out of the kindness of his heart, to make a charitable donation to you for sixty dollars to end this."

Old man Lussier heard the amount and quickly agreed. After he got the money he was right back to a grumpy old geezer. As he stuffed the cash into his pocket he said, "You better watch yourself sonny boy. I've got my eye on you." He started to head for his shotgun but the constable told him, "Leave it! We will drop it to your house soon."

As he started to pull out, Deputy Donato went over to the girls and said, "Okay, break it up! Nothing to see here! It's all over," like he was breaking up a large crowd.

Mark was telling the constable that he could not wait to get home and tell his girlfriend Beth all about his day. The high speed drive to

Wauwinet, turning on the flashing lights, and pulling his gun, controlling the situation, this was big, he thought. Really big!

Mark thought to himself that he might even call the Inquirer newspaper and fill them in on the radio call. Maybe do an interview with them about today's events in depth.

The paper might want to take some photos, maybe an action shot with the deputy pointing his gun. Front page news he figured!

Kosmo picked up the shot gun and checked the cartridge. Just as he thought. It was empty. He shook his head and let out a slight chuckle. He did not want to take the wind out of his deputy's sails so he kept it to himself.

Deputy Donato finished his shift around 5:00p.m. and went home, took a long shower, changed into his civilian clothes and headed into town. He first went into the Rose & Crown. There were only two other people besides the bartender there so he decided to move on finding it too quiet. He walked over to the Atlantic Café and again the same thing. The place was almost empty only a scattering of people at the tables with only two people at the bar. Next he decided to wander over to The Tap Room but instead he found himself climbing the stairs of Cioppinos.

Greg LeBlanc was bartending. Andy, a local mason and Kerry an artist were sitting at one end along with Michael Shannon who was the Chef-Owner with his partner Joe Pantorno of the Club Car Restaurant. At the other end of the small quaint bar was Duff Meyercord.

Hoody was standing at the mantle across from the them drinking what looked to be a nice bottle of red wine. He sent a glass of his wine to Duff.

"Day off today?" Mark asked Hoody.

"You got it," Hoody replied.

"So of all the places you could go," Mark asked, "why come here? I mean you tend bar here five nights a week."

"This place has the best wine list and I get an employee discount on top of it. Besides this is like being with my family when I am here." Right then Susie the owner walked in. "Hey Mark how's it going? Anything big happening lately?"

"Well now that you mention it." He puffed up his chest and hooked his thumbs into the waist line of his pants. Duff chimed in, "Yes - Heard a couple kids got their tricycles stolen," and everyone started laughing.

"Hey Greg?" Hoody asked. "Get me a glass for Mark. You're going to love this. It's a great California Cabernet." With the wind taken out of his sails, Mark then started again, tying to tell the story of the big day. He said, "We had a pretty good day. It's one of the days when your glad your packing heat."

Michael Shannon, who everyone called Shannon, had not heard the whole sentence, just something about the heat said, "Yup - It was pretty warm out there today. Going to be like that the rest of the week."

Again the deputy was deflated but not discouraged. Mark said, "It was pretty exciting out there today."

Again Duff chimed in, "I know what you mean. I had a pretty exciting day myself. I caught a thirty-eight-pound tuna before noon. Can you imagine if every time I went out fishing I caught a fish like that?"

Now the deputy was getting agitated, as he could not break into the big event that happened during the day.

The deputy was determined to get the story told. He began, trying not look like he was bragging, as he started one more time to express the events of the day, everyone seemed to be listening when Colin Keenan and Sean Divine walked in. "Hey everybody," Sean belted out and next thing you know everyone was lost in conversation. Everyone started talking at once. This was too much for the deputy. He sucked down his glass of wine. Draining it and walked abruptly out the front door.

Back at Trevor's job, Emily and Maureen had just left after dropping a hot meatball sub from Pi Pizza. His crew sensed something was bothering him. One of the guys finally approached him and said, "Everything okay with you Trev?"

"Ah, it's that clown, Chris Meyer. He's flirting with Emily and he won't stop. They both happen to be working on the same property. It's bugging me, big time."

"Trevor, everything's going to be fine. Emily is head over heels in love with you and she can take care of herself. Chris is just a jerk. He's full of himself at times, with his good looks and all, but everyone thinks he's more like a big bag of wind."

Trevor was sure of his and Emily's relationship being solid. Thinking back, he remembered proposing to her. They had gone to the Jetties Beach Bar. His plan was to wait just until about the sun was setting, walk with her down to the ocean's edge and asked Emily to marry him but things did not work out as planned. The sun was glistening off her face while they were sitting at the bar and she looked almost magical. He got off his bar stool and asked her if she would like to become Mrs. Trevor Smith Obrien.

Marshal Thompson, the owner was standing near them and overheard the proposal. After she said yes, Marshal was so overjoyed he said, "You must have the celebration here. I will toss in a case of French champagne!"

As Emily and Maureen drove back to town, after leaving Trevor's job site, Maureen told Emily, "Look that guy Chris has nothing going on for him. He owes money all over town. He hasn't got a pot to piss in. I don't know why you are so nice to him?"

Emily said, "I feel sorry for him. He's like a lost puppy dog."

Maureen replied, "I know, when he looks at you with those deep brown eyes of his, you know he's just a lost soul."

"Don't you try and tell me you don't have feelings for him Maureen. I watch you when he's around. You get all soft and googly eyed. And I know he thinks you are pretty. He's just afraid to tell you."

"I do not have feelings for him!"

"Do too."

"Do not!"

"Do too."

Maureen also knew that Chris was always checking her out but it was still tough to compete for Chris's attention, especially with Emily, the beauty queen, with high cheekbones, dark brown eyes, her long tanned legs and a great personality.

Then of course there is Karen, his latest arm candy, which was just that, killer eyes, beautiful smile, olive complexion, and a butt you could bounce a quarter off of. It seemed that anyone who ever came in contact with Karen adored her. Maureen just didn't feel confident enough to think she could compete with her, even though Maureen was considered a 'hottie' with her auburn hair and such an outgoing personality. Unfortunately, she privately only had eyes these days for Chris Meyer. It was just so hard to compete against those two for Chris's attention.

Chris did like the fact that Maureen had a new BMW convertible, always seemed to be flush with cash and she owned her own private wedding consulting business. But still his mind always seemed to be on someone else and not Maureen.

Two days later, Emily and Trevor were enjoying drinks at DeMarco Restaurant on India Street prior to their 7:00pm dinner reservation at Company of the Cauldron, which was right next door. Chris and his two friends Sean Divine and Colin Keenan walked in. Chris walked right up to Trevor and Emily, slapping Trevor on the back and said, "How's the two love birds getting along?"

Trevor said, "Just leave us alone and we will be fine."

"Look you Irish chicken," Chris blurted out. Trevor started to get out of his seat but Emily calmed him down. "That's right," Chris said, "have your girlfriend protect you."

Emily said, "Why don't you just go and join your friends Chris?" He looked into her eyes for a second and quietly walked away.

Chris called the bartender over and said, "Buy those two a couple glasses of champagne."

"Sorry Chris but before I get you anything I am going to need to see some cash or a credit card from you," the bartender stated.

"Here," Chris said and pulled out a wad of cash. "All my bills are current everywhere in town." A few minutes later the bartender came back over and said, "The couple declined your offer."

Chris yelled over. "What's the matter you Irish scum bag, Champagne too rich for your blood?"

Trevor got off his bar stool and Emily felt a fight brewing. At that point Constable Kosmo who was enjoying a nice bowl of linguine and clams got up from his table, approached Chris and his friends, called the bartender over and said, "These guys were just leaving. Can you get their tab in order?"

Constable Kosmo escorted them out the front door. Chris yelled out,

"You're just a peasant here. Taking our jobs and ruining this islands economy!"

WARRENS LANDING

For the last couple of days, it was only Steve and Uncle Zach staying at the house. Everyone else was back in Columbus for family and school obligations except for Jessica who was in Switzerland at a private school for six months.

Steve had asked Chris if the wine racks on one side of the cellar were sturdy enough to start stocking some wines. He had three cases they brought back from the New York Finger Lakes District and four other cases that had been shipped to him by Bill Heifner, which were all French Bordeaux. Chris explained that the racks were totally secure and maybe he and Steve could rack them together.

Later on in the afternoon Steve brought down the cases of wine that were still up off the back entry of the kitchen. Chris suggested one section for the New York whites and an area for the reds. Then another section dedicated to the Bordeaux and one area for California whites and reds and so forth as he began to build his inventory.

Steve and Chris set about the task of getting the wines in place. Steve asked, "When are going to finish that one section over by the coal chute?"

Chris, trying to think fast about the delay, told Steve, "Well while you were gone I ran the hose several times around the outer upper lawn area of the chute. I just want to make sure if you have a long, heavy downpour that the chute will stay dry. You don't want to have water running into it. If it sits and collects in a pool on the bottom of the shaft it could possibly become an uncontrollable mold source. If that happens, it could cause a huge problem. It will become a real mess and the whole section would have to be torn out and rebuilt again as mold, just like rust, never dies. I've been watching to make sure that it is water tight."

They put the New York State wines away. They were mostly whites with a few bottles of rose. Steve loved the way it looked on the racks. Then they broke out the French wines Steve's friend, Bill Heifner, had shipped from Ohio. Bill loved Bordeaux wines. He had a cellar with over forty cases back in Ohio. Several times, after having dinner at Bill's home, he and Steve would head down to the cellar, break out a bottle of wine and light up a couple of cigars. Steve kept telling Bill that someday he would have his own cellar.

"How many bottles do you think this will hold when it's finished?" Steve asked.

Chris told Steve, "I figure at least two hundred cases. Maybe put a nice table with four chairs right there in the center. This space has plenty of room."

As they were putting the wines on the racks, Chris shared with Steve his knowledge of French wines. Explaining all sorts of stories about different chateaus. He pulled out one of the bottles of Chateau Beychevelle from Saint Julien that they were stocking and explained how on the label the sails were lowered at half-mast because when they sailed past the Grand Admiral of France's private estate they did this as a salute to the Admiral. That's what was depicted on the label. Chris also told Steve the story of the different artist's paintings on the Chateau Mouton Rothschild labels. They were sanctioned by the Mouton family to famous artists and, if they were selected, they received two free cases of the vintage along with their painting featured on the label. He also told Steve that Bordeaux was the largest wine growing region in France and the red wines were usually a blend of five different grapes but mainly Cabernet with the exception in Pomerol and St. Emilion. Merlot grew much better there than Cabernet. Chris also pointed out other fun facts about the Grand Dame of Champagne, the Widow Clicquot and in Burgundy they make such a small amount of wine their motto is 'let them drink Bordeaux.'

They started to put away the Chateau Haut-Brion from Graves when Chris started to tell Steve a bit of Irish folklore. "Many years ago, as the legend goes, the Chateau," he stopped when they heard someone coming down the stairs. "Hello?" Diane was saying as she was headed downstairs into the basement. "Hell-o-ho?"

"Hey Diane." Chris welcomed her.

"Hi Diane. How's Luna?" Steve added.

"We are all good. My little angel is sitting in the front seat of the car looking out the window for Marshmallow. I just saw Uncle Zach. He was heading to the Wauwinet Inn. He told me you were down here. I just brought you over a loaf fresh of baked honey nut bread. Right out of the oven along with two jars of my freshly made Beach Plum Jelly. It's on the kitchen table. Wow, this is really looking nice. When are you going to finish up that section?" she asked Chris, looking at the six-foot area by the coal chute.

Again, Chris knew he had to get the lock and the lip cut off. It was becoming obvious he was stalling. He had better get moving and complete the job but where was he going to store the goods?

Uncle Zach had kept his distance from Chris ever since the blowup at the Rose & Crown. He knew if he got too close to that loser he was going to deck him and the poor kid might not get back up. Zach had briefly mentioned the beer situation to Steve with the girls and he knew it would never happen again. This kid Chris was way too scared to try another move like that again.

Zach had found a spot in the basement where he could secretly observe Chris when he was supposedly working in the wine cellar. The work did not seem to be progressing around the one area of the coal chute. "Why?" was the question floating around in Uncle Zach's mind. The door was almost finished. The electrical and lighting was in place. The sink and the plumbing were ninety-five percent installed. All except the wall with the coal chute. The dirt pile was still off to the side with the old cut lock in it. What was this guy up to? Zach was determined to find out!

After puttering around working on the door the next day, Chris looked around to make sure he was alone and felt above the wall in the left corner of the almost completed wine room, not noticing the large figure standing out of sight near the washer and dryer. Chris removed something that Zach thought was possibly a key, he got down on the floor and opened the lock to the chute, lifted up the heavy steel covering, placed the pin in the side bar to keep the lid open and reached in. It was fairly dark looking in the room from where Zach was standing but he could still make out what Chris was doing.

Chris pulled something out of the chute, unwrapped it and took something from what looked like a small bag and placed it onto the floor. He then removed something else and wrapped the rest of it back up placed it back inside and locked the chute.

He slid whatever he removed into his pocket, put the key back up on the top of the ledge on the wall and headed upstairs.

All Zach had to do was wait until Chris left the property which the way this kid worked might be any minute now. Zach now knew where the key was hidden and hopefully Steve would still leave the house and have his 4:00p.m. meeting with his accountant. Zach figured he only needed a few minutes to get the key and search the chute and lock it back up. Looking at his watch it was only 1:30 so he had plenty of time.

He figured he would stroll down to the Wauwinet Inn and enjoy a cold beer tor two. He was in no rush to see what was behind the steel door but he was extremely curious. The more he thought about it he was becoming more and more curious. Was it drugs?

BRANDT POINT

"Nantucket Police Department. What is your emergency?"

"There's blood - blood everywhere!"

"Excuse me?"

"I think he's dead!"

"Who's dead?"

"My carpenter! He's been working on my house doing repairs. I have blood on my hands! My shirt! It's awful! Send help!"

"Okay sir, slow down. Whom am I speaking with?"

"Germain - Steve Germain."

"And what is your location sir?"

"Umm - I am - I'm at my house here in Wauwinet."

"What's the address?"

"It's ah – its - Oh God! I can't remember. I just bought the place a few months ago. I know how to drive here but the house address? I can't remember."

"Okay sir, who did you purchase the house from? What road are you located on?"

"I bought it from - um - um, Tom Kendrick of Kendrick's Real Estate on Main Street."

"No Mr. Germain. The person who owned the house."

"Oh, I can't remember. Only thing I remember is signing the papers in the lawyer's office. We are located on Wauwinet Road about a mile and a half down on the right. There's a big rock out front with a red mailbox. Now I remember. His name was Cate. The last owner."

"OK. Mr. Germain. Stay on the line. Sit tight. Don't touch anything. Help is on the way."

Beth English, who was the dispatcher on duty when the call came in was flustered. Beth had never expected a call with such urgency to ever be taken by herself. She dropped her tuna fish sandwich that she was enjoying right out of her hand landing on the desk where she was reading a magazine.

Beth had been on the job as a part time employee for the last four months and had taken the position at the request of her boyfriend Deputy Donato, who had told her that it's really easy nothing dramatic ever happens here on Nantucket.

When she got the call she instantly became flustered. Trying to remember the code numbers for certain radio dispatch information to give out. She had never expected anything like this. "Oh My God!" she said to herself looking around for the code booklet. She then knocked her coffee all over herself and the switchboard. Everything else on the small desk also became scattered in her haste. Knocking some of it on the floor as she looked around in vain for some help but the station seemed to be deserted of other employees. They were all in a late afternoon meeting.

Knowing she better remain calm and move quickly she reached for the portable handset, pressed the call button and started yelling into it. "Chief! Chief!"

A moment later Constable Kosmo radioed back, "What is it Beth?"

"Oh My God Chief! There's been a murder!"

"What do you mean a murder? Calm down and slowly tell me what's going on," Kosmo said with a stern voice.

"It's at the old Cate house on the Wauwinet Road next to old man Lussier's house. You were there a few times this week. Mark had told me!"

"Okay. Okay. I am on my way. I will put this out on the radio. You remain calm. Call me if anything else comes in. Is the caller still on the line with you?"

"Yes. It's a Mr. Germain. I have him holding on the phone."

"Tell him I will be there in under ten minutes." The constable quickly got Deputy Donato on the radio. "Switch to channel five." he quickly told the deputy. Seconds later the constable heard Deputy Donato. "I'm here Chief what's up?"

"We have just received a call from a Mr. Germain out at the old Cate Estate on Wauwinet Road."

"Oh?" replied the deputy. "Old man Lussier acting up again Chief?"

"No it's much more serious than that. It seems that there is a dead body somewhere on the property. I could not get much more out of Beth. I am going to get her back on the radio now. Meet me there ASAP. Move it Deputy!"

Deputy Donato started shaking and feeling for his gun blabbering away. "I'm on it Chief. On my way!" Doesn't it figure of all the darn luck? Here he was way out on the farthest point of the Madaket Road talking with a very upset Dolores Frechette about her dog, Teddy who had wandered off as in the many times prior. Why couldn't he have been at the rotary sitting in his patrol car about a few miles away from the scene? If he had been, he could have been one of the first responders to the crime scene. Secured it, and hopefully located the suspect. He could then take the suspect into custody and probably gotten his name and photo on the front page of the paper. Then his friends and fellow officers would be so proud of him. But no, here he was with a missing dog call. He told Mrs. Frechette, "Your dog issue is going to have to wait. I got a big call. A real big one and I have got to go!" Mrs. Frechette was tugging on his arm, "What about Teddy? My poor baby!"

The deputy was so excited he fired up the siren, squealed the tires sending sand everywhere and started charging down Madaket Road. He had only gotten about a quarter of a mile when a flock of ducks were crossing the road blocking traffic in both directions. "Not now!" he said. He leaned out of his window and yelled, "Get out of the road."

People on their bikes were stopped blocking all the cars taking photographs. "This can't be happening," he said out loud. "NOT! NOW!" He jumped out of his car shooing the ducks across the road. "Out of my way! Big police business here. Move off the road!" He was yelling, "Clear a path!" telling the people taking pictures. Right then one of the heavy set kids who was on his bike fell over and skinned his knee. One of the adults, a female, laid her bike down right in front of the line of cars that were already blocking the road and looked at his knee and said. "Hunny? Here let me get my handkerchief. I can use it to attend to this scrape."

"Move it! Deputy Donato said getting out of his car again, "MOVE IT! MOVE IT! MOVE IT!"

As he finally made his way around all this commotion he was thinking, "Do I have my bullet proof vest? How many bullets do I have with me?" He felt around looking down for his handcuffs. "Check!" he said to himself as he almost ran off the road.

125

When Deputy Donato finally arrived at the scene, he ran up to the constable and started rambling quickly. "What do we have Chief?"

The constable was talking with Steve Germain.

"Where's the body? Who was murdered? Were they shot? Strangled? Bludgeoned? Who do you have here? Did he do it? Want me to cuff him? He's got blood all over him looks guilty to me. Let me take him into the station. I'll sweat the truth out of him in no time!"

"Calm down deputy. I just arrived and am analyzing the scene. The body I have been told, is in the basement. I am headed there now. "Mr. Germain just wait right here. Don't go anywhere. Is there anyone else in the house Mr. Germain?" Constable Kosmo slowly and calmly asked.

"I don't know. I just returned home about fifteen minutes ago. Right then another patrol car arrived with its sirens blaring.

Hearing the commotion out in the driveway Uncle Zach woke from a short rest. He and Diane had met at the Inn. After consuming three beers at the Wauwinet Inn bar they headed back to the house about thirty minutes prior. Diane dropped him off and he figured a little siesta was in his future.

"Deputy, you cover the back of the house." He then told the other officer Patrolman Jaksic, "Place Mr. Germain in the back seat of your car."

"Should we hand cuff him Chief? Deputy Donato asked.

"No." replied the constable, "Patrolman Jaksic, please, just place him in the back of your car. Make sure he's comfortable."

The deputy quietly mumbled to himself sarcastically, "Maybe we should get him a soda as well."

"Deputy, I am going to head inside the house through the front door and go down to the basement. I want you to check out the back part of the house. Look for any signs of blood on the porch. Then cautiously enter the house. Make a quick sweep of the main floor and make your way up to the top floor. Carefully check all the rooms and closets. See if there's anyone inside, then work your way downstairs. Meet me in the basement. Patrolman Jaksic, I want you to do a walk around the outside of the property. Look for anything suspicious. A blood trail, a weapon, anything out of the ordinary. If you find something, don't disturb it. Come find me."

Just then a fire truck and an ambulance arrived. A crowd started to gather and everyone started acting like they were in charge whispering and making up accusations. "What's happening?" someone whispered. "I think a whole family has been murdered." another person remarked. "Might have a hostage situation." another mentioned. "Heard that lots of shots have been fired. They've got a sniper on their hands." "Oh - the Chief has his hands full on this one. Wonder if he called in the State Police as back up?"

Ted Hudgins, the harbormaster who kept a police scanner in his old Willy's jeep, had heard the original broadcast over the radio from Beth at the station. His friend, John Vega was sitting in the passenger seat. He pulled out his megaphone, donned his old civil defense helmet from the floor of the back seat, telling John, "Sorry I don't have one for you," and headed towards Kosmo's direction. When Kosmo saw Ted the only thing he could say under his breath was, "Not Hudgins. Not now. Of all things."

"I got you covered Chief!" Ted told him. "I heard there's been sniper fire from the east. Want me to draw fire away from you?"

"Ted, there's no sniper fire. Don't go getting everybody all worked up. Best thing you can do is head back to town."

"I got it!" Ted replied. "I will handle crowd control and have everyone stay behind the fire trucks just in case of stray bullets. Do you have an extra bullet proof vest Chief? I also have my good friend John Vega here, he's a licensed lawyer from Naples Florida and if were talking hostage situation he could be the negotiator, if needed."

"Ted! Calm down. You are going to get everyone all fired up around here. It will be like a riot scene." Realizing that Ted was not listening to him, he said, "I really need you to do the crowd control." Kosmo opened his trunk, pulled out several rolls of yellow police line tape and handed it to Ted. "Stay clear of any sniper fire and tape off the entire area," he said shaking his head. At least this would keep Ted from interfering any further. Ted gave Kosmo a salute. "And tell your friend to stay out of the way."

Deputy Donato was getting ready to enter the back door of the house and head up the stairs. The constable was inside waiting for the deputy to make a sweep of the first floor before heading downstairs. When the deputy and the constable had entered the house all seemed quiet. Just then they both heard a loud floor board creak above them. The constable held two fingers to his lips to let the deputy know to be still and quiet. "Well it sounds like we have company," he whispered very quietly to the deputy.

Deputy Donato shaking, reached for his gun, looked over at the constable who started making hand signals implying that the deputy should quietly sneak towards the kitchen and see it there were back stairs leading to the upstairs. The constable would head up the front stairs. Very slowly with his gun drawn the constable started upstairs. The deputy went to the back kitchen area and looked around. It seemed the only way to the second floor was the way the constable ascended.

Right when the constable reached the top of the stairs a door opened down the hall. "Hold it!" shouted the constable. "Put both your hands slowly outside the door."

The deputy hearing that started bolting up the stairs. He missed a step, tripped and almost fell backwards down the staircase. He recomposed himself and was glad that the constable did not see his actions.

"Slowly exit the room!" the constable said. Out came Uncle Zach. "Hold it," the constable ordered. "Hands where I can see them. Slowly step all the way out into the hall." as the constable watched a rather large form of a person fill the hallway.

"What's going on?" asked Zach.

"I was going to ask you the same thing," the constable replied.

"I am staying here. Just took a short nap. I am Kim Germain's brother. My brother in-law is Steve Germain."

Just when the constable was assured about this, Deputy Donato came the rest of the way up the stairs huffing and puffing. "Should I cuff him and take him into custody Chief?"

'No, all is good." he told the deputy. "Deputy, please escort this gentleman downstairs and outside to Patrolman Jaksic. Then return and meet me in the basement."

"What's going on?" asked Zach for the second time.

It was total chaos out around the house. Ladders were being unhinged, the fire chief, Dan Connor, was shouting out orders over a megaphone, two fire fighters were running a hose to the nearest fire hydrant and the ambulance crew, seeing Mr. Germain covered in blood, were approaching the patrol car thinking he possibly might have been shot as that was the gossip flying around.

Zach, seeing Steve in the back of the patrol car, was trying to figure out what the hell was happening. As he got closer he could see what looked like red blood stains on Steve's shirt and his hands which he was holding up to his face. Steve lowered his hands and his face was smeared in blood as well.

"What the heck?" he tried to ask Steve through the open window.

"Hold it there sir," said Patrolman Jaksic, "No one is talking to anyone until I get a green light from the chief!" Steve wanted to tell Zach how he had just gotten back from the accountants and wanted to see if Chris had managed to hang the new door on the wine room when he found him lying on the ground stabbed, with a knife coming out of his abdomen.

Steve had knelt down to see if he was breathing and had reached down and slowly started to pull the knife out of his body but he was not moving or breathing. Steve then freaked out and ran upstairs and dialed 911 and that was how this whole scene started.

The constable and Deputy Donato were now making their way to the basement. As they got to the bottom of the stairs, Kosmo asked quietly, "Do you have your flashlight?"

"Right here Chief," the deputy said slapping the side of his belt.

"You search the rest of the basement and I am going to check on the body. Mr. Germain said it was in the wine cellar."

As Deputy Donato opened a few side doors that were small storage rooms he was trembling, his gun in one hand and flashlight in the other. All was quiet, at least he thought that was the case. As he opened up one of the slatted wood closet doors that was slightly ajar and peered into the dark. Right at eye level, about a foot inside, were two beady eyes staring right back at him. Startled beyond belief, trying to shout for help but no words came from his mouth, he dropped his pistol. When the person made a move towards him, he fell backwards. Marshmallow let out a big meow and jumped out of the closet landing on him, thinking this was yet another game.

Constable Kosmo entered the wine room and checked the body, laying before him, for signs of life but to no avail Chris Meyer had taken his last breath. The constable shook his head. Such a loss at a young age. He figured Chris must have been about in his late twenties.

The constable noticed one strange thing as he took a few moments to review the scene. It looked like the stabbing happened on one side of the cellar but the victim had crossed over to the other side of the room. Blood drops from the floor showed a pattern. Why wouldn't the victim head towards the door and yell for help? And why was he cradling a bottle of wine in his arms? Was his idea to use it as a weapon to attack his assailant as he left the cellar?

Constable Kosmo climbed the stairs ever so slowly thinking. What is going on here? Why would someone murder this young man?

The constable always remembered in his thoughts that sometimes slow and steady in thinking wins the race for clues and facts.

He went out to the front porch and stood back for a moment, standing off to the side of all the chaos. What a mess this scene turned into. These overzealous idiots. Back in Boston he never ran into this problem.

People were trained and retrained in Boston and every second counted in times of homicides, accidents, or fires. Well thought out plans were rehearsed using different scenarios so that when it happened people were prepared.

He looked around. People were gawking behind the yellow caution tape that was draped around the house. At least this wasn't in the heart of town so the crowd was much smaller. He reminisced his thoughts to a few cases in the past like this. It almost looks open and shut. There are finger prints on the knife he was sure would belong to Mr. Germain. Kosmo had to find a motive and that's what his next move was. A short interview with him and the other man, Zach here, while it's still early on at the scene and a more thorough one at the station. At this point Deputy Donato was still bossing everyone around. Telling anyone that would listen, "Get moving along. This is a dedicated crime scene".

Kosmo went to the patrol car where Mr. Germain was seated in the back seat and the deputy quickly approached. "Should I cuff him Chief? I got my card. I can read him his rights word for word."

"Hold on Deputy. Slow it down. Let's do this by the book. One step at a time not like this cluster of a mess going on around here. Let's see if you can get this place under control. Deputy, send the fire trucks back to the station. Have Patrolman Jaksic start clearing the crowd out. Tell the ambulance driver to remain until we get the coroner here. And get that megaphone away from the harbormaster! He making it sound like a bomb went off and the house is going to collapse."

"Mr. Germain? Please step out of the vehicle and lets you and I move to a quieter place and see what the facts are." The constable looked over to Zach, smiled and quietly led Steve to a place where they could talk in peace.

"Start from the beginning Mr. Germain. Where were you, say, from 8:00a.m. until now?"

"Well I was here at the house. I got up made coffee had a muffin, talked with Zach, told him I was headed to my accountant's after lunch. It's Frank Berger's office on Old South Road. I had to sign some tax papers that were in reference to the purchase of the house. I stopped at Egan's garage filled up the car with gas prior to that. Zach, my brother in-law, told me his only plan was to walk down to the Wauwinet Inn for a beer later on after lunch and he would be back soon after."

"So what time did you leave the house?"

"It was just after noon I believe," Steve told him.

"And who was here on the property at that time?"

"Zach and Chris Meyer. He was working in the new wine cellar."

"And what time did you return?"

"I guess around two-thirty?"

"Did you stop or talk with anyone else after you had finished up you're meeting with the accountant?"

"No, I headed directly back here."

"And who was here then?"

"Well I got out of the car, went into the kitchen, started to make a sandwich and I thought I would offer one to Chris if he was still working. His truck was still parked right over there. So I headed down to the cellar and that's when I discovered the body."

"And he was laying right where he is now?"

"Yes, I was kind of freaked out. I mean I have never seen a dead person, not even at a funeral."

"Then what did you do?"

"At first it took me a moment to take it all in. Then I knelt down and thought I would see if he was breathing. I don't know, then I thought I should maybe pull out the knife. I put my hand on it and started to but then thought better of it."

"So you touched the knife with your hand?"

"Yes."

"Which hand?"

"My right one."

"And how far did you pull out the knife?"

"I don't think I even moved it. I was too freaked out. I really don't know. I am still in shock I think. Then I ran upstairs and dialed 911."

"So have you had any unpleasant dealings with Mr. Meyer?"

"No - Not really."

"What do you mean, not really?"

"He did give my daughter and her girlfriend some beer a couple of weeks ago. My daughter Jessica told me about it so I met with Chris and I told him pretty firmly to stay away from them and keep his mind on the job at hand."

"Did you witness the girls drinking beer?"

"No but Zach told me he had come back to the house a few weeks ago and he mentioned that he had seen three empty glasses on a table where my daughter Jessica and her friend were laying out in back of the house and the glasses were still chilled and smelled like beer. Zach caught up with him at a bar downtown and warned him to stay away from them because they are underage. I guess it got a little heated, the whole episode and conversation. One of your off duty officers broke it up. But that was it. I also mentioned to Chris he needed to spend more time working and less time going to town for so called supplies, flirting with our gardener, and hanging around my daughter and her friend. I told him that they are off limits to him. I also brought up the subject that my wife Kim has been going over the bills from Marine Hardware, Hardy's Paint Store and Island Lumber, and she pointed out a few discrepancies that I needed to discuss with him sooner than later. He did not seem to be very keen on finding a time to go over them with me."

"I am afraid that we need to go back over your movements in the house from when you arrived back and your phone call to 911."

Deputy Donato came over and was off to the side taking some notes. His own hand writing was so poor at times, he had a hard time reading his own notes and he had to squint his eyes at times to try and make out some of the words. He was still shaking slightly after all the excitement that had just happened which did not help with his note taking.

As the deputy reviewed a few things he had already written down, he knew deep down that if the constable would just allow him a good thirty minutes alone with Mr. Germain he could break the case wide open. He was thinking to himself. There was the daughter and her friends' incident, also the padding of the bills and his milking of the hours on the job itself. To the deputy it was black and white. It was an open and shut case. The way he saw it had been played out was that Mr. Germain confronted Chris Meyer in the wine cellar and things just escalated from there. If he could play the good cop routine, he figured Mr. Germain would play right into his hands.

The deputy knew and respected the constable's approach. He was aware of his outstanding past history as a lead detective in Boston and then, over time, he was promoted to Chief of Police up in Boston prior to his accepting the job on Nantucket.

The deputy was starting to see the headlines now.

132

'Deputy Donato of the Nantucket Police Department Cracks open the First Murder on the Island in over Twenty Years'

In his mind he saw the interview and the photo of himself in his dress uniform on the front page. Beth would be so proud. Possibly he would also be receiving a medal.

"Okay Mr. Germain. Who else was in the house upon your return?" Kosmo continued.

"Well I am not sure, possibly Zach. I didn't hear anything when I was in the kitchen but if he was back from the Wauwinet Inn he might have been taking a nap. You would have to ask him personally."

"That we will, but first let's walk you through the arrival back home until you dialed 911."

They started to move from Steve's car to the house. The deputy snapped out of his daydream and started to follow the constable and Steve staying back about three or four feet.

"Were you carrying anything with you?"

"The only thing I had was a manila envelope with copies of my tax information from Frank Berger."

"Where is that now?"

"It's inside on the kitchen counter."

"Okay, let's head inside. Was the front door open or closed?"

"Open I think?"

"Did you see anybody driving or walking away from the house when you arrived?"

"No - Not that I recall."

"So you entered the front door, you headed directly to the kitchen, placed the envelope on the counter top?"

"Yes," Steve replied rubbing his bridge of his nose.

"Then what?"

Deputy Donato was becoming frustrated. He could have moved this interrogation along much quicker and possibly with a little more authority. By now he would have had Mr. Germain confessing to the whole incident. He would have placed him in the back of a patrol car and in a short time have a signed and sealed confession already done down at the station. The deputy could envision it now. The Inquirer and Mirror reporter would be waiting patiently for an exclusive interview with the deputy. Everyone would be patting him on the back congratulating him on his fine detective work and the fast and swift action he took but there was nothing he could do but take more notes.

The three of them walked into the kitchen where a loaf of bread lay opened and a plate was close by on the counter top. Next to it was a plastic deli bag with sliced cheese and another plastic bag, with what looked like to be sliced ham, a mustard bottle and a jar of mayonnaise along with a regular dinner knife. The phone on the wall in the kitchen was covered in blood.

"This was where I was going to make the sandwiches when I thought about Chris so I headed downstairs to the cellar to see if he might like one as well. It would be more cost effective for me to feed him and keep him on the job then Chris taking another two-hour disappearance from his job here."

"So this guy Chris was really getting on your nerves. The old boy was milking the clock. Seen that dozens of times myself," Deputy Donato chimed in looking directly at Steve.

Kosmo looked over and said, "Just take your notes for now Deputy."

"Just eats right away at your gut doesn't it?"

"That's enough Deputy!"

"Excuse me Chief," Patrolman Jaksic said as he knocked on the back screen door to the kitchen. "Everyone has more or less cleared out. A reporter from the Inky Mirror is hounding me with questions and the coroners van just arrived."

"Okay patrolman. I need a few more minutes here. Just tell everyone to be patient and tell the reporter no statements will be made until after we are at the station, as this is still an ongoing crime scene and where is Mr. Germain's brother in-law?"

"I have him sitting in the back of my patrol car at the moment."

"Good. Let's keep it that way for now. Now, Mr. Germain. You headed directly down the hallway stairs from here to the basement?"

"Yes. That's correct."

"Okay let's head downstairs. At this point you still did not hear anyone else in the house or possibly outside?"

"I did not hear anyone inside or outside."

Now the deputy was sure of it. Mr. Germain is trying to cover his tracks.

At the same time, he is digging himself into a hole. "No one else is in the house?" he thought to himself. "And the body is still warm? He's the only person around? Guilty. Guilty as sin."

As they reached the bottom of the stairs, Kosmo again noticed the bloody footprints on the floor of the wine cellar and told Steve, "Please step around them so we can preserve it for evidence. Now without stepping into any of the blood surrounding the body, can you re-enact your moves when you discovered the body?"

He said. "Like I already told you, I came directly down the stairs. I walked into the room. I do not recall hearing any sounds not even a saw or a hammer. Then I went like this," Steve knelt down near Chris's body as close as he felt comfortable doing. He was shaking pretty badly. Without touching the knife again, he did his best to show what transpired when he found Chris.

"Yeah right!" the deputy thought to himself. "The good caring person image. He is guilty as sin and its plain as day. The guy offed him. Pure and simple."

"Another question Mr. Germain. It looks like the struggle started over there where the blood is on the floor. Then the body ends up here. It's almost five feet away over to where he's laying now and Mr. Meyer is clutching a bottle of wine in his hand. Does that make any sense to you? It's puzzling as why would he do that? Any ideas or thoughts on that? Did he think he had enough strength to hit the attacker with it?"

"I have no idea. Like I told you, this is how I found the body. Can we now get out of here? I feel like I am going to be sick."

"Just a few more questions then we can leave. Have you ever seen that knife before? The murder weapon?" The constable watched the reaction on Steve's face.

It remained passive as he replied, "I have never seen it before."

"Do you know of anyone that might want to see Mr. Meyer dead?"

"None," replied Steve.

"One more question. Did Mr. Meyer have any visitors while he was working here not counting the other employees he had working with him?"

"The only other person that stopped by a few times was a girl that I assumed he was dating."

"Did you ever meet her?"

"Yes. He introduced me to her. Her name is Karen - Karen Grant. We chatted for a short time once and she's quite attractive. She told me she was originally from someplace in Maine."

"Okay let's let the coroner do his job. They will need to take several photos of the kitchen and the phone as well as parts of the murder scene. Mr. Germain, we will need to do a photo documentation of you as well. Then at the station you can clean yourself up. I am also going to need to question your brother in-law for a few minutes here and also at the station. So Deputy, you take Mr. Germain down to the station after we get a few photos of him and his blood stained shirt. Get him inside as quietly as possible. Do not speak with anyone about the case. Place him in the interrogation room and leave him alone. No one is to speak to him or question him. I will be there in a while. Get him some water. Make him comfortable."

"Again with the comfortable part," the deputy thought to himself. "We should make him uncomfortable so he might trip himself up on a re-examination of the facts. This is not a Country Club we're running here!"

"Could I make a phone call?" Steve asked.

"Okay, Deputy upon arrival at the station let him make his call."

"Hey Chief. I just remembered something."

"Can it wait Deputy?" Kosmo answered looking down and shaking his head.

"Well it's about Mr. Germain's brother in-law."

"Okay, keep it to yourself. We can discuss it at the station."

As they headed outside the constable noticed Zach sitting in back of the patrol car with an attractive tall female standing off to the side. He approached the patrol car. Kosmo asked Patrolman Jaksic to let him out of the back seat. The constable then asked Zach, "May we have a word in private? Let's step over here. May I have your full name and date of birth?"

"Zachary Cisco," he proceeded to give him all the information and his Phoenix address.

"Now Mr. Cisco, please tell me you're whereabouts since this morning."

"Well I was around the house all morning. I had coffee with Steve. I went out to the back porch and read some magazines. They should still be on the porch table. A while later I called a friend of mine in Phoenix. We talked on the phone for about twenty minutes."

"What did you talk about?"

"I don't know, just small stuff. I told him what a unique place Nantucket was with the cobble stone streets and how after the sun sets the temperature drops rapidly just like Phoenix."

"Was the deceased also on the property the same time you were here?"

"I believe so but I did not pay much attention. I mean he's been here for several weeks working or, shall we say, half assed working! Then Diane, the pretty lady who is standing over there, and I headed to the Wauwinet Inn around noon, she drove us there and back."

"Who's Diane again?"

"She's the neighbor. That's the peak of her house over there," Zach pointed through the trees.

"Was your brother in-law here when you left?"

"No he had already left for the accountants, about thirty minutes prior. Diane had stopped by just as I was planning on walking to the Inn. She decided to join me and drove us there."

"What time was that?"

"It must have been around 1:00p.m."

"So you're stating that you and the deceased were the only two on the property for about close to an hour?"

"I am not sure if we were the only two as there is usually guys working upstairs above the garage."

"What time did you return from the Inn?"

"We each had two beers out on the deck so I would say close to two. You can ask Diane. She might have the exact timing."

"Did your lady friend come inside?"

"No she dropped me in the driveway. I went inside and directly upstairs to take a nap. I didn't leave my room until I heard all the commotion happening and saw you in the hallway."

"Have you had any problems with Mr. Meyer?"

"No! None at all but I was not a fan of his work ethics."

"Okay. Did you enter the basement anytime today?"

"No."

"Do you know if your brother in-law has any beef or grudges with the deceased?"

"None that I know of."

"Okay, well that's all for now but I need you to remain on the island until this investigation is finished."

"I have no plans to travel anywhere in the near future as I am pursuing that fine philly over there," he said with a grin looking over to Diane.

The constable went over and asked Diane a few short questions and then went to his car. As the constable was pulling out of the Wauwinet property, he caught the glimpse of someone hiding in the deep scrub off to the side of the house. He got on his radio, contacted Deputy Donato, told him he spotted a person hiding in the scrub bushes behind some trees about a hundred yards off to the east side of the house. He instructed the deputy to quietly turn around, park about a quarter of a mile short of the entrance of the Germain property and told the deputy to quietly flank the area from the east. The constable would enter from the west off the road where he had pulled over. They were both to head into the scrub quiet as church mice.

Within five minutes the deputy had arrived. He radioed the constable and gave him his 10/40 as they both approached the area. Kosmo spotted the subject. His back was to them. The constable moved up fairly close then he yelled out, "Don't move! Drop your weapon! You're surrounded! Stand up and raise your hands high above your head."

At first the person did not move. The deputy had his gun out shaking as he pointed it towards the figure. Again as they moved closer, the constable repeated the order and again there was no response.

The constable in a low tone told the deputy, "I am going to circle around towards the front of him so I can get a better view of the suspect. He looks like he's just squatting there."

"Maybe he's loading up on ammo Chief! Better be cautious."

"No it looks like he's frozen with fear," Kosmo replied.

The constable circled around to the front of the suspect and almost started laughing. There was old man Lussier sitting propped up against a tree quietly snoring. The constable walked up to him, gently removed the rifle that was laying on the ground next to him and then gave him a slight tap on his shoulder.

Mr. Lussier jolted awake and said, "I'll have a hamburger." At that point the dazed Mr. Lussier focused his eyes and looked lost in thought for a few moments then realized where he was. He had been watching all the action going on at the Germain property. All the excitement made him a little tired and he sat down and had fallen asleep. When the constable woke him up, he was dreaming that he was at a restaurant.

Kosmo had moved the shotgun a good five feet away and helped him to his feet. The constable was considering questioning him on what he might have witnessed but thought better. He would be better off to let him go home. He had plenty of time to interview him the following day.

TOM NEVERS HEAD

"Okay Mr. Germain, here's the phone. You got one phone call so I would make it a good one," the deputy explained.

Steve dialed the number from memory, the law office of Mr. William Heifner. "Debbie Otto speaking. How may I help you?"

"Hi Debbie. It's Steve Germain. Can I talk to Bill please?"

"One minute Mr. Germain."

"Hey Steve. How's Nantucket? The wine cellar finished yet? Did my five cases of Bordeaux show up all in one piece?"

"Yes, everything is fine except I have one small problem."

"What's that Steve?"

'Well Bill, I am being questioned about a murder that happened at the house."

"Murder? Did I just hear you say murder?"

"Yup that what I said."

"Who was murdered and are you in custody?"

"Well it was the carpenter who was working on the wine cellar and other projects. I came home found him and called 911."

"So why are you being questioned?"

"Well I knelt down and tried to pull out the knife that he was stabbed with."

"Why would you do something like that?"

"Look Bill, I need you here to help me sort all this out. Get here as fast as you can and don't tell Kim."

"Okay Steve, but you know that it's not that easy to get to the island. First let me try and get someone to represent you before I get there. Just hold tight I will help sort all this out. I know a guy Walter Lesnevich. He has a home on Cape Cod. Let me try and reach him. He's a very good criminal attorney. He practices in New York. I know he spends a lot of time at his home on the Cape. With any luck he's there now. And Steve, no more talking to anyone about anything until you have legal representation and I mean no one! I doubt they will hold you over night but then again it's a murder case and I am not sure how they handle things in that part of the country. They can't hold you if you have not been charged and they can't make you talk without a lawyer present if you ask for one. Have they read you your rights?"

"No not yet, nothing like that. They just want to get to the facts of the murder scene and seeing as I am covered in blood; I make a pretty good candidate."

"Okay well just tell them you would feel much more comfortable with legal representation present. Call me when they release you. I am not licensed or certified to handle law in the state of Massachusetts but I am pretty sure Lesnevich is. I think he told me once that he's licensed in New York, Connecticut and Massachusetts."

As Kosmo sat in his patrol car still on the Wauwinet Road, he re-read his notes and what he had jotted down so far. There were no other suspects at this time. One thing he ran through his mind was the time Mr. Cisco was alone at the residence. This allowed him ample time to commit the murder but he did not seem to have any motive to commit murder. But then again, if it was that easy all homicides would almost be an open and shut case.

He started his car and headed back to the station. Upon arrival word had begun to spread around town. It seemed to spread like wild fire. There was already a small gathering of at least twenty people at the front entrance to the station. A few people had cameras. Mostly by-standers with nothing else to do but see what the gossip was about.

As Kosmo got out of his car, he was approached right away by Mrs. Frechette. "Excuse me Constable, what are you going to do about my missing Teddy?"

"What?"

"My missing Teddy,"

Kosmo, with a very bewildered look on his face, said, "What are you talking about?"

"My dog Teddy!" Mrs. Frechette replied.

"Your dog? I don't know what we are going to do about your dog. I am sure he will come home when he's hungry. Don't you worry, dogs know their way around pretty well."

He then stepped closer to the entrance of the station when someone from the small crowd said, "Is it true that there was sniper fire in Wauwinet Chief?"

He looked around and spotted Ted Hudgins, the harbormaster, still wearing his old civil defense helmet, along with his sidekick Mr. Vega from Florida. His jeep was parked right in the middle of the road with his four way flashers still blinking, blocking the side street. This is all he needed, fuel to add to the fire.

The harbormaster had his megaphone and started off, "Let's clear the area. Give the chief some room here."

Someone from the crowd said, "If there's a sniper out there I've got to warn my grandmother! She's always sitting out on her front porch at sunset! She lives nearby in Pocomo."

"No! No! No! There was no sniper fire in Wauwinet. Will everyone just relax and just go home? We are in the middle of an investigation and I can't really comment but your all pretty safe."

He started to walk into the station when he over heard someone say, "It was a bomb scare. Someone was planning on blowing up old man Lussier's house, the old goat! He's got lots of enemies that one."

The constable entered the station and told the front dispatch person, "Place an officer out front and disperse the crowd. Don't let anyone into the station and especially Ted Hudgins. Have someone make him move his old jeep out of the road. No one in no one out unless it's official business and don't say anything about what's going on!"

As he headed into his office, he called for Deputy Donato. "So what's the situation here?"

"I have the suspect in the interrogation room. I gave him some water and a pad of paper just in case he wanted to write his confession Chief, and he made his phone call."

The constable went into his office and made a few notes on a pad of paper reading;

MOTIVE?
Suspects,
    Steve Germain
    Uncle Zach, (Cisco)
    Albert Lussier
    Roommates
    Jealous Boyfriends/girlfriends
Was he a drug dealer?

After that he drew a blank. "One step at a time," he thought to himself.

In his mind he thought that Mr. Germain was an upstanding, law abiding citizen as much as he knew about the man. He made a mental note that after the interrogation to get background checks on Mr. Germain, Mr. Cisco, and Mr. Lussier and on Chris Meyer. Also, he thought to himself, there is no rush for unspecified answers. It will all come out in due time. One other idea in the back of his mind was a jealous girlfriend or husband. One never knows who Mr. Meyer might have jilted. He wrote that angle down on a side bar of his notes.

He called for Deputy Donato to join him and they entered the room together. Steve was sitting at the desk and asked, "Can I change my shirt now and go wash my hands?"

"Certainly. Deputy please escort Mr. Germain to the men's washroom. Oh and Deputy, don't forget to get an evidence bag for the shirt."

Steve went into the men's room and spent about twenty minutes scrubbing off the dried blood. He washed his face, his hands, arms, even ran cold water through his hair. Steve looked into the mirror with water dripping off his face and thought, "How could this be happening? One minute I am doing my taxes and the next I am being questioned about committing a murder."

When he returned to the interrogation room he was just wearing his tee shirt and quietly sat down. The deputy started the tape recorder and told Mr. Germain that this and all future conversations would be recorded.

"Okay Mr. Germain, we want to get your thoughts on the murder that took place today at your home on Wauwinet Road. The deceased being Mr. Chris Meyer. His date of birth to be added to the record and relatives to be notified. So starting at the beginning, please tell us your exact moves since you awoke this morning."

"Well Constable, since I made the call to my personal attorney who is going to contact someone to represent me in this line of questioning, at this point, I will not discuss anything relating to this episode until I can be advised by counsel."

"Now Mr. Germain, if you are innocent then the truth will prevail and you have nothing to worry about."

"I understand that," Steve replied, "But I will wait until I have proper legal representation and if I am not being charged with anything I would like to go home."

At this stage of the investigation Deputy Donato really felt strongly about Mr. Germain's guilt. He's upstairs making a sandwich. It's brewing in his mind. All the things that Mr. Meyer had been doing like padding the bills, flirting with his daughter and giving her beer among other things and it began eating away at him so he opens a drawer to get a knife for the mayonnaise. At first he pulls out a regular butter knife. He notices the green inlaid knife and then his blood starts to boil. Those thoughts start running over and over in his mind and he grabs the murder weapon. He conceals it in his back pocket and goes downstairs to the wine cellar. Confronts the victim. Their conversation escalates and Mr. Germain, who is quite upset thinking about this guy trying to get his daughter drunk, snaps and next thing you know Chris is stabbed. It's pretty open and shut. If he was truly innocent, he would have just gone over all the facts as well as he could but this lawyer tactic just made it seem like he was hiding something. Something big! Like guilty!

The Deputy thought to himself that the constable should have pressed him harder but his response was, "We will release you on your own recognizance but do not make any plans to leave the island."

Steve got up and went to the dispatcher and asked if someone could arrange a taxi for him.

Constable Kosmo went to his office and started running a background check on Chris Meyer of Nantucket, Zachary Cisco of Phoenix Arizona, and Karen Grant, from Maine.

He put the information he had into a national data base and figured within six hours everything would show up for a print out. He also put in the name Steven Germain, Columbus Ohio.

"Okay Deputy," Kosmo said, "let's call it a day."

"But Chief, don't you want to bring in that guy Zach now while the case is still hot?"

"I am going to head over to the coroners in a while and see what personal items Mr. Meyer had on him at the time of death and I need to go back out to the Germain house and search Chris's truck before calling it a day. At the least I can hopefully find a current address for Mr. Meyer. See if he has any roommates and if so do they know of any family members we can contact. But for the most part I want to sit back and think on this a bit. There are a lot of variables to ponder. I will head home in a while and take my mind off this. Sometimes it helps me think more clearly if I step back from a situation and clear my head for a short while. Then I will look at all the options with a different point of view. The one thing that is bothering me is why would Mr. Meyer go over to the other side of the room and pick a bottle of wine out of the rack? But not just the nearest bottle available but one from the top part of the rack. That just doesn't add up. I am also going to go over all the crime scene photos tomorrow to see if there might be any other clues we might have over looked. I am still puzzled at the reason for the bottle of wine. Was he going to use it as a weapon to protect himself? We should start making out a witness and suspect's board. Write down any unanswered questions and place it on the board. I think you and I should perform a complete search of the premises where Mr. Meyer lived tomorrow. I will also search his truck one more time tomorrow morning and I need to inventory the personal belongings that were on his person at the time of the murder. We also need to locate any relatives to notify, sooner than later. Anything that I find in his truck tonight, like his registration, may not match with his current address so let's see if we can run it through the Department of Motor Vehicles. Deputy, you will need to get the names and D.O.B. of his roommates, if he has any, as well as who his landlord was."

"Oh by the way Chief, I wanted to tell you this earlier. I made a small note in my daily log a few weeks back."

"Referring to what?"

"I was at the Rose & Crown and I broke up and altercation between that guy Zach and Mr. Meyer."

"Really? That must be the one Mr. Germain was referring to earlier."

"Yes they were going at it about Mr. Germain's daughter and her friend. Seems that Mr. Meyer was giving them beer when no one was around."

"Were there any threats made?"

"Well this guy Zach was saying in a loud agitated voice that he was going to rope him and skin him and Mr. Meyer said he plays for keeps where he came from. That's when I separated the both of them. The guy Zach left and Mr. Meyer said to his friends that he was just about ready to pummel him."

"Interesting, I am going to have to have a word sooner than later with Mr. Cisco."

Steve returned home finding yellow tape still strung around parts of the porch and inside blocking the hallway stairs leading to the basement. Uncle Zach was sitting in the living room and Steve had a million questions for him. Zach answered almost all of them and then Steve said, "I need a hot shower and some rest."

After his shower he called Bill Heifner and told him what had transpired so far. "And also, let's not mention this to Kim. It will just make her upset and worrisome. I will sort this out and then find the best way to break the news to her. I only hope she doesn't want to sell the house after all this mess. Bill, if this guy Lesnevich is around, you don't have to come running out here. I can only imagine that Kim is going to blame the whole thing on the fact I wanted a wine room. I can hear it now, '*Steve if you and Bill had not gotten that stupid idea of a wine cellar none of this would have happened!*'"

The next morning Steve was having coffee, not sure of how or what he felt like. Was he angry? Upset? Confused?

The phone had rung the night before and it was Mr. Lesnevich, the attorney from Cape Cod. Steve told him every detail that he could remember about the murder and Mr. Lesnevich said, "Please call me Walter. I will take the morning boat and arrive around noon tomorrow."

Steve looked out of the double kitchen windows that morning. Two deer were off in a distance. A few birds soaring overhead and sun was shining in the cloudless sky. Marshmallow was hopping and running through the tall grass when he heard a car pull into the driveway. His heart sank. He did not want to talk with anybody at this time.

Steve looked out of the side window off the kitchen and saw it was Diane. She was carrying what looked to be a pot of some sort, covered in tin foil. He could see her dog Luna sitting in the front seat.

Steve went to the front door and opened it up managing a smile on his face.

"Hi. I just wanted to drop this off for you and Zach. It's a richly flavored beef stew. I know you have a lot of things on your mind and I am sure cooking is not one of them. Just set the pot on the stove, place it on low, add some water and let it simmer for thirty minutes. Make sure you add at least a cup, if not more, of water otherwise the potatoes will absorb all the juice."

"Thanks," Steve said.

"Zach has my telephone number if there's anything you need. Got to run. Ciao!"

As Steve carried the pot into the kitchen the phone rang. "Now what?" Steve muttered to himself.

145

"Good morning Mr. Germain. This is Constable Kosmo."

"Good Morning or I hope it's going to be a good morning."

"Mr. Germain, we would like to talk with your brother in-law today. Do you think we can set up a meeting here at the station sooner than later?"

"Well our attorney, Mr. Lesnevich, is arriving today on the noon ferry. The three of us could come directly to the station. So let's figure around 12:15?"

"That works out perfectly. See you in a few hours."

After Steve hung up Zach came downstairs asking, "How did you sleep?"

"I tossed a lot but I am okay. You?"

"About the same. You know Steve, I am cut from a different cloth than you are. Scenes like this are more of a common place for me but still I know it's terribly upsetting for you. And Kim, well, I don't know how well she's going to take this news."

"Well for now, I am not mentioning it to her."

"Smart move. I wouldn't either."

When Zach and Steve arrived at the ferry they spotted Mr. Lesnevich right away. He had described himself to Steve saying he was over six feet tall, wearing a tan overcoat, a navy blue tie and he would be carrying a briefcase. Steve told him about their 12:15 appointment and Walter, as he preferred to be called, said, "Well that's not going to happen. Is there a place we can sit and go over some facts of the case? I need at least an hour with the two of you."

"Yes we can go to the Atlantic Café. It's close to the Police Station."

"Good. Before we have our sit down at the restaurant I will stop in the station and introduce myself and give them a new time line of 1:30p.m. How are they treating you?"

"Pretty good except they would not let me change out of my blood stained clothes yesterday until after several photos were taken of me. I was in their interrogation room for a short time after, I mentioned that I needed to seek counsel from my lawyer before proceeding. The constable seems to know his way around a murder investigation but the deputy, he gave me the feeling like he thinks I am guilty."

"Well that usually how it goes, good cop, bad cop. We can sort all this out over time."

146

STEPS BEACH

When they arrived at the Atlantic Café, the whole bar seemed to be talking about the murder. They overheard bits and pieces.

"It looks like the guy who owned the house offed old Chris Meyer. Stabbed him like - twenty times."

"I heard the guy went nuts and was firing bullets all over the place"

One guy added, "He was about to torch the house to hide the evidence."

Steve was grateful that he did not know anyone in the crowd that hung around the bar there. No one paid him or Zach any mind.

The three of them slid into the farthest back booth of the restaurant and Steve again went over the whole scenario.

Walter chose to look towards the front of the restaurant so he could see if anyone was coming close enough to be able to over hear their conversation and also to keep Steve and Zach from possibly being recognized.

Walter spent a few minutes telling them both of his experience and that he had a very good success rate.

After hearing the story from Steve, he turned his questions to Zach, his relationship with Steve, and to the deceased etc.…

"Any suspects you might know about?"

"No." the both of them nodded.

Right before they finished up he looked at both of them and said, "Are we going to find any skeletons in the closet here? One more thing. Did they ask you if the knife was yours? And was it?"

"Yes, the constable asked if I was the owner of the knife," replied Steve. "I told him I had never seen it before."

"I mean if anything is being hidden, now's the time to bring it up!"

Steve gave a nod and was wondering what Zach would say.

"No," was all that Zach replied.

"Good then. Let's go get this thing done!"

The five of them; the constable, Deputy Donato, Steve, Zach and Walter sat in the interrogation room. They talked briefly then Zach was led out to wait his turn for his interview. Things went smoothly.

Deputy Donato was operating the tape recorder. Adjusting volume control and pretending to look busy. He knew in his mind that Mr. Germain was the killer but there were proper protocols that had to be followed.

Constable Kosmo had made light of the background check stating that it looks as if Steve had a solid background as an up standing citizen. After Steve had again, for what seemed like the twentieth time, retold the events of the day leading up to the discovery of the body, he was sent out of the room and Zach was brought in.

After a few simple questions, Constable Kosmo looked straight at Mr. Cisco and asked, "What line of business are you in?"

Zach knew this was coming and nonchalantly replied, "I raise horses."

"Really? That's you whole source of income?"

"Yes."

"Well I ran a background check on you and called a detective by the name of Seth High, in Phoenix. It's reported that you might also be connected with a few people in the underworld and that one of your other sources of income is that you're a collector for the mob. Isn't it possible that racketeering, strong arming and murder are not out of the question in that line of work? Actually, you have been questioned in the past in Phoenix on all sorts of questionable deaths, loan sharking and so forth."

"I have never been charged with anything."

At this point Mr. Lesnevich said, "If nothing has ever been proven, it has no bearing on this case." Then Mr. Lesnevich said, "We need to take a break here so I can confer privately with my client."

Walter sat with Zach alone in the room and Walter quietly said, "I asked you, not one hour ago, if they were going to find any skeletons in the closet and this pops up?"

"It's really nothing. I have some friends that ask for my help in certain matters but I have never been charged."

"Well I hate to tell you how this looks," Walter responded. "But I am pretty sure I can get us around it. Anything else I need to know before we head back in? This guy Kosmo is no slouch. I will have his background checked out tomorrow first thing."

The rest of the interview went smooth enough but now Deputy Donato started thinking maybe they were in it together. Zach and Steve, they both took Chris Meyer out. His mind was racing, playing out different scenarios in his head. "Oh this was big. Really big!"

After their meeting, Walter checked into Martins Guest House, reviewed his notes and walked to the North Shore Restaurant which was just a few blocks away. He ordered a bowl of steaming hot clam chowder and the special of the day, the slow roasted prime rib with a jumbo baked potato and green beans.

Walter tried to make as much sense of the facts as possible. The part about Zach being associated with the mob certainly did not help matters as he was on the property at the time of the murder. This was not good for his defense strategy.

Meanwhile Constable Kosmo, keeping matters close, had not revealed the findings of the search of Mr. Meyer's car or the items that were on his person at the time of the murder.

That morning, the day after the murder, Deputy Donato and the constable had located the house where Chris Meyer lived, and the Constable was correct. His driver's license and his truck registration were both listed under different addresses. "How did the constable know that was most likely the case?" Deputy Donato wondered.

He had roommates and they talked with all three of them. In the deputy's mind they all seemed like sleaze balls. Just what this island needed now is more low-lifers. The deputy searched Chris's room which did not turn anything up out of the ordinary. He had a sense that the minute the roommates found out about the murder, the first thing they did was rifle through his stuff looking for anything of value.

One of his roommates looked as if he was stoned and definitely half in the bag. There was an opened bottle of vodka, a quart of orange juice, and a few ice cubes still floating around in the pint glass sitting on the coffee table along with what looked to be some pot seeds in an ash tray that was directly in front of the couch where he was laying. One of the roommates mentioned that Karen, his latest squeeze, was going to take care of his dog, Socrates.

After the interviews with Steve and Zach along with the earlier walk through at Chris's residence, Kosmo headed home. He sat in his kitchen enjoying a bowl of cold left over pasta from the night before. He had the clear plastic bag of the things that were in Chris Meyer's pockets from the coroner. It contained two hundred dollar bills, three twenties, two tens and two five dollar bills, four one's, along with several assorted business cards. Most looked like they were from prospective clients. One was from a pawn shop in Mashpee. There were a few pieces of scrap paper with girl's numbers written on them. One with a big smudged lipstick kiss on it with a number and a name that read Inga.

Kosmo was holding the thing that puzzled him most in his hand and he was turning it over and over, a beautiful red stone, clear and bright. What did that mean and where did it come from? Was it valuable? In the search of his car, there was nothing of importance. Several old beer cans, lots of old paper coffee cups, old newspapers, a few ball caps, two full oil cans and three empty ones. A car registration that did not match the address of where he was living now and three unpaid parking tickets dated over a month old.

Nothing stood out except two things, one was the pawn shop card and the other was the gemstone. Not knowing anything about jewelry, he had no idea if it was a cheap costume piece or not.

He went over to his phone and called Marty Texeria, the owner of Main Street Jewelers. His wife Sue answered the phone.

"Hey kiddo. It's Kosmo."

"Hey stranger. Where have you been hiding? How have you been? It seems like ages since we have seen you. Nasty business about that poor boy being murdered in Wauwinet yesterday."

"Yes it's a tragedy and I am wading through all the mess."

"What can I do for you Kosmo?"

"Well Sue, I have a stone and I am not sure if it's a costume piece or a valuable one."

"Bring it by, either Marty or I can take a look at it."

"How long will you be at the store?"

"At least another couple of hours. With the good weather we've been having lately, been staying open until 7:00p.m. but the latest marine weather report states that a pretty powerful nor'easter is headed our way."

"Yes I heard that on the marine radio this morning as well. It's moving at a pretty good clip. The harbormaster, Ted Hudgins, is already preparing for it. I have a couple of things to clear up then I will head down to your store. I'll see you shortly."

Deputy Donato was also at home. His plans for the evening were to take Beth down to the Wharf and enjoy a cocktail. His mind was still racing. He wanted to tell her his theory about Mr. Germain and his brother in-law both committing the murder of Mr. Meyer.

He told her to meet him at 7:00p.m. at the Tavern. He headed out early and stopped by the Club Car Restaurant. He walked in very casually. He had already been stopped in the short time it took for him to park his car having walked by several people wanting to know if there were any developments on the case. "Sorry I can't comment at this time. It's an on-going investigation but we should have it wrapped up pretty soon."

Mark found a seat at the end of the bar and Joe, the proprietor, came over and said, "Please get Mark a drink. Whatever he would like and place it on my tab. So how's the case going?"

"Well I am not at liberty to say much Joe. It's all still pretty hush hush at this point in the investigation but the constable is following up on a theory I have about the case. I laid it all out for him earlier today and he seems quite impressed. When it cracks open you will be one of the first to know." He finished his drink and walked down the cobblestone street to meet Beth.

When she saw Mark she started beaming, which was always the case. Beth was still shaken up that she was the one who had gotten the call and not knowing the proper code numbers to read out. When she had finished yesterday's shift she took the 'Call Code' book home with her and studied it front to back twice.

Mark filled her in on his latest theory of how the murder had taken place and the motive. Beth said, "Oh Mark. You're so smart. I am sure the constable recognizes your foresight and wisdom. I am so proud of you. Maybe you will get a raise if you solve the case."

"All in due time, my dear. All in due time!"

Kosmo entered the jewelry store on Main Street. He was also getting bombarded with questions every other minute as he walked down to the store.

"Hey Kosmo."

"Hey Marty."

"Sue told me that you were headed over here. Long time no see."

"I know. We need to get together soon. Let me finish this case and we can enjoy a Sunday lunch at the Galley. My treat."

"Okay so what's on your mind Constable?"

"Well I came across this stone recently and I want to know if it's real or costume jewelry."

"Okay let me get my loop." Marty slipped the strap over his neck put the stone under his jeweler's light, took a minute turning it over and over ever so slowly, took his eye loop out and asked, "Where did you say you got this?"

"I came across it in an old box I found in the attic last week. You know I was clearing out some junk. You never know how much stuff you need to get rid of until you start looking."

"Well where ever this came from, it's a beauty."

"Really?"

"Oh - yeah really! Yes, it's a genuine ruby about four carats."

"Well that's nice to know."

"And that's not all."

"What else is there?"

"It's flawless. I mean a real beauty. I have not seen a stone like this in fifteen years, maybe longer."

"So what would be the value on something of a stone like this one?"

"Well if you sold it loose maybe it would fetch twenty-five hundred. If you made it into a pendant with diamonds or a ring it could easily triple."

"Are you looking to part with it?"

"Not at this time. I am still trying to find out where it came from. It's a mystery to me."

"Well if you are ever looking to unload it, I would gladly take it off your hands and would get you three comparative prices so you know you are getting top dollar for it."

"Thanks Marty. Give my best to Sue."

The next morning Walter called Steve at home. They discussed their options and Walter said, "Let's just see how this plays out. It's early in the investigation and I know they are working on the blood type on your shirt to match it with the deceased. Also, it will take them several weeks to get a finger print evaluation off the knife. Listen, I received a call here at the hotel from my contact in Boston. The constable, well he is pretty sharp. He was a patrolman on the Boston Police Force for five years, climbing the ladder and making detective, and then he was promoted to the Violent Crimes Unit. Kosmo moved up the ranks and became the Chief of Police. He has a very impressive record and treats people fairly not jumping to conclusions. He goes by the book and believes in reviewing all the facts.

His father was also a police detective on the Boston Force for most of his working life. Everyone thought Kosmo would become the Boston Police Commissioner when he talked about possibly retiring. They say he saw the Police Chief of Nantucket job was going to open up so he applied and was very quickly approved by the Town Selectman.

Steve, I was planning on taking the noon boat back over to the Cape today but I was informed by the inn keeper here that they sent the 8:00a.m. boat out but looks like the rest of the boats are canceled until further notice, due to the storm blowing in. I think I will wander the town. Maybe head over to that really quaint book store, Bookwork's I think it's called, and see if I can find something fun to read while waiting out the storm. Can you recommend any good places for lunch or dinner? If I am going to be here for a few days might as well enjoy my time."

Constable Kosmo was coordinating with several of the departments of Public Works about the approaching storm. Latest reports were sixty to eighty MPH winds with stronger gusts. There were high sea advisories and local flood warnings, mainly in the downtown core of Brant Point. Ted Hudgins, the harbormaster, was bringing in extra reserves to be on standby. The Coast Guard was on High Alert from southern Maine to the Cape and Islands. Reports coming off the marine radio were that it was coming down from the Canadian Maritimes and the temperature was going to drop by thirty degrees and remain in a stalled state for up to three days directly over the Nantucket Sound.

With all this going on, a fresh murder on his hands, the wellness of the local residents, hospitals up to full staff, and additional rescue crews he was buried in phone calls and Emergency Management meetings and of course, nonstop phone calls from old man Lussier. He was calling at all hours of the day asking about the murder and if they have any suspects arrested yet.

QUAISE

By late afternoon the winds started to pick up at a pretty brisk pace and the temperature started dropping rapidly. Reports were coming in via Coast Guard radio, Marine radio and a steady flow of calls into the Police Station.

Mrs. Frechette had called the day earlier to thank the constable and Deputy Donato, as they were correct. Teddy, her dog, did return home after taking the deputy's suggestion and placing a bowl of his dog food out on her deck but he was covered in sea water and seaweed and it was a good two scrubbings in her kitchen sink before she got the damp musty smell off him. She also inquired if she should move into town with her Teddy. She was concerned about Madaket being so open to the outside forces of any storm.

Constable Kosmo had no time to deal with her so he had Beth call her and relay the message that town might not be a bad idea, if she had a friend that they could stay with, or perhaps the Jared Coffin House Hotel would be good, as it had a restaurant right on property and a small park across the way for Teddy if she needed to take him out.

He left another note for Beth to contact Lori Caputo, the nurse at the hospital. She was the one in charge at the nurse's station and to please inform her, as he was sure she already knew, that due to the inclement weather that was approaching, there was no way any helicopter service was going to be available so Med Flight was out of the question and all physicians should be notified that they should all remain on standby for emergency medical service.

The storm hit with a vengeance. The winds were relentless for almost three days. The waves were crashing over the docks and boats that had been moved in from their moorings to the docks. They were being tossed around like they were weightless. Lower Main Street was two feet underwater as it came running down from upper Main. Brant Point area was now getting huge surges. At least three feet of water from the storm was flooding the area. Several people were out in kayaks and canoes in some areas where the streets were flooded and there was no time to even review any facts or clues on the death of Chris Meyer.

Walter Lesnevich had found two good books to read. He had gone to Murray's Toggery Shop and bought some rain gear and a pair of Eddie Bauer waterproof boots like the ones he had back home on the Cape. He had been spending time on Cape Cod for nearly thirty years and knew the havoc these type of storms could bring.

His plans were simple. Enjoy breakfast, go back to his room to review the murder file and then he would head downstairs to sit in front of the fireplace in the living room of the Inn. Maybe even snatch one of the cookies that were on a communal platter on a side table and read a book.

He had purchased two books, 'The Deans Death' by Alfred Lawrence. It was written many years earlier and then using the basis of the book, made into a television show called 'Colombo'.

He also he purchased 'Silence of the Lambs', the second in a series about Hannibal Lecter. He enjoyed the first one 'Red Dragon' about a young female FBI agent that Hannibal requests to befriend him.

After a while he returned upstairs, put on his foul weather gear and trudged out for a long leisurely lunch. Walter really enjoyed this type of weather once in a while. It added adventure to the day.

It was around noon when headed out and walked around the corner to Cioppinos Restaurant. This was one of the spots Steve had recommended to him. As he entered he was told that they were completely full, the one table left was already reserved. The bar was packed. There was no way he was even going to be able to squeeze in there.

Walter was ready to turn around and walk away. Directly behind him were two gentlemen that had walked in and overheard his plight. They knew that it was almost a sure bet that the restaurant was booked so they had called and made a reservation. Brittany, the hostess said, "Hello Mr. Rubin. We have your table all set."

"Wait a minute Brittany, how many seats are at our table?"

"You're at the four top in the corner by the window."

The man turned to Walter and said, "Hi, I am Bob and this is Manny. Would you like to join us?"

"That would be great. Name's Walter - Walter Lesnevich."

Bob replied, "Great let's make the best of it."

Walter then said, "I am visiting from Wellfleet over on the Cape."

"My name is Bob Rubin and this is Manny Golov."

"This might be a fun lunch," Manny added as they shook off the water on their coats and got settled at their table.

Bob asked, "Would you enjoy a glass of wine if I were to order a bottle?"

"Sure," Walter replied.

"White, red or both?"

"I am wide open. I have no plans for the next couple of days but to read a couple books I purchased yesterday and enjoy a few lunches and dinners."

"Oh, you should get 'Murder on the Sconset Express'. It's a really fun read and it was written by a friend of the owner here. Rumor has it that the author, Hunter Laroche, spent several afternoons in this place writing the story about some of the local island characters in the book."

"Do they sell it across the street at Bookwork's?"

"Yes they do and they say it's hard to keep in stock. It's very popular."

Bob said, "I am featured in it. That's why it's a best seller."

"Yeah right," Manny said laughing.

"Really?" Walter said, "Good to know. I will get one this afternoon."

"It's an easy read. The book is penned by Hunter Laroche."

"So what part do you play in the book? The murderer?"

"No, it references me about my business. I own Ruby Wines in Boston."

"Hey, I have heard of you. I practice law in New York and Boston. You know, I think we have a mutual friend Alex Gambal. You know of him, don't you?"

"Yes I do. Alex and his wife Diana are very good friends. Alex has one of the most remarkable wine cellars in Boston. His cellar is so old that part of it runs under the street out front of his old brownstone on Clarendon Street. While you're down there drinking wine you can hear the cars driving over one of the old storm drains. It's really pretty unique. Let's just hope they never decide to dig up at that spot. That would be a big surprise for the road crew," Bob said laughing.

Walter asked, "Have you heard the rumors that Alex might be headed to France to purchase an old winery in Burgundy? He had told me that he looked at it last fall and is getting close to making a decision soon on whether to purchase it."

"Yes," Bob said, I spoke to Alex and he is moving ahead with the deal."

"So – Bob, I know you are in the wine business but what made you decide on that line of work?"

"Ruby Wines in Boston is ours," Bob said. "It has been in our family for years and years. Manny and his wife Karen own a store here on the island, The Eye of the Needle on Federal Street and also another one in Palm Beach. Well what a small world we live in. In the book I am the wine merchant for Ruby Wines but you will have to read the book to find out more about it."

Bob proceeded to order a bottle of white and red Burgundy and mentioned to the server, "Don't be too far away as we might run dry."

"So what brings you to the island Walter?"

"I am here representing the owner of the house where the murder happened a few days ago."

"Oh really? The island is buzzing with rumors about who did it. Everyplace you go, the stores, the restaurants, people are talking about it. The paper comes out tomorrow and I am sure it's going to take up the whole front page."

"Well it's got some twists and turns that I have to sort out. One thing is for sure. I am quite impressed with the Chief of Police here on the island.

"Ah, old Kosmo. He's a friend of both of ours as well."

"How are you connected with him, Bob? I can understand Manny here as he's a business owner on the island."

"Well we had met in Boston on several occasions. Kosmo is actually quite interested in wine. He took several courses in Boston. Evening college classes and I had done a few impromptu discussions for them and met him there. So how's it progressing? The case?"

"As of now it's in the very preliminary stages. No one's pointing fingers as of yet but I am sure that's next. I have handled over thirty murder cases and it takes a good amount of time to sort through all the facts and the leads that will come in."

They ordered lunch and were the last to leave the dining room around 4:00p.m. The bar was still packed with people who were there when Walter had arrived. Bob Rubin picked up the tab for lunch and the next thing you know they were making plans to meet for dinner next door at the Languedoc around 8:30. "Only if I am buying!" Walter put into the clause.

Walter left Cioppinos and walked across the street to the bookstore in a torrential downpour that had not seemed to let up at all during the day.

The winds were whipping up Broad Street from the ocean. He entered and asked if they had any copies of 'Murder on the Sconset Express.' He was directed over to a table off to the side, where the book was on display. A lady standing nearby saw Walter pick up a copy and made a remark to him, "It's a great read." He promptly bought a copy that had a sticker on it that said it was signed by the author.

Later on that evening he rejoined Bob and Manny at the Languedoc for another wonderful get together. Lunch plans were also discussed for the following day at the Club Car Bar. "If it's not under water," Manny said.

For the next forty-eight hours the lunches and dinners continued for the three men.

Constable Kosmo never had a moments rest. Deputy Donato was fending off calls along with Beth as best he could. Steve Germain had kept the fireplace going at the house in Wauwinet. Kim had called three times that day and each time Marshmallow let out a loud meow prior to the phone ringing. Steve was dumbfounded and just started laughing every time it happened. Kim was worried about the storm. Steve never let on about the murder as of yet. Diane and Zach were enjoying long lunches at the Wauwinet Inn and afternoons either in front of her fireplace or the one at Steve's home.

Marshmallow had found the best seat in the house, on the other chair next to Steve on her blanket, in front of the fireplace.

Steve could not believe that he was actually holding small conversations with Marshmallow at different times of the day. He was still trying to understand how, ever since Marshmallow arrived on the property, she always seemed to be near the phone letting out a big meow every time it rang when Kim had called. No other times had she made a peep when it was someone else on the line, strange he thought, very strange!

Hunter Laroche was on the island residing at a rather large private home as guest of the owners who were on an extended stay in Europe. They left him with a full wine cellar and a staff of three. Hunter had heard a few things about the murder that happened a few days prior when he had been in town. The first time was when he was sitting with John Krebs, the owner of the Ship's Inn. This got him thinking of a new idea for his next book. He jotted down some notes while enjoying his time at the estate in Monomoy.

Out in 'Sconset at the Summer House Restaurant, Emily and Maureen were into their second bottle of Pinot Grigio. The winds and the rain had not let up. They both thought it might be fun to head out to 'Sconset in the storm, sit by the fireplace and drown their sorrows. So they hopped in Maureen's BMW, slipped in a Linda Ronstadt cassette, and made the eight-mile drive.

Emily could see Maureen was visibly upset about the death of Chris. In her own private thoughts, so was Emily.

Emily had liked Chris a lot, privately on the inside. She also enjoyed his boyish wild charm and never let on that she enjoyed his flirtatious manner towards her. She was engaged to Trevor. With his jealous temper she could never reveal that to anyone, not even Maureen.

As they were drinking, trying to ease the pain of Chris's death, Maureen broke down and the tears started flowing. She said, "You were right Emily, I did have a thing for Chris. Well actually I am, or shall I say, I was madly in love with him. I just had to keep it my secret. I could not stand if I let my feelings be known and then be totally let down by him. I mean he's like a Rolling Stone, a real playboy!"

"Emily gave her a hug. "It's going to be all right. You will find the right guy. You're such a warm hearted, genuine person."

"No – No – No," Maureen said, as the tears rolled down her cheeks.

"I have done something terribly wrong. It's terrible," Maureen remembering the evening she left a note on Karen's car.

"What could you have possibly done that's so bad?"

Right then Maureen felt like she had slipped up, pulled away and said, "Oh it's nothing, just my emotions talking and the wine."

Mid-Island at the Faregrounds Restaurant, Karen Grant was also drowning her sorrows sitting at the bar with Jimmy Jaksic, who was in his off duty clothes. "It's unbelievable. One minute your loving life and the next, WHAM-O, their boxing you up for your next journey out of this world." Jimmy said.

Karen went on to say how she and Chris were just so happy together. "I didn't see us going on forever but what a great, fun summer we were enjoying. He was certainly charismatic. Always wanting to go out and do something. He truly loved life. I know all sorts of women were vying for his attention. Just last week I got a note. It was almost like a hate letter all about, who did I think I was, and Chris was just using me, and how it was never going to last, yada- yada- yada."

"Wow that's strange," Jimmy mentioned. "What psycho wrote you that?"

"I have no idea. It was on the windshield of my car under the driver's side wiper blade when I went out one morning."

"Bunny boiler?" Jimmy said.

"Chris had recently told me his aunt had passed away a few months earlier and left him with a good amount of funds to hold him solid for many years to come. He said he was going to get the money in several installments over a few years. He went out and bought a cassette tape of Jimmy Buffett and played the song 'He went to Paris' over and over. It put him into a daze. "Well, we all know he was a dreamer," Jimmy chimed in.

"He had a plan. One where he wanted to take his good friend Doug Amaral and me to Paris. I mean he was talking about doing it next month. All he kept saying was it was going to take a little while longer for him to have the money settled into his account from his aunt's estate as her Will was going through probate but the attorneys had sent him a nice fat check to hold him over." Karen finally pulled out of the pity party that she had going. She looked around and asked Jimmy, "When the hell do you think this storm is going to pass. It's like the whole island is holding one of those Florida hurricane parties. I mean, just look around, it's a drunk fest going on."

Jimmy agreed shaking his head, "Boy don't you know it. The bars have been packed for two days straight now, and it doesn't look like it's going to slow down anytime soon, the storm or the boozers in the bars! The drunks on this island are so happy to have someone to talk to."

HIDDEN FORREST

The fourth day after the storm had started, the residents of the island awoke. Still many without power but the sky was clear. Kosmo had his hands full with meetings involving different town officials and departments surveying all the damage on parts of the island that took him through most of the afternoon.

Later that day, he called Mr. Lesnevich at Martins Guest House asking if he could stop down at the station before 6:00p.m. or before noon the next day.

Kosmo now started to regroup all his facts on the murder. He wanted to do this privately without meddling personal around and no annoying meaningless phone calls.

He told his staff to just write all the messages down with the time and date and whom they are from and he will sort them out every few hours.

He then headed home taking his file on the murder with him. His first agenda was to most likely cross out Mr. Germain as a suspect. Not one hundred percent but his gut feeling was telling him Steve was innocent. He thought maybe he had just got caught up in the crossfire, wrong place wrong time, and he did not fit the profile of a murderer.

His next issue was Zachary Cisco. He had dealings that were documented by Deputy Donato about an angered and heated conversation with Chris. Was there more to Mr. Cisco than met the eye? He did seem to have some sort of mob related history.

His history of being a possible fence, possible racketeering and mob connections would make him a perfect candidate for murder. Kosmo needed a stronger motive to prove his involvement. So Zach got a big red circle around his name with a few questions listed next to the circle that he needed answered.

Next, he thought to himself, "What about old Man Lussier? He has had several run ins with Mr. Meyer." Even though he was an older male, he was built like a linebacker. Six foot' two weighing in at about two hundred forty pounds. He had a stocky build but was solid and was just mean enough to let his feelings get in the way of reality and confront Chris. He could have gotten carried away enough to commit murder. His name was followed with a red question mark.

Now who else was there?

Diane, the woman that Mr. Cisco was flirting with, she was with him around the time of the murder so maybe there is a connection there?

Karen Grant, his girlfriend, was she the only one or one of many?

Emily Dutra, the gardener, what was going on between her and Chris Meyer that got her fiancé so upset?

Trevor Obrien, fiancé of Emily Dutra, who Kosmo had witnessed an altercation between him and Mr. Meyer at DeMarco Restaurant. Kosmo would have to go back and get some background information on Chris's roommates to see if there was any bad blood there.

He then added to his questions on the yellow legal pad.

A Jealous husband in the mix?
A jealous girlfriend in the mix?
A Jealous boyfriend in the mix?

For a small town, this case had a lot of suspects. He also needed to check with any disgruntled past employers that Chris might have done work for or even suppliers. Did he own money to them? Did he have any gambling debts or drug issues?

Kosmo knew that one by one the pieces would fall into place. It was all just a matter of time. Which clue might answer all the questions? Some of them later than others but you did not want the case to go cold.

Kosmo also knew that Deputy Donato meant well but had a vivid imagination that interfered with a clear logical train of thought. His inexperience was a major factor in getting the details straight.

The following day, Walter went to the Police Station at 9:00a.m. to meet with the constable. Kosmo more or less told him where he was in the interview process. The constable told Walter that his gut feeling was telling him that Steve was innocent and also his thoughts on Mr. Cisco, which were not so favorable. Zach sure seemed to be a logical suspect as he was at the house during the time of the murder and he had a run in at a public bar with the deceased that was broken up by his deputy.

Walter made a few notes and he was slightly agitated with Zach as he never mentioned any of his past history in Phoenix or the confrontation at the bar. Zach was not all that forth coming when Walter asked about any facts that he should know about so that no surprises would arise. This bar issue was now number two of the surprises that landed in his lap.

He asked Kosmo if there was a written or documented detailed report on the altercation between Mr. Meyer and Mr. Cisco.

Kosmo opened his file and pulled out a copy of what Deputy Donato had written in his daily log for that Wednesday July 14th 1975

A verbal altercation was witnessed at approximately 4:30p.m. at the Rose & Crown Restaurant on Water Street which was witnessed personally by me, Deputy Donato and Liz Leblanc the bartender, as well as several (unnamed) customers at the bar between a Mr. Chris Meyer and, as known to me, an unknown person who's name I did not acquire.

While Mr. Meyer was at the bar with three other of his drinking buddies, Sean Devine, Colin Keenan, and one party I did not recognize, the unknown man approximately six feet' two, a large framed muscular body, two hundred pounds or so, clean shaven wearing an Arizona Cardinals logo cap and a jean jacket had walked into the bar. I observed him as that's the natural training I have. I watched him walk directly up to Mr. Meyer and grab his arm and spin him around. The conversation I observed seemed to be in a fairly agitated voice and went, as best to my knowledge, as follows;

> **"Hey you jerk face. Who do you think you are?" (UNKNOWN)**
> **"What are you talking about cowboy?" (CHRIS MEYER)**
> **"You know what I am talking about." (UNKNOWN)**
> **"Get lost, I know who you are, you're a friend of Mr. Germain's, the guy's house I am working on in Wauwinet." (CHRIS MEYER)**
> **"I am not his friend I'm his brother in-law and I know about the beer that you evidently gave to the girls, one is my niece and the other is her friend. They are both seventeen years old! What kind of pervert are you, giving beer to two young girls! I ought to knock your block off. Right here and now." (UNKNOWN)**

"Oh yea! You try it cowboy and I will pummel you." (CHRIS MEYER)

"Well where I come from we rope and hog tie punks like you in seconds." (UNKNOWN)

"And where I come from in Pittsburgh we play for keeps. I grew up on the streets." (CHRIS MEYER)

Right then I got up from my dish of fried clams and went to the other side of the bar and stepped in between the two men. I separated them, the larger gentleman apologized, backed down turned and walked out. I went back to finish my clams then thought I should put this in my daily log. I was off duty at the time.

Deputy Mark Donato July 14ᵗʰ 1975 1800 hours

"Well I think I need to have another conversation with my client. I was planning on heading back to the Cape on the noon ferry tomorrow. When will you be talking with him again Constable?"

"Within a day or so."

"Okay give me enough of a time frame. I will be present at all meetings."

"Hi Steve. It's Walter Lesnevich calling. I just spent about an hour with the constable. Looks like you are going to be cleared of any wrong doing for now. But with Zach, well we seem to have some issues that need to be cleared up, one being with Zach and Mr. Meyer having a confrontation at one point. There are some new unanswered questions that were brought to my attention by the constable. I was planning on taking the noon ferry back over to the Cape tomorrow. Do you think you could get Zach to meet me at the Martins Guest House around 11:00a.m. tomorrow? If you have any other requests for either of you to return to the station by the constable, do not do so without me being present. That goes for both of you."

"Okay. I will get him there tomorrow. We will meet you around 10:45 at your guest house in the lobby. You can fire all your questions at Zach and I will make sure he answers them clearly, and truthfully. Walter, he does have a checkered past but I am sure, no matter how it looks, he had nothing to do with Chris's death. What he does in Phoenix is his own business. I have known him forever and he would not bring any ill will to our family."

After Steve got off the phone he went up to Zach's bedroom and knocked on his door. When Zach opened the door Steve explained that

Walter had just learned a few things about a confrontation he had had with Chris and was now more aware of his other life in Phoenix.

Steve told Zach they had to meet with Walter the next morning at his guest house as he was leaving the island that day on the noon ferry. Also that Zach had to come clean so that Walter could work his magic to clear them both off any wrongdoing. He also explained to Zach that it looks as though one of them was off the hook, and it wasn't Zach.

Zach said, "I can straighten all this out and I also have got to let you know, I had nothing to do with the death of Chris. I might not have been a big fan of his but trust me they have nothing on me. My Phoenix life is just what it is. It's not all they playing it up to be. Period."

SMITH'S LANDING

The next morning, Steve was talking to Zach in the kitchen, "Well for what it worth, let's go. You have to lay all your cards on the table. Bill Heifener says that Walter is one of the best at what he does so let's go and finish this up and don't hold back. Tell him everything, he's on our side."

They arrived at Martins Guest House and met in the library living room area and were grateful that they were alone for privacy reasons.

Walter asked Zach to outline the details of his meeting with Chris Meyer at the Rose & Crown, which he did. Walter did not let on that he had a copy of the incident report in his hands and was reading it as Zach was replaying the story. After Zach was finished, Walter showed him the report and said, "Well, it matches what the deputy had filed. So that's one good thing. Zach I wished you had told me about this incident earlier on but we can get past it. Now fill me in and don't skirt around the edges. I want the whole story, all of it, regarding to your life in Phoenix and remember it doesn't matter what you discuss here, it's a hundred percent confidential."

Zach told him, "I work for a certain not to be named powerful family with ties to - let's just say - not all above board dealings and leave it with that. I have been questioned several times in the last few years about some issues which have arisen being associated with this family but no charges have ever been filed. Besides my job is raising horses. The other is just a little side job that I do from time to time and I get results. It's not a nine to five job that you can just walk away from. I get the call. I have a meeting with the head of the family but the most harmful thing that comes out of it is a little roughing up here and there. Nothing more than that. It just comes with the territory. Now when it comes to Chris Meyer, I was not a huge fan. He pissed me off with the beer issue but I got over it quickly, right after I walked out of the Rose & Crown, as when I have a conversation with someone in that manner it usually sticks soundly in their mind."

"Now one final question, and Zach I need the truth, not part of the truth but one hundred percent accurate."

"Okay fire away."

"Did you have anything to do with the murder of Mr. Meyer, or have any knowledge of who did, or take part in the murder in any shape or form? Remember, if you lie to me, I will drop you as a client."

"I can truthfully answer that. I, Zachary Cisco, have no knowledge or any information of who killed Mr. Meyer and I was not involved in any way at all. I truthfully can say I wish it never happened to him."

"Okay, well I think we are done here. If the constable requests another interview with either of you, let me know as soon as possible. I will be there. Neither of you are to speak about the case with anyone or talk to any law enforcement person without me being present."

After their meeting with Walter, Steve and Zach went to Mignosa's Market on Main Street and ordered two of the sour dough maple syrup BLT'S while sitting at the counter at Les's Lunch Box.

"Well I am glad we got that straightened out. Let's hope that's the last of those meetings" Steve said relieved. "Wow! These sandwiches are great. I think I better order one more," Zach said.

"Hey let's go hit a matinee," Steve said. "We need to get our minds off this mess. 'One Flew over the Cuckoo's Nest' starts in fifteen minutes. It might be a good laugh. Jack Nicholson is the main actor."

That evening as Steve was reading some sales reports that had been overnight express mailed from the dealership in Columbus, Marshmallow let out a loud Meow. A moment later the phone rang. He looked over at Marshmallow and said, "Really? How do you know that it's Kim calling?"

He picked up the receiver and not waiting said, "Hello Kim."

"Hi Steve. How did you know it was me?"

"Long story. I will explain it when you get here."

"Okay, Well I am planning on arriving in four days as long as the Nantucket weather agrees. Sandy and Bill are going to join me. He mentioned he wanted to come out last week but then held off for some reason."

Steve thought, I guess it's now or never. "Well we had a little issue here and I had to call Bill last week."

"What type of issue?"

"You might want to sit down Kim before I get into it. Everything is fine now but this is what happened," Steve said and continued to tell her the rest.

"Murdered! He was murdered? Oh My God! Who did it? Are you and Zach all right? Murdered in our basement? In the wine cellar? I knew that wine cellar was going to be trouble."

"Calm down Kim."

"Well. We are going to have to sell the house and find something safer."

"We are not selling the house and when you get here everything will be back to normal. You won't even know it happened."

"I don't know if I can sleep in a house that someone was murdered in."

"Look, the boys will love the story. Maybe not so much that it was our carpenter. When you all get here, we will go to the Boarding House Restaurant and have a really nice dinner. I will explain everything to you. Now calm down and relax."

After Steve hung up with Kim, Zach said, "I am out of here. Diane is picking me up in a few minutes and we are headed to town for dinner. She wants to take me to the Brotherhood of Thieves. Say's they have someone playing music so we are going to grab a couple burgers and beers. Want to join us?"

"Thanks but you go and enjoy. I am just going over some sales figures for the Ford store. Let Diane know that Kim is arriving with Bill and Sandy on Friday and we are planning on dinner at the Boarding House, maybe you guys can join us and Diane can keep Kim calm."

"Oh, so you spilled the beans, I take it?"

"Oh yeah and she's not a happy camper about this whole issue."

After Zach left, the phone rang and this time Marshmallow did not make a peep. "Well I guess it's not Kim," Steve said as he looked over at Marshmallow.

"Hi Mr. Germain. It's Rusty Riddleberger."

"Hey Rusty. How's things?

"All good on this end. How are you making out with all the headaches that I am sure you're going through after Chris's unfortunate death?"

"We are plugging along."

"Well Mr. Germain, the reason for the call is since the garage apartment is only about ninety percent finished and your wine cellar is about seventy-five percent completed, I would like to offer my services. I have done quite a bit of finish carpentry. I work hard and attention to detail is what I like to see. I could have the apartment completed within a week and the wine cellar in about two weeks. So within three weeks, everything would be one hundred percent completed."

"Rusty, first off, call me Steve. I believe the crime scene is finished. If I call the constable and explain the Kim is arriving with guest's maybe it's possible for you to get into the wine cellar and make it look like nothing ever happened. I mean, can you make it so there's no trace of blood stains and so forth?"

"My advice is get the call to the constable as soon as possible. If you get the go ahead I will come over, make an assessment and do exactly what it takes. Also, I will get a nice lock set and door hardware and we can close it up. That way if Kim has to go downstairs, she won't be looking in the wine cellar. Nothing better than the old saying, out of sight out of mind. One thing I was so curious about in the cellar was why Chris neglected that one area by the coal chute. When we were both working in there, he just seemed to ignore that spot and work around it. I know at one point he wanted to run the hose down around the top of the chute from outside the house but all he had to do was cut the safety lock off and pull up the hatch to see if it was dry inside. They made coal chutes pretty water tight otherwise the coal would absorb the moisture and not ignite very well. It just seemed so strange to me but I guess we will never know his reasoning behind it. I mean he had all the finish work done on seventy-five percent of the cellar."

"Okay Rusty, why don't you call me tomorrow morning around 10:.00a.m. I will get an early call into the constable and see if I can get the go ahead."

"I will ring you at 10:00. Have a good night!"

COATUE

Uncle Zach arrived back at the house around 10:00p.m. Steve was still sitting in the leather chair in front of the fireplace enjoying a glass of red wine. Marshmallow was also still curled up on her new favorite blanket on the floor next to him.

"Any more wine left?"

"Yup. Grab a glass it's sitting on the counter in the kitchen."

"What are we drinking?"

"It's a Zinfandel from Steele Vineyards. I got it down at Hatch's. Pretty tasty."

As Zach sat in the other leather chair, Steve said, "That was a pretty good movie today. I am glad we went. It was good to get my mind off all that's been happening the last few days."

"That Nicholson, he played a really good part and that other guy Martini, he cracked me up," Zack chuckled.

"Rusty the electrician called me after you left. He does finish carpentry work and said he would be glad to complete the apartment above the garage and also he is going to clean up the wine cellar if I can get the go ahead from the constable. Also finish the new door and put a lockset and handle on it so that way Kim won't freak out if she has to go downstairs."

"That makes sense. Is he also going to finish up the one wall with the cover of the chute finally?" Zach asked, "It's about time. When is he going to start?"

"Well if I get the go ahead the first thing is the door and I know he wants to open the chute to see if it's dry or needs some water proofing."

"Well I am sure when it's all completed it will be nice. Diane wants to meet me in Phoenix when I return home. She's a horse lover so it might work out well having her come stay at the ranch for a while. I think as soon as I can get the constable to let me take off, I will head out."

"Well you are welcome to come and go as often as you like. You know that."

"Thanks Steve. I do."

"Okay, well this wine is tasty Steve, but I am heading up. I have some things I want to get done early tomorrow."

"Like what?"

"Just a little shopping. Maybe some flowers for Diane. We are also almost out of beer and running low on stuff for sandwiches in the fridge."

"I am also thinking of heading into town. I want to either call the constable or stop in at the station. I can grab the beer if you want?"

"Perfect. Why don't you head in early, pick up the groceries then when you get back I will take the car in and get the flowers and some other things. That way if you get the go ahead for the wine cellar you can meet Rusty here."

"Why don't we just head in together?" asked Steve.

"Well, I – um," Zach did not see this question coming from Steve and he really needed to be alone in the wine cellar to find out just what was hidden in the coal chute. "I thought I would hang around here for a while sit out back and catch up on that pile of magazines and enjoy the great fresh Nantucket air and the morning sun. When I go to town, I might stop in the Tap Room and have lunch. If I do, you wouldn't be here in time to meet with Rusty."

"Sounds like a plan Stan. See you in the morning."

The next morning Steve called the constable. Kosmo told Steve he could move forward with his plans. He now had the crime scene photos and that's all he needed for now. He had also received a call late last night from Mr. Lesnevich. They touched upon several facts on the case and that Zach had sworn to him that he had no knowledge of who or why the murder was committed. He was not involved in any way shape or form. And he also discussed the incident at the Rose & Crown which Zach said he always seemed to get the point across by meeting it head on and then just walking away. People usually got his message loud and clear and sharing a beer with two underage girls is not a reason to commit murder. The Constable also had to agree with the last point.

Steve headed into town. Right after he heard the car pull out of the driveway, Zach headed to the basement.

171

After the constable hung up, he started going through all the crime scene photos he placed them in piles but what most intrigued him were the ones in the cellar. If there was a clue, it was there. He mulled over all of them one by one. He turned them sideways, upside down held them away at arm length, laid them side by side comparing them and looking closely but what was he looking for? Something was there, some clue but what?

After about twenty minutes using a magnifying glass, he turned them all face down and gave it a break. After a short time, resting his eyes, he would turn them back over and re-visit them again, just like the crime scene. He sat and thought, what was it? It was happening to him again; it almost always did. His sixth sense was kicking in. He could see something. It was a vision but not one that would connect with his brain. How he hated when this happened but he now knew it would soon come to him, but when?

A day? A week? A month?

He went out to the common area got himself a fresh cup of coffee and went back to his desk. Kosmo then pulled out the personal property bag, dumping everything out. The stone was not in the bag anymore as he had removed it to keep it away from prying eyes. This was one of his aces in the hole but not knowing anything about where Chris had obtained it.

At this point he was thinking maybe he lifted it from one of his past jobs. Could it have been discovered and the rightful owner tracked Chris down at the Germain Estate?

He had Deputy Donato meet with him so he could put him on a project to research Chris's past jobs. When the deputy asked Kosmo, "How am I going to know where the past jobs were that he worked on?"

That's when the constable taught the deputy something, "First go to the bank and see where his last three months of check deposits came from. If his jobs were paid to him by check, there is a name on each one. Then you know who he was working for. Get the names and go question them."

"Wow! That's real detective work. Nice idea Chief!"

"Next stop by Island Lumber and Marine Hardware and ask to see what charge accounts Mr. Meyer is allowed to charge on and if he had a personal account. If so, is it to current or past due? They always add a job listing to certain charges for reference if Mr. Meyer needed it for his billing records or the client wanted to see what he was being billed for. Then you go and interview each client he worked for. While you are at the bank get his credit history such as over drafts, bad checks, deposit history and balances for the last six or eight months, so we can see his lifestyle and money trail."

After Kosmo's break from the photos, yet again, he flipped them back over repeating what he had done the night prior and just about thirty minutes ago.

His phone buzzed, it was Beth in the front office, "Chief I still have yesterday afternoons call-in sheet about tips on the Meyer case."

"Okay. Bring them back. I could use a fifteen-minute break before I go over these photos again. Beth brought in the sheet and started reviewing it with the chief.

"Not much to go on here but what is this about Maureen Maher? Do you know of her?"

"Yes I do, sir. She's the strawberry blond. Wealthy parents. They live in Shimmo on the water. She drives that shiny new red BMW with the Florida tags.

"Is she nice?"

"Seems to be. At least I think so. I am not a friend of hers but I see her in passing."

"So this tip that came in, who was it from?"

"It was a woman's voice sir. Sounded like it was from a pay phone in a bar by the background noise. It was on the recorded line. It just says we should look at Maureen as a jealous girlfriend. That we might be surprised what we find out."

"Okay. Let's put Deputy Donato on this as well. It will keep him quite busy, I have to admit, but then again he thrives on it."

CISCO BEACH

Kosmo again picked up the contents of Chris's items he had on his person at the time of the murder. Looking at the pawn shop card, he thought why not give it a shot. He dialed the number. After two rings a man picked up.

"Graham & Clary Pawn Shop, highest prices paid on the Cape. Michael Clary speaking. How may I help you?"

Constable Kosmo introduced himself and asked who he might speak to about someone that might have been in his shop recently.

That would be either myself or my wife, Jennifer, but right now it's just me here minding the shop."

Kosmo asked him if they were registered with the state for stolen articles. Michael stated that they were and had a clean record. Kosmo made a note to verify that.

"Do you have any record, let's say, within the last month or so of any sales to a Mr. Chris Meyer of Nantucket Island?"

"Well, I would have to go through our records but to me it doesn't ring a bell. My wife might have, but we usually discuss our day's coming and goings and our sales and purchases. My wife handles all the books. I am sure she would have mentioned a person from Nantucket as we go there every summer. Is there something I can reference this call to such as an appliance, watch, jewelry or golf clubs? It might narrow the search and I can have my wife go through our records and get back in touch with you."

"Right now we are not sure what we are looking for." Kosmo threw in a slight ringer not giving too much information away. "We received a tip that Mr. Meyer had gone to a store on the Cape and pawned a perfectly good gemstone of flawless quality. Something worth in the neighborhood of fifteen hundred dollars or more."

Now Michael paused and became slightly nervous. He knew in an instant who the constable was referring to. His mind started racing. He had not informed his wife about the stones or the transaction. He had paid cash for the stones and had already tripled his cash lay out on such item. He was hoping the kid would come back again.

Kosmo said into the receiver, "Hello? Are you still there?"

"Yes. Sorry, I just had a car pull up and almost hit our front door."

"So have you had any dealings like that in the last four to six weeks?"

"I am sorry to report we have not had any type of transaction that is even close to something like that. The most expensive item we pawned was for a gentleman. It was an older Rolex watch. That was for six hundred dollars and that's on the high end of our weekly or should I say monthly transactions."

"Could you have your wife give me a call when she returns?"

"Well - um, I guess so, but I don't see any reason for that."

"It's just a formality. I like to speak to all parties involved. I do believe that if he was in your store your wife might remember him being there."

"Well I will have her call you. She's out for a few days, you know, with the flu that's been going around?"

Very convenient timing, Kosmo thought and said, "Understood, thanks for all your help."

After he hung up, Kosmo knew there was more to the story than this guy Michael was giving up. His next call was to the State Regulations Office that kept records for private money loans and pawnshop businesses. He was given a certain person to contact in reference to pawnshop investigations, a Mr. Dane Wooldridge.

He dialed the number and right away the phone was picked up. "Dane Wooldrige, Fraud Division for the State of Massachusetts." Kosmo again introduced himself and asked for any infractions regarding the Graham & Clary pawnshop in Mashpee. He was placed on a fairly short hold and when the Mr. Wooldridge came back on the line, Kosmo learned that in the past five years the Graham & Clary Pawn Shop had been investigated almost ten times for receiving stolen goods and dealing in cash without receipts or any paper trail. They were cited four out of the ten times, as some of the tips were credible. The only way they were discovered was by people trying to reduce their sentencing at trials. They figured it was easier to rat out some pawnshop then spend a longer period in jail or on probation.

Kosmo now knew that he had to get the wife of the pawnshop owner on the ropes and see if he could rattle her nerves. There is no way that Mr. Meyer just happened to have a very fine gemstone floating around in his pocket and at the same time, it just so happens that he picked up their pawn shop card on Nantucket. Too much of a coincidence. He knew, in his mind, that Chris had been to the pawnshop but how was he going to prove it was entirely another matter.

About thirty minutes after the call to the pawnshop he asked Beth to come into his office. "Beth hit *67 and dial this number. That way if this person on the other end has caller ID, our number won't show up. If a woman answers, ask if she is Jennifer. If a man answers, act like you were referred to call Jenifer by a friend about a set of ladies' golf clubs you would like to unload. If he asks who is calling just say your name is Beth and when would be a good time for you to contact her."

"Okay," replied Beth, not asking any questions and dialed. On the first ring a woman answered. "Is this Jennifer?" Beth asked.

"Yes it is. Who's calling?"

"Please hold for a second I have someone that wants to speak with you. Beth handed the phone to Kosmo. "Hi Jennifer. This is Constable Kosmo of the Nantucket Police Department. I am trying to follow up on a lead of a person who might have been in your store in the last few weeks. We are trying to track down anyone that might have actually seen him so we can put a time frame to his movements in the last several weeks. It's nothing really to be concerned about. We are not sure exactly where he visited while in Mashpee."

"I am not sure what use I can be but I will try my best."

"Okay well, he stands about 5'11", weighs about 190Lbs. He's a resident of Nantucket."

"Oh we love Nantucket," Jennifer chimed in.

"Well he has dark black hair, clean shaven and a boyish look to him. He's 32 years old but looks younger and he's what the girls call, and I am only going by what I have been told, a hunk, a boy toy, stud muffin and a head turner, just to name a few. He has very good facial features, dark eyebrows, and blueish eyes." Kosmo not wanting to use the past tense and scare the woman. "If you could tell me if you have a store receipt of what he was selling or purchased it might help. Well at this point we are unsure but it might have possibly been a colored gemstone."

"I am sorry to say we have not taken in any diamonds, rings or colored stones either but we did have someone that fits your description a while back. Maybe a week or ten days ago. I did not speak with him. If it's the person you're asking about, he actually entered the store as I was getting ready to leave. I don't know if it's the same gentleman but the two things that made me think that this might be the person is when you mentioned Nantucket. The person I am referring to was here around 10:30 in the morning as I was headed to the bank. I do all the paperwork and bank deposits almost daily. He was, as you say, very handsome had darkish carpenter style pants on and the main reason I remember him was I noticed his hat."

"What type of hat?"

"It was a ball cap with the Nantucket Whalers logo on it."

"Thank you Jennifer. One other thing, if you could remember the day or date that would help."

"Well I am sure I can remember if you just give me a second. It was not a weekend as our bank is not open and if I can remember the deposit I was making it will come to me. That's how I remember things by the deposits. Most people can't understand my thinking or logic. It's kind of strange."

MADEQUECHAM

"Here's what I will do. Give me some time and I can call you back or you can hold on while I go through my bank deposit receipts. I keep them all stapled in our deposit books. Hold it! I remember now. I remember it was a Tuesday. There was a taxi out front. Must have been waiting for him, I thought, as the driver was parked right in front of our door. That happens often when someone is here to pawn something. They usually don't have a car and need cash. You would be surprised how many people need to get quick cash for bailing someone out of jail. I know it was Tuesday because I had tucked a dollar in my coat pocket to donate to the pet fund jar at the bank and Tuesday was the last day of the pet drive."

"Could you look into your record book and see what was pawned that day?"

"Give me a moment. It should not take long. Weekends are our busy time. Midweek is usually very quiet. Let me just open the ledger. Okay, here it is, Tuesday the 23rd. The only thing we gave cash out for that day was a set of golf clubs eighty-five dollars and a guitar forty-five dollars that was all our transactions for that day."

Kosmo thought for a moment. Maybe Chris went in and just wanted to see what the value would be if he actually was pawning a stone. He had Jennifer check the following day's receipts as well.

"Not much of a difference. We paid out twenty-eight dollars for a chainsaw and fifteen dollars for a bowling ball. Oh, and a kids bike thirty dollars."

"One other thing, how many taxi cab companies do you have in Mashpee?"

"Well there is Bert's and Ships Taxi but it was not one of those."

178

"Of course," Kosmo thought. "If Chris took it from Hyannis the taxi would most likely be a Hyannis cab company.

"Do you remember anything about the taxi waiting for him out front of your store?"

"Oh yes. It was Town Taxi. Five – five – five, five – five – five - five."

"And how do you remember that number so well?"

"I love numbers. It's like a game to me and I always see their taxis around. 555-5555 is a very catchy number. Easy to remember."

"Well thank you Jennifer. You have been most helpful."

Kosmo handed Beth a piece of paper and asked her, "Call this number and contact someone in dispatch. Find out on Tuesday July 23rd if they made a pick up either at the steamship authority or at the airport and went to this address in Mashpee. If so, did they wait and bring the fare back to Hyannis."

Fifteen minutes later Beth knocked on Kosmo's door. Even though it was open she still always knocked prior to entering. "I have the information on the fare. A man with a ball cap got into the taxi at the Steamship dock. The taxi drove him to the address, waited outside for fifteen minutes then took the fare to a bar in Mashpee called Teasers. The person flipped the driver twenty dollars and told him to keep the meter running. He was only going in for a short time and then back to the boat. After about an hour of waiting the driver entered the bar. The rider flipped him another twenty and said he would be out in a while. Well it was about two and a half hours total the driver waited out front. Finally, the guy came out and got back into the taxi and was dropped off at the boat."

"Did you ask for a description of the rider?"

"Yes. Early thirties, black hair, black pants and wearing a ball cap."

"Now the next call I want you to make Beth, is to the Steamship Authority. Get a hold of Captain Andresen. See if he remembers any person fitting Mr. Meyer's description on either the morning boat heading to Hyannis or the afternoon boat returning back to Nantucket. It's a long shot but more information is better than less on the hunch I am working on."

The next day after a very restless night's sleep, Kosmo again pulled out the photographs. There were some answers somewhere he could feel it and sense it but his mind would not register it.

About an hour later as Kosmo kept looking at the crime scene photos on his desk, Beth knocked. "Chief, a person that fits Mr. Meyer's description had to be woken up about ten minutes after the boat had docked here on Nantucket. The Captain woke him up personally, noticed he looked like he was drunk and smelled of alcohol."

"Nothing new for this island," Kosmo added.

Kosmo made a few more notes. He knew that Mr. Clary had lied about Chris being there. "So where do I go now?" Kosmo thought. "Head to the pawn shop and see what answers I can get? No. If there is no paper trail, I have only speculation. I doubt that the owner is going to confess about anything without any security cameras or no real witnesses at the store. If Mr. Meyer had pawned anything, I will just put this train of thought on the back burner for now."

After studying the photos for a while longer he started put them away. Something was there but what? He decided to take one more good look again at them before putting them in the locking drawer. The knife, he felt he had seen it before. Green with some gold in the long slim handle. But where could he have ever seen that knife prior? It almost looked like an antique. So many things were running through his mind but he could not grasp the answers. He knew they would come. He hoped sooner than later. Now back to his notes. He wrote on his pad;

Gather information and background checks on
Maureen Maher, Trevor Smith Obrien.
No others at this time.

"Deputy where do we stand on your findings?" he asked Deputy Donato, who had been working diligently on digging up information about Chris Meyer's cash flow and jobs.

"Well he was running low on funds for quite a while, at least six months. He was always late on his rent to his roommates. They had already told him that he was going to have to move out. He was way over his credit limit with Judy Brownell at Hatch's Gas Station for a few months. He was bouncing checks, owed Island Lumber and Marine Hardware and he had some unpaid bar tabs at several restaurants. But recently he seemed to clear up all his overdue bills in town and as of now he's current on his bills since the last two weeks and his balance in his checking-savings account at Nantucket Bank is two hundred seventy-five dollars and some change. I reviewed as many of his invoices that I could gather together. I looked over the information on his job invoices from Marine and Island Lumber. I did some back tracking and made calls all day yesterday. Not one complaint except that he was late on getting some of his jobs finished in a timely manner. All in all, everyone I talked with was pleased with his work. So Chief, my feeling is, he finally got a lot of his last payments in from his past jobs. Almost like he sat down one day, did all his billing, and in the last few weeks everyone paid him."

"One thing," Kosmo asked, "did you go through his statements looking at his most recent deposits?"

"Well no. I - I mean, I looked at the balances."

"Well Deputy, go back and see if the deposits were cash or by check and were they over several weeks or all at once? That will give us a background history of his recent transactions. And Deputy, why don't you go through his statements with Beth."

"Why Chief?"

"Well for all the years I have been doing police work, one thing I have found out when it comes to paper trails, a woman's instinct, eyes and ears seem to play favorably towards results and answers."

"If you say so Chief."

"I do say so," replied Kosmo, slightly grinning.

The next day they took a trip out to see Al Lussier. Kosmo had to cover all his bases. Prior to leaving the station, Kosmo filled in the deputy about the background information he had gathered on Steven Germain and he felt that avenue was a dead end. Wrong place at the wrong time.

Deputy Donato himself had slowly come to that conclusion but not admitting that his first theory about Mr. Germain was wrong and that his second theory, which he had divulged to Beth about both Mr. Germain and his brother in-law were in it together, was now not correct either. Again, he had to revise his story. It was still possible that Zach could still be a prime suspect.

The deputy still was trying to find a way to look ever so important in Beth's eyes. He knew how he would handle it. He was going over it in his mind. He would point out to her that one had to have a very open mind and theories were just that, theories. All of which were subject to change at any time as new facts and evidence showed its hand. He would also present Beth with his latest theory. The one about Zach committing the murder or the fact that they had found old man Lussier hanging around the Germain's property the day of the murder hiding in the bushes. He had motive, I tell ya! Motive. He would explain to Beth how you always got to keep an open mind, or you will never advance your train of thought.

ALTAR ROCK

As they pulled into Mr. Lussier's driveway both the Deputy and the Constable's radio came alive. "Constable we just got a call from Mr. Lussier. I know you are on the way out there. He complaining about some kids on skate boards making too much noise."

"Okay Beth. We are here now and will handle it."

They approached his front door ready to knock when it opened. "Well that was quick," Mr. Lussier said. "What are you going to do about all this ruckus Constable?"

"Calm down Mr. Lussier. They are only kids out on the road past your house. They are just having harmless fun. There's no law against that."

"Well they are making a huge ruckus."

"Look Mr. Lussier, they are way over there. It can't be disturbing you."

"I was trying to take a nap."

"How could you say that?" asked the Deputy. "I can hear your TV blaring all the way out here."

"What we are really here for Mr. Lussier," Kosmo stated. "Is we have a few questions for you about the murder of Mr. Meyer."

"Why are you bothering me with this issue? I have no knowledge of any suspects regarding his death."

"Well your one of our suspects," the deputy chimed in.

"Me? What are you talking about you insignificant dweeb?"

"Well Mr. Lussier, we have to differ with you on that. You did say you were going to shoot him at one point," Kosmo mentioned.

"That's rubbish! I don't remember ever saying anything like that."

"Don't you remember showing up at the Germain residence with a shotgun about two weeks ago? You said, and we have it on a recorded call at the station, that you were going to kill him."

"I don't remember that. I never said anything like that. I am seventy-five years old. I forget things. Get off my property you young whipper snapper," he snarled at the deputy.

"Calm down there Mr. Lussier. We don't seem to be getting anywhere here."

"Yea well, I am going to sue all of you for defamation of character!"

"Now Mr. Lussier, if you don't calm down I am going to cuff you and take you to the station where we can get you under control."

"Don't you even try to lay a hand on me. I will sue the whole town if you do. That punk, whatever his name was, deserved to die. He had it coming to him."

"Mr. Lussier, why do you say that?"

"Oh get lost both of you. You're on private property."

"Mr. Lussier, I think this would best be handled down at the station. So you have two choices, either you follow us to the station…"

"I am not following you anywhere! I am going to sue the whole town if you touch me."

"The other option, Mr. Lussier, is I call the hospital and we have an ambulance come out and we place you in a straitjacket. Then take you to the hospital for a competence evaluation unless we can get you to come to your senses. So you make the call here."

"Oh, this is all horse rubbish. I will follow you in my car. Let me go inside and get my keys."

"I will accompany you inside, if you don't mind," Kosmo told him.

While Mr. Lussier went inside with the constable, Deputy Donato waited on the porch and thought of what Mr. Lussier had just said, "*That punk deserved to die*".

While they were walking into the house, the deputy overheard Kosmo saying," Mr. Lussier, I would not go around saying things like that about Mr. Meyer deserving to die. It only implicates you more with all the things you have said in the past. Let's not go and make it worse," the constable stated.

Now, as this was overheard, another theory started to form in the deputy's mind….

SANKATY

Mr. Lussier located his keys and followed them downtown. When they all arrived at the station, Mr. Lussier was still rambling on and on about what a set of buffoons ran this island, the selectman, the police, the tax collector, everything was wrong and if he had his way and was a few years younger, he would show them all how to do things properly. While he was in the interrogation room, he started on the federal government and how they were spying on everyone. "Ever since JFK had been assassinated, the whole county has been deteriorating at a rapid pace." He then started in with, "Just last week I was attacked by a group of young men. They surrounded me."

"You were?" asked the deputy. "Did you call it in?" As the deputy reached for his note pad he started thinking, "This is big! Really big."

"Okay Mr. Lussier, give me the facts I will put an APB out and see if we can't round up these hooligans'. What day did this happen?"

"It was Saturday at the A&P, in the morning, right in the parking lot!"

Hearing that the constable let out a little chuckle and said, "That's okay Deputy you can put your pad away."

"What do you mean Chief?

"Well as I recall Saturday was the school's annual car wash held in the grocery store parking lot from eight in the morning until three in the afternoon. Was that what you're referring to Mr. Lussier?"

"They surrounded my car and when I said I don't need no stinking car wash they asked for a donation. Don't they need a permit for something like that? Are they paying taxes on the money they raise?"

"Okay now, calm down here Mr. Lussier," the constable told him. "Let's get back to the business at hand. We just need to go over a few issues while we are here about the murder of Mr. Meyer then you can go back home and brood all you want about anything and everything that you think is wrong with our island, our state and our country, but now let me ask you a few questions." The deputy started the tape recorder.

"First, did you kill or have any knowledge about the death Mr. Meyer?"

"What? No way. I might have not liked that idiot, he was nothing but trouble I tell you - trouble, but I didn't kill him. I thought about it a couple times but I did not do it. He was a nuisance I tell you - a nuisance! I think you should have locked him up a while ago. He still might be alive today if you two bozos had done your job!"

"Well Mr. Lussier, you are laying out all sorts of innuendos that make you more and more of a suspect. Are you sure you don't want a lawyer to help you through this line of questioning?"

"Lawyer? I don't need no stinking lawyer. Do you know how much those vultures charge? I still remember the crook who handled the closing of my house when I bought it over forty years ago! Crooks all of them! Crooks!"

"Okay then, let's proceed. Do you own a long thin knife with a greenish in-laid gold and pearl handle?"

"No I don't own a knife with any such stupid design. The only sharp knives I own are steak knives in my kitchen and a hunting knife made of real galvanized steel. Owned it for fifty years. Not like the cheap junk they make today. The blade is strong enough to skin a deer with. I should have skinned that Meyer kid. Taught him a lesson. I tell ya!"

"Calm down Mr. Lussier! We are just getting some background information and your additives of speech here are not helping your case."

As the questioning went on Deputy Donato was off to the side with a yellow legal pad making his own conclusions. Jotting down notes.

Skin Him?
Nuisance?
Owned a hunting knife, means he had the skills to kill?
Total dislike of Mr. Meyer

He now knew they had their man but why could the constable not see it loud and clear. Maybe the constable did and was trying to trap him into a confession. The deputy could see it now. If he could be left alone with Mr. Lussier for a short time he could sweat the truth out of him. He was sure of it. All he needed was some time. He would not be so soft on the old man. Go in with vengeance and end up with the confession. Beth would be so proud of him. He could just envision it now. The newspaper printing the front page news with his picture directly atop of the story.

"Deputy Donato Cracks the Chris Myer Murder Case wide open!"

Quoted in the paper, it would read really well and Mark would be the town hero. He could see it playing out like that. He could almost envision a home town parade with the him sitting on top of the back seat of a convertible waving to the onlookers!

Old man Lussier would be trembling when he was placed all alone with the fearless deputy in the interrogation room. The story would continue on to say, "Deputy Donato pressed Mr. Lussier hard in the line of questioning. In less than thirty minutes the deputy had him writing his confession."

"Deputy? Deputy!" the constable said. Mark snapped out of his day dream. "Yes Chief?

"Please get Mr. Lussier another glass of water. Would you like something to snack on?" he asked Mr. Lussier. "Did you eat breakfast earlier today? You are looking a little pale."

"I am fine and I will be a lot better as soon as you release me and let me get back to my gardening."

The deputy thought to himself, "Maybe I can run and get him a lobster roll on a toasted bun. My God man! Let's just sweat him. Sweat him good. Make him uneasy. Then he will crack and confess. Why doesn't the constable see the clues and realize the facts. They are clear as day!"

The interrogation continued for another forty-five minutes. Most of the time Deputy Donato was jotting down useless notes on his pad. Several times he had scribbled the word "GUILTY" in capital letters but then he would make it unreadable by changing some of the letters and scribbling over it.

After Mr. Lussier departed, the constable went into his office and shut the door. He needed to review his notes in solitude.

Beth had left earlier on for the day and called the station a few hours later and asked for the deputy. "Hi hunny. Want to meet me for lunch at Mignosa's Market? Today is pastrami day and it's been weeks since I have enjoyed one."

"Sure. I really could use a break. It's been kind of hectic around here. Big interrogation. Lots of stuff to go over. Maybe a change of scenery would do me good."

"Meet me out front of the station in fifteen minutes."

When Beth arrived Mark was already standing out front of the station on Water Street. "Hi hunny." he greeted her. "Ready for one of Les's famous mouthwatering hot pastrami sandwiches?"

"You better believe it." Beth replied. "I've been salivating for one since I mentioned it to you."

They entered Mignosa's Market as Rita, the owner, was just heading out. She said, "Hi-ya Deputy. Hey Beth, how have you both been?"

"Great Rita," Beth replied. "How's Don?" Beth inquired.

"He's good. He has been working all day out at the house in Pocomo with Rusty Riddleberger. Chris Meyer was helping Rusty with our new addition on the house but now with Chris's passing, Rusty has more work piled on his already busy schedule so Don is giving him a hand a few hours every day. Hey it's packed at the counter and the booths due to Les's famous hot pastrami day. Let me walk you both back and you can have the roped off booth. You know, I thought Don was nuts when he put a rope on the last booth and keeping a reserved sign on it but he knew with Les taking over the lease on the lunch counter he would flourish with business and Don said we will never be able to sit and have our coffee and manage to do some of our paper work. So now we keep the booth reserved for ourselves and our staff. They take a break at different times of the day and they deserve a place to sit and relax. If we are not using it for lunch or entertaining friends it's theirs to use. Here let me get you situated there."

As they entered the area of the crowded lunch counter, everyone seemed to have a question or comment for the deputy. Mark was all smiles but also very serious saying, "Sorry I can't comment. This is an ongoing investigation and all the questions will be answered soon enough."

As soon as they were seated, Les had come over to ask them if they might like a beverage. They both ordered Cokes and settled into the booth. Neither of them even glanced at the menus. The deputy was amazed at the number of people lined up waiting for seats and ordering for takeout.

"So how did your interview go today?" Beth asked.

'Well," the deputy sat back in his booth and stretched his arms out wide, "I have it pretty well figured out."

"You do?"

"Yup, had it figured out pretty early on in this stage of the investigation."

"Oh Mark, you're so smart. Does the constable know about your thoughts?"

"Well it's not quite that easy," the Deputy said as he hooked his thumbs into his suspenders. "I don't want to cause any rifts with the constable. He likes to review and go over the facts when they are really right in front of him. I mean, it's plain as day. If I had the shot and was left alone with old man Lussier, I could sweat it out of him in no time."

"Mark you're just a genius."

"Well I guess it goes with the territory. My grandfather told me when I was young that I had a gift. He told me I was a smart little one and I would go far in life. Did I ever tell you he was on the fire department and when the big calls came in they chose him to drive and navigate the route to the call as he was so quick witted?"

"Didn't your grandfather live in a really small town in Vermont? It had about three hundred residents, I thought you told me once?"

"Well it's complicated as there are several towns all connected."

"Excuse me! Les?" he said quickly wanting to change the subject. Mark signaled him over. "Les we're ready to order."

GREAT POINT

The constable knew deep down that Mr. Lussier did not commit the crime. He might be an old grouch but that's about as far as it went.

He had done background checks on Karen Grant, Maureen Maher, and Trevor Obrien, and they all came up clean.

So now where did this take him? Back to square one? He knew the answer would come but if he rushed it, the answer would evade him.

Constable Kosmo mentioned to Mark and Beth that between all the extra hours that everyone had put in, along with the stress factor in last few weeks with the storm damage and the murder, that an evening out was the answer. No shop talk. Just a nice dinner amongst friends. That afternoon he contacted Patrolman Jaksic.

He then placed a call to the Languedoc. "Thank you for calling the Languedoc. This is Eddie Grennan. How may I help you?"

"Hey Eddie. Kosmo here. I want to see if we can make a reservation for tomorrow evening at 7:00p.m. A party of four?"

"Most certainly Kosmo. You're all set."

"One more thing, is Neil around? I would like to discuss possibly setting up a special menu."

"Yes, he's in the kitchen. Let me go get him."

"There's no need for that. I am down here at the station. Tell Neil I will walk up in the next thirty minutes or so. Thanks Eddie. I look forward to seeing you tomorrow."

A short while later Kosmo was in the kitchen of the Languedoc. He and Neil were discussing old times and how they needed to get together in the fall. Kosmo asked, "Do you think we could have a set menu so when my staff sit down, they would not have to order anything?"

"Sure thing," Neil assured him. Neil and Kosmo selected the menu together. A large bowl of clams steamed in garlic and white wine with a basket of nice toasted garlic bread followed by four individual cheese soufflés. The main entrée would be the, simple but classic, steak frites with sauce béarnaise on the side. Last, but not least, Neil would send out an assorted dessert platter.

"Neil could you just have Al tally up the bill adding the tax and tip and send the bill to the station?"

"Without a problem," Neil told him.

"Oh and for wine. Will Allan be here tomorrow?"

"Yes he will."

"Great so can you have him pick out a bottle of white and red for us to have and if anyone wants anything extra it's not a problem. Since it's going to be Mark Donato and Beth English, along with Patrolman Jaksic, can you try to seat us at a table that's upstairs, more out of the way of the public eye? It might make us all more comfortable than having people stop by and start asking a lot of questions about the ongoing murder case."

"Consider it done Chief. See you tomorrow."

The next day, Kosmo went over the crime scene photos yet again. He took a few more notes. On one line he wrote Chateau Haut-Brion and circled it. Why did Chris Meyer reach all the way to the top of the shelf's racking when he could have just grabbed a bottle from the lower part of the wine rack? It did seem to have a unique shape to the bottle. Maybe Chris thought it was a better bottle for its shape and grip if he was going to use it as a defensive weapon.

Kosmo picked up the crime scene photos and left the station with them. He drove to Hatch's Liquor Store and asked to see Judy Brownell. "Hey Kosmo," came a cheery voice from the back storage area. One thing Kosmo could always say about Judy was that she had a great attitude towards life. She gave him a big hug and said, "If you don't start stopping by here more often for a cup of coffee or if we don't get together for a dinner sooner than later, you're going to be on the naughty list. And you know what that means. A cheap bottle of Christmas wine instead of a good one."

"Ah - Judy, it's always a breath of fresh air to see your smiling face."

"What brings you by the store, Koz?" (Judy was one of the only people who could get by calling Kosmo by that nickname.)

"Well, I have question and wanted to know if you might be able to clarify it for me. Do you know this wine?" He had written it on a piece of paper and removed from his top pocket. "I have heard of it in the past. I was just trying to get some information about it. Sort of a different point of view. Chateau Haut-Brion."

Judy told him, "It's a great bottle. One hundred percent French grapes from Bordeaux. Are you looking for a good vintage? Funny enough, I have a bottle of the 1929 vintage in my Queens Quarters. That's where I keep the good stuff. I actually obtained it two years ago from Tracy Root. You know him don't you?"

"Yes I know him pretty well."

"Actually if you wanted to know more about any wines he is the go-to guy. He was the sommelier and maitre'd at the Chanticleer forever until they brought Denis Toner on board to take the major role of sommelier to relieve some of the pressure off Tracy's shoulders. The Chanticleer is such a popular restaurant. At one point they had over fifteen-hundred wine selections so if you wanted to know something about a certain bottle on the massive list Denis and Tracy were the guys to ask. They had to be on their toes at all times as Chef Jean-Charles is a real master. Not only of the cooking but all the wines which he personally selected for the list. I swear that man has a memory like an elephant when it comes to food and wine. Not even to mention Cognac and Armagnac and, wow, can he cook. His wife runs the front of the house and has an eye for detail that's why the dining room was always looking so grand and flawless. If you really want to get the information on this wine, stop by Cioppinos and have a chat with Tracy or see if you can get ahold of Denis Toner or Jean-Charles. One of them should have the answer you're looking for."

The next day Zach was with Diane and told her, "I have to head back to Phoenix soon."

"How soon?" was her question.

"Next day or two. I thought I would take the ferry to Hyannis, rent a car and drive back. Take my time and see some sights."

"What are you crazy? Drive all the way to Phoenix?"

'Sure, it's not a problem. Fresh air will do me good."

"Well you have had the best fresh air right here on Nantucket. You know I could go with you, me and Luna."

"I know you could, my little daffodil, but with cheap hotels along the way, and my snoring, you would be miserable. Here's my plan. When I get back, let's say, in about ten days from now, I will send you a plane ticket. You can get someone to watch over little Luna and we can have a blast. I will take you to Scottsdale and Flagstaff. We can go hot air ballooning. I think you would really enjoy it. I will show you all my horses and we can take one for a ride. Stop by the library here and research Arizona and whatever you'd like to do. Let's see if we can plan it out. But right now, I need you to take me to a store. I need some new suitcases. I have collected a lot of stuff since I have been here."

"Okay I know just the place," Diane replied.

They headed into town and they parked in front of the Boarding House Restaurant. As they walked up India Street they passed the Company of the Cauldron, a quaint thirty-five seat restaurant. Zach stopped and took a peek inside. "Hi there. I'm Andrea the owner. What can I do for you?"

"I was just taking a look around." Andrea turned and noticed Diane. "Hey Di. How are you? Is he with you?"

"Yes Andrea. This is Zach Cisco from Phoenix. Zach, Andrea also has horses. Zach has a pretty big stable in Phoenix."

"Nice to meet you," Zach said. "This is a pretty nice spot here."

"Yes. We do a set menu nightly. The meal changes every evening and we do two seating's. People usually stop by as we have the menu printed up with about a two-week preview for customers to take with them so they can call to make reservations."

"Well I'm departing back to Phoenix in two days so probably not much of a chance for us to dine here. What's on the menu tomorrow?"

"We are starting with a corn and lobster chowder followed by a Bartlett Farms' tomato salad with crumpled blue cheese with a sherry vinaigrette. The main course is an eight hour slow roasted bone in prime rib of beef and dessert is death by chocolate. If anyone has dietary needs, we are always ready with alternate choices for each course. Lots of picky eaters out there these days.

"That menu sounds great. Can you sign the two of us up?"

"Earlier or later? We seat at 6:00 and 8:15."

"Put us in for the later seating."

"And Mr. Zach, I will see if I can make sure to get you a table with enough elbow room for you."

Zach and Diane continued on to the Hospital Thrift Shop. Zach asked, "What are we doing here?"

"This is where we are going to try and find you some luggage."

"Really, at a thrift shop?"

"Trust me Zach. Just trust me."

Fifteen minutes later they exited the thrift shop with one suitcase and two heavy duty, sturdy duffel bags laughing as Diane said, "Best nine dollars you ever spent."

"I mean that was so cheap, I felt like making a donation for the cause," stated Zach. "Hey we might have time to catch the afternoon movie. I saw 'The Eiger Sanction' was playing starring Clint Eastwood. Let's go grab some popcorn and a couple of Cokes and enjoy a show."

COBBLESTONE HILL

That evening the Constable met his staff at the Languedoc. As they were seated, Jimmy Jaksic said, "I had heard so many great things about this place. I have never been."

Beth chimed in, "Mark and I had our first date in the café downstairs. It's always been a wonderful experience."

Kosmo said that he had arranged with Neil, the chef, to prepare a set menu for them. All they needed now was to speak with Al Cunah about some wines. Right then Al arrived at their table and said, "Hello Kosmo, Beth - Mark and I am sorry but I don't know your friend here."

"That's Patrolman Jaksic. It's his first time here."

"Hi, I'm Jimmy Jaksic. Nice to meet you Allan."

"Welcome," Al said to him. "Hope it won't be your last."

"Al, we need some wine for our dinner tonight," Kosmo said.

"Yes, Neil told me, so I have two bottles for you. Both are from Steele Vineyards in Mendocino California which are made for us. The white one is called Remember February. A wonderful Chardonnay and the name refers to an inside joke around here. The second one is Grey Lady Pinot Noir which is only available at Cioppinos and here."

"Well we are anxious to try them. Can you tell us a little about the tastes we should expect?"

"I can do better than that. Give me a second." Allan went over to another table and had a quick conversation with a gentleman. A minute later the man came over with a wine opener in his hand. He introduced himself as Jed Steele, the wine maker of both of the bottles of wine. Mark who sitting down looked up at him and said, "Just how tall are you?"

"Just shy of six-feet' six," he replied.

They had a nice discussion about the wines and Jed explained how the Remember February was named. It came down to the fact that no matter how busy or crazy it became in July and August, the sign posted right above the phone in the reception area read remember February, meaning there was no business!

As dinner progressed, every plate was completely emptied, baskets of bread were consumed and dipped into the sauces, one bottle of white and two bottles of red wine were consumed. After dessert, Neil and Allan joined them for a nightcap. Jimmy Jaksic said, "If I ever choose to get a second job this is where I am coming to apply. It was over the top."

"Hey Al," Kosmo said, "are you around tomorrow? I have something I would like to run by you."

"Sure thing. What time?"

"Let's plan on around 11:00a.m."

That evening the constable had a very restless sleep. He kept seeing a letter opener laying with its tip inside of an opened envelope like it had just sliced through it. It was a foggy scene playing out in his dream he could not make any sense of it. There was a scattered pile of mail, a folded copy of Yesterday's Island newspaper, a few pencils with teeth marks on them, some crumpled up pieces of paper and what looked like a parking ticket obscured below the letters. He woke up twice during the night and kept trying to make sense of the dream but it faded away quickly.

Walter Lesnevich called the station the next afternoon, from his home in Chatham on Cape Cod, asking for updates on the case. The Constable told him he was narrowing it down but as he did he was crossing off suspects. If the ones he still had left did not pan out he was going to have to dig deeper, a lot deeper.

Kosmo called for Beth and when she stepped into his office he asked her to look up a file that was in the left hand side of the dispatcher's desk and asked her to bring him, the file named 'Petty Cash Checkbook'. When she brought it in he reviewed it and saw that his allotment had grown to twenty-six hundred dollars. The last draw that had been taken out of petty cash was about six months prior. It was for a lunch at the White Elephant with Fire Chief Dan Connor of Nantucket and Fire Chief Tom Brielman from Boston and actor John Shea. One of the movie companies, Beacon Films from Los Angeles, was interested in doing a new movie starring Mr. Shea who resides in Quaise and Los Angeles. The filming would take place in Boston and on Nantucket. So Kosmo figured even with what they spent a few nights' prior at the Languedoc, there was quite a bit left for him to spend any way he saw fit.

Kosmo figured that at the end of this whole ordeal of the murder, if and when they could catch the murderer, he was going to enjoy another dinner out just like they had at the Languedoc and he made a mental note to do that on a regular basis as it was good for moral. He was surprised at what a great evening they all had.

Kosmo left the station. Deputy Donato wanted to join him on his visit to the Languedoc but the constable suggested that he finish up with the banking information on Mr. Meyer. "The sooner we figure that part of this investigation, the sooner we will be one step closer to possibly getting some answers."

"You got it Chief!"

Allan offered Kosmo a cup of coffee while they were standing at the bar downstairs at the Languedoc. "I might indulge in one."

"Better yet," Al asked. "How about a cappuccino?"

"Now you're talking," Kosmo said. They made small chat about the dinner that they enjoyed the night prior. Kosmo mentioned, "I want to know if you could give me some background about a wine? It's called Chateau Haut-Brion."

"Oh that's a very nice French wine from the Bordeaux region. One of the great Grand Cru's of Bordeaux. As I remember," Al was saying, "you're pretty well versed in wines yourself, correct?"

"Yes and no," Kosmo replied. "I enjoy wine and I read articles about it when I find the time. I did take some fun night classes on different wines of the world back in Boston. I went to the Athenaeum yesterday and tried to get some information on this particular wine but there wasn't much, so here I am."

"The most I can tell you is it's one very old Chateau. It was owned by an American banker for many years, Clarence Dillon. We carry the wine only keeping six bottles of it in stock due to the high cost. One of our very good customers, Hunter Laroche, enjoys a bottle or two when he's in town. Otherwise it doesn't really sell due to the high price tag. It runs two hundred twenty-five dollars per bottle on the list. "You know Kosmo, go see Tracy next door at Cioppinos. He knows a lot about French wines or you can head out to 'Sconset and see Jean-Charles at the Chanticleer, as he's the real master of French wine."

When Kosmo left Allan, he stopped by Cioppinos to see if Tracy was available. Two minutes later he was seated in Tracy's office. The conversation started off with Kosmo's questions on the French wine. Tracy filled him in on the history and the grape composition. That it was from the commune of Graves, specifically Pessac. He started to tell Kosmo a fun story related to the Chateau many years ago which most likely wasn't true but it was a fun story.

"It was that the Irish…" Right then, Kosmo's radio came on saying there was a person that wanted to speak to him at the station about the murder. Kosmo not wanting to lose the moment, radioed back, "I will be there in a few minutes. Move the person into the interrogation room. Sorry Tracy, I've got to go."

As the constable was walking back to the station he thought, "What was the Irish story about this French Bordeaux?"

He entered the station and went into the interrogation room. Deputy Donato was standing by with the tape recorder and a pad of paper. "Hi. I'm Constable Kosmo. I am sure you have been introduced to Deputy Donato. And your name is?"

"Stephanie Silva and the reason I am here is I am not sure if you're aware of a Ms. Maureen Maher. She was quite infatuated with Chris Meyer and if you're looking for a suspect, I would take a good look at her."

"What is your relationship with Ms. Maher?"

"I know of her from the many times she sat at my bar."

"Which bar is that?"

"The Galley. Our family has owned it for years. You see our bar is very small and so over hearing conversations is par for the course. Even at the tables across from the bar you can hear almost everything that's being said, and on several occasions over the summer Maureen has sat there. Numerous times I have heard her say that if Chris would just give her a chance she knew she could make it work between them. She would often say that he would love to be driving around with the top down in her BMW. Much better than his old truck. She also mentioned that she could get him some new tools and all sorts of stuff. I have heard her say the only bad part is he's got eyes for the gardener, Emily Dutra, even though she's engaged to the carpenter Trevor Obrien. She also carried on about how Chris flirts with Emily every chance he gets and the fact that he's got that arm candy, Karen Grant with him twenty-four seven. On more than one occasion, she has shed a few tears, mainly after a couple glasses of wine. So it kind of put's her in a prime position."

It was like a light bulb went off in Deputy Donato's head. He started scribbling wildly on his pad. He began sweating. He was hanging on every word that was being said. He knew it. Why didn't he spot it earlier on in the case? Chris Meyer is flirting all over town and it's eating away at Ms. Maher. First it's the gardener who's beautiful and Chris is all googly eyes for her. That stings Ms. Maher. Then he's flirting with every pretty female in town, maybe even some of the married women at the jobs he's working. That's another thorn in Ms. Maher's side. Then of course, there's that girl Karen with her aqua blue eyes, long tan legs and a smile that just radiates when she walks into a room. Now the deputy, with all his notes, was starting to see it. The headlines;

"Murder Case Breaks Wide Open"

Deputy Donato sweats the truth out of jealous island girl. Front page news! His photo in his dress uniform! Oh how everyone would be patting him on the back. It might even make the Boston and Providence papers. Maybe a book deal!

"Deputy?"

Mark snapped out of his day dream. "What? Oh sorry Chief. Just summarizing what's going on here."

Kosmo walked Ms. Silva out to the front office and had the dispatcher get all the particulars of her contact.

He went back to his office and right before he shut his door so he could have some privacy and think about what was just told to him, the deputy leaned against the door frame. "I have a theory chief."

"Well deputy, let's do this. Head to your office and write down all your thoughts as I am going to do right now as well. Then tomorrow morning after I have a night to sleep on it, we can compare notes."

That night the deputy had to celebrate. He was going to bust this case wide open. Boy will Beth be proud of him. Maybe he would receive a medal!

Mark made reservations at the Second Story Restaurant for 7:00p.m. that evening. He had called ahead and ordered a bottle of Perrier Jouet champagne to be on ice waiting at their table when they arrived. Mark and Beth climbed the stairs arriving promptly. On the way to the table Mark saw Bob Rubin along with Karen and Manny Golav. Stopping to say hi, Mark was all smiles. "You're looking chipper," Bob said.

"Well I can't really talk about it but I think really soon I might just have all the answers to the murder sewn up."

"Really?" asked Bob.

"Yup," Mark said. "Tomorrow the constable and I are having a private meeting. He's really anxious to get my views on the case. I can't really discuss any more with you about this but it should be big news real soon. Don't change that bat channel," he said referring to the batman show, as they walked away.

As their server approached the table he said, "Your bottle of Champagne is compliments of Bob Rubin." The server added, "He wanted to say thanks for supporting his company. That champagne is one of his wines."

Beth and Mark clinked their glasses. Mark quietly told Beth the scenario about all those issues of other women, and how the rage just overcame Ms. Maher, and how she drove out to the Germain's home and found Chris working in the wine cellar. She confronted him and an argument ensued. She stabbed him. Its blind jealous love. That also explains the intricate knife used as the murder weapon. Someone who has money and thinks using an expensive antique knife like that was nothing. Most people would have just grabbed a regular kitchen knife but that would have been too bulky for her to conceal. It was a woman scorned. A jealous rage. I thought of that angle right from the beginning but with so many suspects it just kind of slipped away."

"Oh Mark, you're so smart," Beth replied.

"Just a careful deduction. Quite elementary my dear, quite elementary!"

HUMMOCK POND

The next day Diane arrived at the Germain's house. Zach was on the front porch. Steve was standing with him. "Well looks like your rides here. How many bags of luggage do you need? I mean - you arrived here with one and now you have four?"

"Yeah well, I bought a lot of stuff. All sorts of neat things that I would never find back in Phoenix as well as tons of gifts."

"Let me help you." As Steve went to pick up one of the duffel bags, Zach stopped him and said, "Grab the suit case. I have some fragile stuff in the duffel's." When they were all packed in the car and ready to go Steve said, "I can't believe you're driving all the way to Phoenix."

"Hey it's going to be an adventure. See you in Scottsdale! Ciao Steverino!"

When they arrived at the boat, Zach asked Diane to see if there was a cart he could load the luggage onto. She responded, "I can grab a bag." As she went to pull one out of the back of the jeep she said, "Whoa! What do you have in here, bricks?"

"Just a lot of books and they weight a lot."

"You're not kidding," Diane mentioned.

Kosmo met with the deputy and they compared notes. The constable was trying to calm the deputy down. He was almost ready to get a rope and hang the latest suspect without a trial. "Slow down Deputy, we have to investigate this deeper and we will bring Ms. Maher in for questioning when the time is right. So here's the plan of action, go to a few of her stomping grounds, restaurants and bars. Maybe her hair salon, as there is always a lot of the latest gossip floating around at salons. When you go to the restaurants and bars try to get there before they open. That way you will have more privacy and the person you're meeting with might be more open to talking freely. Ms. Maher is quite wealthy and I am sure she enjoys places like the Opera House, White Elephant, Summer House Bistro and upstairs restaurant. See what you can find out."

That night Kosmo had the same reoccurring dream, the knife, the envelopes, but it became clearer. All the items were on the dashboard of a truck as seen through a dirty window. The headlines of the Yesterday's Island paper were clear to him. He could read the headline; *September is only a month away.* There was a parking ticket partially covered underneath the letters and the newspaper. Kosmo could just barely make out the image of the white hood of the auto and front of the windshield.

The next morning the constable entered into the station and asked the dispatcher to get with Patrolman Jaksic and sort through all parking tickets for the month of July. "What are we looking for?" asked Patrolman Jaksic.

Kosmo told them, "Any tickets that are written with Massachusetts tags. Place them in piles by the date. I will be back after lunch. See how much of this you can get sorted out. If it runs too long, take a break, grab lunch and then keep at it."

Kosmo left the station and headed out for lunch. As he was sitting at the counter of Les's Lunch Box which was located inside of Mignosa's Market, Tracy Root approached and sat right next to him. "Hey Kosmo."

"Hey Tracy. What brings you in here? Run out of food at Cioppinos?"

"Not yet. I think we are good to open tonight," he said with a chuckle. "Les used to work for me prior to him taking over this lease. I helped him out with a small loan and a business plan and the rest is history."

"Well it's nice to see you in a different environment. Hey - I have a question. You were going to tell me a story about the wine I had asked you about."

"Well Kosmo, there are so many different folklore stories on wines. I remembered one the other day about Zeller Schwarze, a German white wine. Where the vintner and owners were tasting different casks of the same wine but a mix of different blends, when a black cat jumped atop the large vats and walked back and forth and proceeded to settle on top of one in particular. Next thing you know, they chose that for their premier wine and added the word 'Katz' to it and hence the wine was named Zeller Schwarze 'Katz'. So, in regards to Chateau Haut-Brion, another folklore story is that way back in the sixteen-hundreds, they say that the Chateau was owned by the Irish and it used to be named Chateau O'Brien or that's how they referred to it. But when the French took it over, they changed it to Haut-Brion, a play on the Irish name."

Right then it came to Kosmo, the clue he was searching for. He thanked Tracy and said, "You have been a big help." Kosmo finished his lunch and headed back to the office.

"Patrolman Jaksic, I want you to go to the motor vehicle office and have them run the name and plates for Trevor O'Brien. Get the make and model of his vehicle and bring that information directly back to me. Don't mention anything about this to anyone else."

Kosmo started to put it all together. He knew he had seen that green inlaid knife somewhere and if his hunch was correct, it was on the dash board of Trevor O'Brien's automobile. What had caught the constable's attention was when he was walking past Murrays Liquor Store awhile back. He caught the site of the parking ticket on the right hand side of a dashboard. Thinking to himself, "There goes another unpaid parking ticket. How people did not realize that it caught up with them in the long run when they tried to renew their license or tags."

Upon Patrolman Jaksic's return to the station, he went into the constable's office and handed him the information that he had obtained. The constable wrote down the license number and the information that was presented to him and had the patrolman and the dispatcher look for any ticket that they were sorting through that might have been issued to that reference.

Within about twenty minutes, Patrolman Jaksic knocked on Kosmo's door and brought in a ticket that had been issued to the very automobile that Mr. O'Brien owns. Kosmo wrote down Mr. O'Brien's home address and radioed for the deputy to return to the office.

A short time later Deputy Donato came hurriedly into the station. There were two elderly women talking to the dispatcher along with a small dog on a leash sitting right in the middle of the walkway that led back to the constable's office. Seeing the ladies and the dog blocking his way he said, "Out of my way, official business. Let me pass! Let me pass." With that the dog thought that this meant the deputy wanted to play and started jumping up and down on him running around and getting the deputy all entangled in the leash. The woman who owned the dog was saying, "Isn't that cute. He likes you and wants to play."

"Not now," the deputy said. "Official business. Now move it! Move it!" he started yelling.

Kosmo, hearing all the commotion came down the hall and saw the deputy all tangled up in the leash. Trying not to start laughing asked, "What's going on here?"

The dispatcher said, "I have no idea Chief. The deputy is all flustered."

Mark was now all red in the face and said, "Get your dog off of me!" The whole time the pooch was having a great time.

Kosmo took the leash from one of the ladies and untangled Mark and asked again, "What's going on?"

"Well Chief you radioed that you needed me pronto and I figured it's got to be important so I rushed here."

"Okay, let's all calm down." He handed the leash back to the lady in the red hat, patting the dog on his head. "Follow me Deputy." He ushered the deputy into his office and shut the door. "I think we have a break in the murder case."

"You do? I mean, we do?" Mark asked excitedly. "I mean - I have not even finished up investigating all the avenues with Ms. Maher and there are quite a few. You see I made a detailed list…"

"Hold it Mark. It's not that avenue I'm looking at."

"What do you mean Chief? It's pretty open and shut. I mean the writing is plain as day."

"Well sit down and let me explain it to you." A few minutes later Mark looked like a deflated balloon withering away. The color was leaving his face. He looked like a deer lost in the headlights.

Kosmo then said, "We need to take a ride. Give me about ten minutes then meet me at the dispatcher's desk," he told Mark.

Mark went into his office and shut his door. Not all the way but enough for some privacy, where he turned towards the corner and clutched the sides of his face thinking, "I just celebrated with Beth. I had this whole case all figured out. What am I going to tell her now?"

Kosmo sensed the deputy's depression when he explained all the latest facts to Mark and knew he had taken the wind out of his sails. Kosmo needed to do some damage repair and quickly. He truly respected all of Mark's hard work, dedication and talent he always displayed. That's why he told Mark he needed a few minutes before they headed out of the station. Within a few moments he had it figured out. He went to Mark's office and could see he was turned towards the corner and seemed to be quite upset that his latest theory of the suspect, again, did not pan out. Kosmo gently knocked on the deputy's door. Mark quietly said, "I'm almost ready."

The constable waited outside of his office without entering. A few moments later Mark opened his door and forced a weak smile. Kosmo then said, "You know Mark, if it wasn't for you we would have never come up with this angle."

"What do you mean Chief?"

"Well it was your idea awhile back in this investigation about Trevor O'Brien. You were the one who mentioned maybe it's the gardener's boyfriend. At that time, I was so over whelmed with the nor' easter blowing in, the murder, Steve Germain covered in blood at the murder scene, and Zach Cisco possibly being mob related, that I lost my focus with so many things going on. I am always so grateful to have your input. You're so level headed and calm. Always thinking of different points of view, which is so refreshing. I mean, you're the one who's really responsible for possibly cracking this case open and after we tie all the loose ends together, I am going to call a press conference with the Boston Globe and the Providence Gazette, even the Hyannis and New Bedford papers. I'll let them know what an outstanding job you did."

"Really Chief?"

"You better believe it. We would have never followed the leads that solved this so quickly without all your hard work Deputy."

Mark saw it now. His picture and the headlines. Yes, Beth and everyone will be so proud of him.

"But now we have some work to do you. Ready Deputy?"

"You bet Chief." Mark was grinning ear to ear. "Let's go and round up the bad guys," he said as he tapped his side arm. "So where we headed Chief?"

"We are going to do a very casual drive around the area where Mr. O'Brien resides. We don't want to go spooking him. We just want to do a little reconnaissance."

"What do you want me to keep my eyes peeled for? You know Chief, I have twenty-twenty vision."

"Let's just see if his truck is parked in the area for starters."

As they rounded the corner on Miacomet Avenue, Kosmo told the deputy, "His house number is one seventy-five. We will do a drive by slowly but remain at a steady speed. If we see his vehicle we will then make our plans."

FAT LADIES BEACH

The deputy and Kosmo made their drive pass. The only bad part was the driveway was blocked from the street view by dense hedges. After a drive by in both directions, they realized that there was no way they would be able to see if there was a truck that might be parked on the property.

"What are we going to do Chief? It's impossible to see anything from the street. I could go back to the station and get changed into of my camouflage gear. We could come back when dusk starts setting in and I could do some recon."

"No. Let's just head back to the station. I have another idea. I need you to contact Beth. We might have another way to skin a cat! First thing tomorrow I want you to go to Marine Hardware and Island Lumber. Pull the last two weeks of any job listings that Mr. O'Brien has charged on as well as his personal charges and have Beth meet me at the station at 10:00a.m."

That afternoon after returning to the station the deputy called Beth and said, "Big news. Special undercover operative stuff going on! Let's you and I meet at the Tap Room at 1600 hours. We will take a table off to the side and I will fill you in on what's going on. Oh - and dress inconspicuously."

"Wow - really?" Beth asked.

"Yes and if you run into any of your friends, play it cool. This is tricky stuff we are going to engage in."

"What time is 1600 hours?" Beth asked?

Deputy Donato was the first to arrive at the Tap Room. June was at the hostess stand. "Hey Deputy," she blurted out. "Hey June," Mark said quietly. "Try to act like we are having a normal conversation but I need a very private table off to the side out of ear shot of others and try to act normal June. No sudden moves. Maybe throw in a little laugh like we are talking just as old friends." June, always ready to play along, whispered, "Okay - Like secret agent stuff?"

"Yes, something like that," replied Mark also whispering.

"Do I get a secret decoder ring?" June asked. "Or is there a secret handshake?" Mark just rolled his eyes and said, "Just take me to the table."

Fifteen minutes later, Beth thinking that this was a fun new date night ploy that Mark had dreamed up, arrived in a short skirt, black boots a leather jacket, dark sunglasses, and a large hat. June said, "Hi-ya Beth. What's new?"

"Hi June. Actually you can refer to me as Natasha for tonight. I am an undercover spy!"

"Well if you're looking for Inspector Clouseau, he's on the far side over behind the stair case. By the way, you look great. Enjoy your evening!"

As Beth approached the table Marks eyes opened wide, catching a view of Beth he had never seen before. She promptly sat down, still thinking that this was a new play date idea, and was excited and determine to fill the part. She said in her best Russian accent, "Good evening darling. I am your contact, Natasha from Russia." Their server approached the table and Mark was just about to order two iced teas when Beth said, "I will have a very cold Stolichnaya martini, shaken not stirred, three olives, served straight up and a tin of your finest caviar."

"Beth?" Mark sputtered out.

Beth then said, "And bring my comrade the same thing and make them extra chilled!"

Mark again said, "Beth! What are you doing?" Beth, playing the part as best she could, took her foot and started rubbing the inside of Mark's leg under the table.

"Beth! Knock it off." Which made her reply, "Why darling, who is this Beth person you're referring to? A lover back home? Forget about her. Tonight you have me, Natasha, and when I am done with you she will be a distant memory!"

"Beth. You don't understand. This is real police business."

"Interpol?" Natasha replied.

"No real police business."

"Is it CIA? FBI? Secret Service?"

Right as Mark started to protest their drinks arrived. Mark who had never in his life had a martini, took a sip not knowing what else to do. The server broke into their conversation and told Natasha, "I am sorry but we don't serve caviar here." Natasha looked up and said in her Russian accent, "Away with you," and dismissed the server.

Mark was now on his second or third sip of the martini looking over at Beth. He was starting to really admire her and thought, wow! Who would have ever thought his prim and proper girlfriend could ever look so hot? "Oh darling, we must cheers to an operation involving two of the world's cleverest spies meeting here on Nantucket." By now Mark, not realizing it, had finished off his martini and Beth had ordered two more. At this point, Mark had almost forgot about why they were meeting. He started to broach the subject when Beth slapped her hand on the old worn table and said, "Enough Boris! Tonight we will drink like royals, dine like sheiks and make love on the beach until the sun comes alive."

Now, after the second martini was finished Mark did not recall much more.

The next morning, Mark awoke in his own bed with all his clothes on and a rather banging headache. He got up and headed to the bathroom to splash some water on his face. He looked into the mirror above the sink which was covered in part with a big red lipstick kiss and an XO Natasha.

Mark headed into town to meet up with Kosmo and Beth. As he was walking past Mignosa's Market on Main Street, Sean Divine and Colin Keenan were exiting the store. They spotted Mark and yelled out, "Hey Boris! Where's Natasha!" They both started rolling with laughter.

Mark thought to himself searching his mind, "What did we do last night?" He tried in vain but could not remember. He was walking on Water Street when he passed by the Opera House. David, the bartender said, "Hey Deputy. Natasha was looking quite hot last night. Looks like you two were having a lot of fun." Mark sheepishly looked over towards David, nodded his head and kept walking picking up his pace.

Mark entered the station grateful that no one else made a comment referring to Boris or Natasha. He spoke with Kosmo and mentioned he was going to get right on the task at Marine Hardware. As he was turning to leave when Kosmo said, "Go get – em' Boris."

Mark felt a jolt of lightning go through him but kept walking. When he got into his patrol car he thought to himself, "Does the whole town know?" He was going to have to speak with Beth. She never forgot any of their evening's events or people's names they had met at different times.

Where did they go after the Tap Room? How long was it going to take him to live this episode down?

About twenty minutes later, Beth met with the constable. His plan for her was to just be herself and go around town to see if she could locate Emily Dutra, Trevor's fiancé. This he thought would not cause any suspicion. Not as if a police officer was out asking questions. She was just to try and see if someone knew which job Emily might be working on. As when it came to females, no one ever thought anything suspicious of girls trying to track one another down. If she did locate Emily, she was to act normal and not rush any pressing questions. Beth would need to concoct a story why she was at Emily's job site so that it would seem normal. Kosmo didn't want to stir up any suspicions. Kosmo needed Beth to find out where Trevor was working.

In the meantime, Kosmo jotted down notes on two separate sheets of paper. One was facts and one was for questioning when they brought in the suspect.

It was not long after Beth had begun her quest, when she noticed Emily's work truck heading out of town on Orange Street just by total accident. Beth came to a stop sign where Emily had just gone through.

"Okay Natasha," Beth said to herself, "let's tail her." The first stop Emily made was at Fooods for Here and There. Beth thought, "Let me play this cat and mouse game a little longer. She might lead me right to Trevor." Emily came out a few minutes later with a small paper bag and two coffees. Natasha thought, "Maybe she went inside to meet her contact and has some espionage trade secrets in the bag. Oh! This was fun," Beth giggled.

As Emily pulled out Beth said aloud, "Two coffees. Maybe she's bringing a snack to Trevor or another underworld contact." Ever so cautiously, Beth still trying to pretend she was a spy, was enjoying her pursuit. Emily arrived at the rotary and headed onto Old South Road where she stopped into Valero Gardening Supplies. Again Natasha pulled in and parked off to the side five cars down. She slumped down into her seat and waited. Natasha whispered, "Another contact? Maybe trading microfilm. Oh-this is fun."

Beth's mind was racing as she continued her secret agent fantasy. Emily came out this time with a larger bag in her hand, put it in the bed of her truck and drove out of the parking lot. Beth still imaging that she was Natasha, a trained foreign spy, followed ever so cautiously. Emily headed back in the direction of the rotary and took a right turn onto Milestone

Road, then took the left turn onto Polpis Road. Natasha could see Emily drinking her coffee. "But who was the second one for? Her contact?"

Beth was giggling to herself thinking maybe she should go to spy school. She felt confident that she was so good at what she was doing. Emily took a left onto Wauwinet Road and finally ended up pulling into the Germain property.

Beth said to herself, "Okay Natasha, we're going to play this cool and keep going past the Germain's. We will allow Emily some time to get herself out of her truck and start working. Let's see who the extra coffee is for!"

Beth drove down the road and parked in the lot of the Wauwinet Inn. She figured when she arrived at the Germain's, it would be the perfect place for her to run into Emily. Not arousing any suspicion as to why Beth was there. She could tell her that she was stopping by to see if Mark might be there doing any follow up work on the murder.

As she was sitting in her car in the parking lot George and Mary Williams, the proprietors, pulled in next to Beth's car. Beth had her driver's side window down. As they got out and saw Beth wearing her dark sunglasses Mary said, "Hi Beth. You looked so nice all dressed up while you were out last night with Mark. Everyone in the bar at the Opera House loved your Natasha and Boris characters that you were playing while enjoying your martinis. Good for you both to break out of this everyday life and have some fun."

"Thanks," Beth said. "We have been reading one of the James Bond novel's over the last few weeks and thought, let's go out and pretend we are international spies."

A few minutes later Beth started up her car and drove over to the Germain's. She pulled in and saw Emily removing a sack of mulch from the back of her truck. Beth got out of her car and began a conversation with Emily. She said she thought she might find Mark here going over some details. Maybe trying to see if there were more clues to be found. Emily said. "He's not here. It's nice to see you though. I noticed you pulling out on Orange Street after I drove through the stop sign. Funny we ended up going to the same places, Fooods, Valero's and now here at the Germain's. At one point I thought you might have been following me until I pulled in here and you went straight."

Beth, caught off guard, saw her Spy Training School vanishing into thin air. "Oh?" Beth replied. "I did not notice that you were in front of me."

"Well that's kind of hard not to do, seeing I am driving this old battered truck."

"Well I guess. So, Mark is not around here? How's Trevor these days?'

He's really good. Really busy but you know you need to make hay when the sun shines."

"Where's he working?"

"All over. One day here, one day there." Now Beth was getting nowhere in his location. She said to herself, "Come on Natasha use your spy training. "Well give him my best." Then as she started to walk away she said, "Emily, I was out in 'Sconset earlier was that Trevor's truck near the Summer House?"

"Nope. He's tied up all day at Reg Marden's house in Monamoy. They are digging up an old cement slab next to his garage and are going to build a work shed so they rented a Bobcat. They want to place new footings along with a new, improved waterproof floor in by the end of the day. His house is beautiful. The guest house alone is three bedrooms, three and half baths. I would love to have that landscape contract but it's already taken by Marty McGowan. He's had the job for years."

"Okay well hope to see you at the Boys & Girls Club fair next week." Beth walked back to her car trying not to rush but she was bursting at the seams with the knowledge she had just learned. As soon as she was on the Wauwinet Road, putting on her four-way flashers, she pressed her foot down on the accelerator. Feeling a slight rush of adrenalin go through her body. As the way Beth saw it, she was on a covert mission and time was of the essence and if by chance she got pulled over she would say, "I am on a private mission with strict direct orders to only report to the Chief." Oh Mark would be so proud of her.

She arrived at the station and ran into the constable's office. She was all flustered and started babbling about how she tailed Emily Dutra out to the Germain's and casually coaxed the information out of her. Beth was talking so fast that the constable rose from his desk, put his hands on her shoulders and said, "Calm down and sit. Let's go over this slowly." He poured her a glass of water from the tray he always kept on his desk with paper cups and a water pitcher, which he requested was filled every morning and again in the afternoon daily.

Beth recounted the story to Kosmo and added, "Did I do okay?"

"Yes. You did very well. Now just sit tight. I am going to radio Mark and have him return to the station. He went out and radioed the deputy and told him to return to base, over and out.

210

As the constable returned to his office with all the information written on his note pad that Beth had told him, he looked up and asked, "Did you and Mark have a fun time last night?"

"Oh yes we did. It was a great fun, exciting evening. I dressed up as a Russian agent named Natasha and I nick-named Mark, Boris. We met at the Tap Room and had Stolichnaya martinis just like the spies do in James Bond movies. We have both been enjoying one of the James Bond novels 'Gold Finger' so I thought that it might add to an interesting fun night out. We stopped by the Opera House and The Club Car. It was a lot of fun! Mark had his first martini ever and maybe his last as they creep up on you fast."

A few minutes later the deputy entered to find Kosmo and Beth laughing about their adventures the night prior. Kosmo filled Mark in on Beth's discovery of where Trevor O'Brien might be. Beth started telling Mark of all the details that led up to gathering the information. Mark was slightly let down that he wasn't the one in the spotlight, but then he told both of them that he was right on the cusp of deducting the same details of Trevor's whereabouts.

"Okay Beth, your work is finished here for the day and remember not a word to anyone about you getting Emily Dutra to give you Mr. O'Brien's whereabouts. This is a small island and we don't need any more gossip forming about how you're a snitch, etcetera."

"Okay, here's the situation," Kosmo related to the deputy. "I don't want to go onto private property to talk with Mr. O'Brien, so I am going to call the permit department. Get them out to Mr. Marden's estate and find some fault with the paperwork or if Mr. O'Brien has even filed for any permits. This would be a good way to get Mr. O'Brien off the property then we can pull him over and bring him in for questioning."

"Wow! That's some good thinking Chief!"

The constable called down to the permits office and spoke with Nicholas Mang. He explained the predicament he was facing. Nicholas was quick to respond. "Give me five minutes. What number can I ring you back at?"

After he hung up, the constable figured that he and the deputy could park at the rotary and wait for Mr. O'Brien to leave the job site to file whatever papers that Nick told him he needed before continuing with his construction project.

A short time later the constable's phone rang, Nick told him that he did not see any permit work requested for the job in question and would head out there directly and put a cease and desist order in place.

The constable instructed Nick to make this sound like all Mr. O'Brien has to do is go down to the permit office and file a request for the work along with a twenty-five-dollar check. After that point Nick would quickly approve the paperwork and he could be back on the job in short time.

"Consider it done," Nick replied. "I should be out at the house in twenty minutes or so. May I ask what this is all about?"

"Nothing really but just act like this is a routine job check. Nothing more nothing less."

"You got it!" Nick stated and hung up.

"Okay Deputy. Let's figure this it out. It will take Mr. Mang thirty minutes from now to arrive where Mr. O'Brien is working. Another ten or fifteen minutes for him to deliver the message and then another fifteen minutes for Mr. O'Brien to come past the rotary. So in about forty-five minutes, if our timing is correct, we might find our suspect driving right into our little trap. Let's go and get set up at the Rotary. We know the make, model and color of his work truck so this should be quite easy to pull off."

Mark asked if they should put on their bullet proof vests. The constable replied, "I think we are good for now."

As they backed the car into the Inquirer and Mirror parking lot, the plan was to follow Mr. O'Brien a short distance before pulling him over and bring him in for questioning. After what seemed to be an eternity, they spotted his vehicle heading right into the rotary. Mr. O'Brien was alone, sitting behind the wheel. As he continued on his way towards town, the constable and deputy slowly pulled out of their parking spot. Two cars were now spaced between them and Mr. O'Brien's vehicle. Kosmo was patient. He knew that Mr. O'Brien was not going to run if he turned on the lights. They followed his truck. Kosmo thought maybe the best place would be just to follow him right to the Permit's Department Building.

They slowly followed him and when he pulled into the Building Department parking lot they parked and approached him as he was exiting his vehicle.

"Mr. O'Brien?"

"Yes?"

"We would like to ask you a few questions."

"If it's about the work I am doing out at Mr. Marden's property I am here to get the proper permit. It was just an oversight on my part. I will have it all cleared up in a few minutes."

"No, it's about something else and we really need to conduct this conversation down at the station," With that being said, Trevor seemed to go from rosy red cheeks to a pale grey.

"What's this about?" Trevor asked.

"We rather not go into it out here in the parking lot."

"But I have to get some papers filled out and get back to my job site."

"Well, that is going to have to wait. Now please get into the squad car. We should have you back out to your job in no time."

When they arrived at the station, they put Trevor into the interrogation room. Deputy Donato had a pad set up for the constable and one for himself. He was also ready with a pen and pad of paper to give to Mr. O'Brien at the right time for him to write out his confession along with the tape recorder. Deputy Donato started up the recorder saying, "Test. Test, one, two, three," and played it back to make sure it was working. Mark was chomping at the bit, knowing if he could get thirty minutes alone with Trevor he could sweat him. Press him really hard and he would have him singing like a bird about the murder he committed.

The constable started with the questions. "Please state your full name and date of birth."

"Trevor Smith O'Brien. My date of birth is October 31, 1950."

"Home address?"

"One Seventy-five Miacomet Avenue."

"Mr. O'Brien where were you on the day of Mr. Chris Meyer's death? "I was working out in Quaise replacing some old windows in the Shea home. Do I need a lawyer?"

"Not unless you request one. Right now we are just gathering as much information as we can."

"Well, I don't think I can be of much help. I really did not know him very well. Just from seeing him around town."

"Wasn't it a fact that he was working on the same job site and always flirting with your fiancé, Emily Dutra?"

"Well a lot of people flirt with Emily. It's tough on her. When you have her looks it comes with the territory."

"Did you have a confrontation with him one evening at DeMarco Restaurant about two weeks back?"

"Well it was not a confrontation as much as me telling him to stay away from Emily. It really was just a short kind of abrupt conversation. But as soon as it ended that was it."

Deputy Donato was dying to jump in and quit beating around the bush. "Sweat him! Sweat him good! Come on Chief. Push him. Use the good cop, bad cop scenario." Mark knew he could make him crack in no time.

"How is your hand? Healing?"

Deputy Donato looked over at the constable wondering what he was asking about.

"Its fine just three stitches."

"What happened?"

"I was using a small hack saw and it slipped. I cut it while on a job."

"Well the reason I ask is it seems as it happened the same day as Mr. Meyer was murdered. I just so happened to be at the hospital the same day and time as you were walking out of the emergency room.

"It must have been. If you say so."

"Have you ever seen this knife before?" Kosmo pulled out the evidence bag that the knife was placed inside of.

Trevor glanced at it ever so casually. "Never seen it before in my life."

"Are you sure about that? This knife is the murder weapon that was used to kill Mr. Meyer. Mr. O'Brien I am going to ask you one more time. Have you ever seen this knife before?"

"I don't believe so."

The deputy wanted to jump on this question and shout out, "Well man, which one is it? You have or have not ever seen the knife? You have never seen the knife or you don't believe so." Why was the constable being so passive on this line of questioning?"

"Well the reason I ask is, we have two different blood types that were recovered at the crime scene. We might need a sample of your blood at one point."

Trever went two shades paler when that was mentioned. The deputy was asking himself where all of this stuff the constable is talking about was coming from? He never heard of any other blood type that was found at the crime scene.

After another twenty minutes of questions, the constable was starting to narrow the playing field but he did not want to reveal all his thoughts too early on so he thought let me give Mark a shot at this. It would be good insight to see how he proceeded. He turned to Mark and said, "Deputy, I am sure you have several questions for Mr. O'Brien. Why don't you follow through."

Mark was caught totally off guard. He looked at the chief, then at Trevor, then down at his yellow legal sized note pad. All he had written on there was a large letter "G" for guilty which had been written over several times and darkened by the black ink from his pen. Spiraling out from the G, it looked like he had made a small devil's design with two beady eyes. "Oh! Well - um, let's see here." He quickly regrouped his thoughts. Mark took in a big breath, puffed up his chest and slowly walked around the desk getting closer to Trevor. He wished he had a large bright light that he could have turned on, like in the old movies, and shine it right into Trevor's eyes. "Now! Mr. O'Brien. Can I call you Trevor? There's no need to be too formal around here. We are just trying to get to the facts of this case."

"Sure Trevor is fine."

"Okay Trevor. That's good. Very good. I mean we are sure you would like to assist in this case and get to the bottom of it. Just as soon as we do then you can go back to your job! Now you said that you were out in Madaket replacing windows in a home. Whose home did you say you were working on?" Mark thought a little switch-a-roo in the questioning might trick him up.

Trevor replied. "It wasn't Madaket. It was Quaise and it was John Shea's home. He can vouch for me as he was working on cutting a tree down near his garage for most of the day."

"At any time did you leave the property? Let's say for lunch or materials?"

"I might have but I don't recall."

"Oh come on now!" the deputy said raising his voice slightly. Kosmo sat back making a few notes and was not going to interfere. It was time to let Mark see what he could come up with. Kosmo did look at this style of interrogation as something scripted out of an old movie and he knew Mark and Beth enjoyed old detective movies and they were big fans of Sherlock Holmes books. If this was his style let it be. One never knows what flips someone's switch to turn on and off.

Mark kept on. "What time did you start your day out there?"

"Trevor replied, "9:00a.m.""

"Did you bring any coffee, doughnuts or snacks?"

"Yes I always bring a full thermos and two doughnuts for my 10 o'clock break."

"Did you pack a lunch?"

"I don't remember. I think so."

Mark slowly went back to his pad scribbled a few things on it and placed it again face down on the table.

"So you say you remember what time you arrived and what you brought along with you but then your mind pulls a blank whether you brought a lunch or not? This is sounding like a classic selective memory Trevor," as Mark gently laid a hand on his shoulder.

"Trevor things will go much quicker and smoother for everyone if you just let it all out. What I am saying Trev, is I understand how you feel having a very pretty fiancé on this small island. Everyone eyeing her and this guy Chris Meyer starts flirting and it gets you all worked up inside. Then he continues flirting with her in plain view every chance he gets. It doesn't help that he's almost model material and people are saying that the two of them, Emily and Chris, would make such a cute couple. Talking about what beautiful babies they would make."

Trevor started to twist a little when the deputy started in on this line of questioning. He was rubbing his hands together. This was the first sign that he was really getting agitated. Kosmo made a note hidden from Trevor's view on his pad.

Jealous motive!

"Trev, I really understand how this can get you worked up. I am in the same boat as you. My girlfriend Beth is also very attractive, she dresses very nice and when she's out and about guys are always hitting on her. Even married men. It kind of eats you up inside. As you can't be by Emily's side twenty-four hours a day to protect her. Your mind starts racing wild with ideas. Wondering if one of these times she's going to slip up and fall for some other guy. And the worst part is that Chris and Emily were both at the same location daily. Working almost side by side half the time. Mr. Meyer with his shirt off strutting like a rooster in front of Emily. Yourself not being around to protect her. With all of the very flirtatious moves Mr. Meyer was making, gets your mind all twisted around not being able to be there to monitor the situation."

Now Trevor was starting to bead up with a little perspiration on his forehead. Kosmo was becoming quite impressed with this line of interrogation that Mark was building on.

Kosmo figured this was a good time for him to jump into the questioning. "Okay Trevor, we now understand how this kid, Mr. Meyer, was really eating away at you. Why don't you tell us your side of the story?"

"Well yeah, I didn't like that clown Chris. I mean, every time Emily and I were out and we would run into him he always had to make some snide comment or flirt with her right in front of me. I mean, he was a real arrogant jerk thinking he was the Adonis of men. Just so he could play the big man for women. It was sickening. He used to make my blood boil. I did my best to avoid him. Several times I would be with Emily later on in the day when we were off work and Emily would always mention something about how Chris was complimenting her on her tanned legs. How he loved her in her daisy dukes. It seemed that she was always bringing him up in a conversation. It really got under my skin. We had several heated conversations about him, even though the way she mentioned it, it was supposed to be sounding derogatory but I think she really enjoyed it."

Kosmo explained that he had overheard a conversation one afternoon of what he believed were some of Trevor's workers mixed into a group of Mr. Meyer's employees sitting at the counter of Les's Lunch box. That it looked like a showdown was coming between you and Chris. Then they all started in by saying who would win the fight if it came to blows. "They all agreed that you would be the victor, Trevor."

"He would not have stood a chance against me. He was a big bag of wind. I saw him get into it with a guy at the Rose & Crown one day not too long ago at the bar. This bruiser of a guy entered and gave him a piece of his mind. Meyer was talking big but if this guy back handed him he would have been out for the count.

Now was the time Kosmo thought to regroup. He said, "Trevor we are going to give you a rest, get you a glass of fresh water and then we have just a few more questions and you're free to go."

The deputy and Kosmo left the interrogation room and retreated to the chief's office. Shutting the door, he told Mark, "It was brilliant the way you handled yourself in there."

Mark, all serious looking, placed his pad face down on the chief's desk as he did not want him to notice that he had not really made many notes. Mark started saying, "Well you know Chief, once I get my mojo running there's no stopping me. I have a question Chief. I don't remember any mention of two different blood samples being found at the scene?"

"Well there wasn't but he doesn't have to know that. It kept him on the ropes. Plus, the fact that he cut his hand on the same day is quite a coincidence. I was at the hospital on the afternoon of the murder. Quaise being a mere mile or two from the murder scene, my thought is that he takes a break from the job. He drives over to the Germain's. Maybe not pulling into the driveway but parking down the road a couple hundred yards or so. Possibly parking at the Wauwinet Inn. He walks to the Germain's home. Slips the knife from the top of his dashboard into his pants pocket. Finds Chris in the basement working in the wine cellar and an altercation ensues. Trevor stabs him in a jealous rage and leaves. Mr. Meyer knowing he's in bad shape thinks in his last dying breath, a clue. He has a very good knowledge about wine and folklore stories about different Chateaus. That's why he took such great effort to reach up high and grab the bottle of Haut-Brion hoping that someone might tie the clue to Trevor O'Brien. Haut-Brion, as it's rumored, back in the fifteen-hundreds the Chateau was owned with some Irish decent and named it Chateau O'Brien."

"Okay. Here's the way I see it playing out," the constable said. "We go back in and you take the lead. Be nice but firm, like your good cop, bad cop scenario. You can work the jealous angle again. Let's give him a pad and pen and tell him we are going to need him to write out his thoughts about Emily and his relationship and the problems with Mr. Meyer, then toss in that we might have to bring in his fiancé. Possibly we are looking in the wrong direction and she has a perfect motive to have committed the murder. After you get him riled up, I will come in with how awful it would be to see her have to go to trial and I will close with seeing the knife in his truck a few weeks earlier and how we traced the owner of the truck back to Trevor with the parking ticket that is still on his dash board.

"We will keep going on with the fact Emily had motive and access to the murder weapon and maybe the other blood found at the scene was hers. He just might spill the beans as he doesn't want her implicated and he will then understand that we tied him or both of them to the murder weapon. It's a good possibility that her fingerprints might be found on the weapon. Let's be firm and straight forward. If the situation arises and fits in, you can mention what they do to pretty, vulnerable women in prisons these days. Okay, again, let's go at this cautiously, straight-forward and firm. Keep an eye on me so we can feed off each other's vibe. Okay let's go."

"Okay, Trevor?" Mark started in. "Can I get you anything? More water, something to snack on?"

"No I am fine. How much longer am I going to be in here?"

"Not much longer," Mark replied.

"Here's a pad and pen just so you can write down any thoughts you might remember that could help us out here. Getting back to Emily, did you notice any change in her attitude or in your relationship together since she and Mr. Meyer were working at the Germain's?"

"No. Not really."

"Well Trevor, we have interviewed several people in this matter, covering many different angles. One thing that keeps popping up in these separate interviews are the fact that on several occasions Mr. Meyer had brought lunch sandwiches and enjoyed them in the garage apartment alone with Emily. Were you aware of that fact?"

"What? You have got to be mistaken. Emily would never have done that."

"Well that's just the tip of the iceberg. Other people interviewed also stated that Emily was wearing short shorts and flirting back with Mr. Meyer. She was also seen in the afternoons with her tee shirt cut low at the neckline and tied in a knot above her tanned smooth stomach. I hate to tell you this but she was falling under Mr. Meyer's well planned spell."

Now Trevor was back to squirming around in his chair. His blood pressure was rising; his eyes not meeting the deputy's or the constables.

"One witness we interviewed was a female. She mentioned that Emily had met with Mr. Meyer. They sat with him in a booth at the Atlantic Café. She was with Emily at the time and her thoughts were that Emily and Mr. Meyer had more going on than met the eye."

Now Trevor was starting to boil. A bead of sweat had formed on his forehead. "No way!" he said. "It's not possible. She would never!" Trevor started stammering in his replies.

"Sorry to say it's true," Mark responded.

Kosmo started in. "Trevor we know how this might end. You see we know that the knife that killed Mr. Meyer was inside of your truck on the dashboard." Trevor looked away from Kosmo's stare.

"Don't deny it. We know it for a fact. Now here's the way we see it. Emily and Mr. Meyer are doing the flirting dance. By the time Emily realizes it, it's almost too late. She is being swept under Mr. Meyer's spell and she needs to stop before it goes any further. She takes the knife off your dashboard and goes to confront Chris. What happens next is, Chris threatens to tell you about the latest developments of their ongoing affair if she doesn't play along. It becomes a crime of passion. Emily can't let this happen. She pulls out the knife, stabs him and it's over. Mr. Meyer is dead the relationship is buried never to surface."

"No way!" Trevor said. "Impossible. She would never get involved with a scumbag like him."

"Well, if she comes forward truthfully, we can go easy on her. We play it out like it became a crime of passion and she might get off with a few years in jail and parole for good behavior, or maybe it was self-defense. Maybe he tried to kill her?"

Mark chimed in, "And you know how tough it can be when you're a beautiful woman inside the big house."

Now Trevor was biting on his lower lip, rubbing his hands together like he was trying to keep them warm. Mark continued, "But there is also one other scenario to this story we have. Interested in hearing it?"

Trevor's mind now racing about what was coming down the pike. "Fire away."

"We also see this as a jealousy issue. If we don't put it together on this second scenario, then we are going to go after Ms. Dutra on murder charges."

"The other way we see it is, you parked your car off site, walked in and confronted Mr. Meyer, a scuffle started, you had your knife out and accidently stabbed Mr. Meyer in the abdomen and you cut your hand in the process, hence the stitches the same day. We are confident that if we take a blood sample from the knife, it will match your blood type. You take this jealousy angle, and testimony of several people who can attest to that fact, along with the knowledge of the knife in your truck, and well things don't look good for you. A matching blood sample along with the fact that I had to escort Mr. Meyer out of DeMarco Restaurant from an altercation you were having with each other still doesn't look very good. It's going to sound a lot better for a jury, if you come clean. Otherwise we are going to drag Emily into this as either the murderer or an accomplice, which would certainly tarnish her reputation as there would always be that question of doubt on people's minds. This could ruin her business and her personal life."

"People whispering as she walks by and shying away from her," Deputy Donato added.

"So Trevor?" the Constable asked again. "Think it over. I am only going to ask you this one last time. If we have to move forward investigating both avenues and spend an enormous amount of man-hours on this investigation, my report to the prosecutor will not be favorable. Right now we are looking at this as an accident gone bad. I will give you five minutes alone. After that all deals are off."

As they both started to leave the room Trevor said. "All right! Let's get this done. I killed him! It was an accident. I never meant to go through with it."

"Okay. Slowly let's start from the beginning and then I need you to hand write and sign a confession."

Trevor went through all the details of how he was never a fan of Mr. Meyer. How over time he kept flirting with Emily, as well as every other girl in this town and it had his blood boiling. When Chris ended up working at the Germain house and so was Emily, it became over whelming. "I mean as the summer progressed, her tan made her look like model material. She started bringing up Chris's name more and more often. I don't think she even realized that she was doing it. Then I noticed her starting to dress, in what I refer to as, in a flirtatious manner. Short skirts, buttoned down shirts that I would imagine her wearing with several buttons undone, even in an innocent manner, or in semi sheer tees. One day I brought some sandwiches over unexpectedly around two in the afternoon. She had her V-neck tee shirt tied in a knot on the bottom. At first she did not notice me pull in so I sat in my truck for a moment. I saw that jerk, Chris, strutting around all sweaty with his shirt off and I caught Emily taking a good long glance over in his direction. I wanted to go over and knock that confident smirk off his face but Emily did not like it when my temper flared up as it had the night before when she brought up his name in a conversation. When I surprised her she seemed taken back like she was caught, like a fox in a hen house. I did not let on that I had been watching her for a few minutes. When I told her I had brought two chicken salad sandwiches from the drug store, she said that was nice but she really wasn't very hungry, which I found really weird as she never turns one down. She loves them. So we made small talk while I ate my sandwich standing up. Mr. Meyer had all of a sudden became a ghost. Nowhere to be seen. To add fuel to the fire she said at one point, I should go check out the garage apartment that Chris was working on. It was coming out really well. She was almost bragging at what nice work he has been doing. After she mentioned that, I think she realized what she had said. She started back peddling saying his work could never compare to mine. I quickly finished my sandwich and trying not to show my anger, I said that I would go check it out.

"I went upstairs and there were a couple of guys working away up there that I knew. We made small talk and one of the guys asked if I was there to keep an eye on my lady. So I told him that I just stopped by to see if she was hungry. Well that's when Miguel told me that I was a little late. That Emily and Chris just polished off a box of fried chicken out back on the porch of the main house. I turned around and walked out. I didn't want to let them all see how angry I was. My blood was boiling.

"That's how it began and it just kept eating away at me until I could not even get a good night sleep. I was having nightmares involving him and Emily. The night before I confronted him in the dream I had. It was so vivid. He and Emily were drinking wine watching the sunset at the Galley Restaurant. They were looking into each-other's eyes and clinking their glasses. He had his hand cupped around Emily's lower back. When I awoke, all morning I was in a foul mood. When I could not stand it anymore I jumped in my truck drove to the Wauwinet Inn from the Shea's home, parked my truck and grabbed the knife. I found him in the wine cellar and told him to stay away from Emily. He told me that her heart would come around and she would soon realize, as everyone in town did, that they were meant to be together. Then I really snapped and that's how it happened. We had a struggle. I only meant to scare him with the knife I was waving around. Next thing you know, he was stabbed and I cut my hand. I ran off and he was still standing leaning against the countertop. I went back to the Shea's house, I pulled out my small hacksaw and made it look like the blade slipped and I cut myself. I worked most of the afternoon with a towel wrapped around it. Mrs. Shea saw it and asked what happened. I told her the blade slipped and I nicked myself. She looked at it and said I needed a couple of stiches, so that's when you must have seen me at the hospital."

"Okay well, we need you to write it out. We have it on tape recorder."

"Can I call my attorney, All?"

"Sure thing. Deputy escort Mr. O'Brien out to the dispatcher's desk and let him make his call."

After the constable read the signed confession and typed up his report, he called the prosecutor. Filled him in on the recent breakthrough and told her that she could come and pick up a copy of the file at the dispatcher's desk.

Mark quickly rushed home after calling Beth telling her, "I have big news. Really big! Meet me in the bar at the Straight Wharf in an hour. We are going to celebrate!"

"What is it Mark?"

"You're just going to have to wait, but its Big! Really big!"

An hour later Beth arrived to find Mark standing at the bar all smiles with a chilled bottle of chardonnay, two glasses and an assorted cheese plate awaiting her arrival.

Beth looked at the wine and cheese plate and said, "So what's the big news? Let me guess, your cousin had the baby? Was it a boy and she named it after you?"

"No much bigger. We broke the case. It was a slam dunk. Kosmo and I started interrogating Mr. O'Brien. At first we went easy and after about thirty minutes I mentioned to the chief that we might want to take a short recess to give our suspect a few moments so he can recollect his thoughts."

The bartender came over and opened the bottle of wine and started to engage them in a conversation. Mark quickly held up his hand and said, "Not now. Deep conversation going on here." Mark went back to his conversation with Beth. He was almost bursting at the seams when John Shea, the movie actor, walked in and approached them.

"Hey Deputy. How's it going?"

Now Mark was perplexed. He loved being recognized by a Hollywood actor and really wanted to look like a big man having John hanging around with him but at the same time he really wanted to impress Beth with the story of the interrogation. Why, of all times, did this situation have to arise?

Mark tried his best to keep John in his presence so that he could show off. Beth was so impressed that she was standing next to a famous actor and her boyfriend was such a close acquaintance of Mr. Shea. She was dying to ask for his autograph. She only wished she had her camera.

After a few minutes of small talk another person entered the bar. John, looking over and saying, "Well what do we have here? Royalty has entered our presence. Hello Mr. Laroche. Hunter Laroche let me introduce you. This is one of Nantucket's finest, Deputy Mark Donato and this young lady is?" asked John as he took her hand.

"I am Beth - Beth English. Mark's girlfriend," her body trembling slightly as John held her hand then kissed it while looking into her eyes.

"Nice to meet you Beth." John and Hunter said in unison.

John then said, "Well we will let you two love birds continue on. Hunter, let's grab a table. Love to catch up on old times."

Right before John and Hunter moved on, Hunter asked, "How's the murder case progressing along? I might want to write a book about it."

"It's just about over and solved. Just a few more hours and we should be able to make a public announcement," Deputy Donato proudly responded.

It took Beth a minute or two to get over the excitement of meeting Mr. Shea. Mark was all smiles. People were looking over his way seemingly impressed, Mark thought.

Beth mentioned to Mark, "I can't believe you know him that well. I mean, you told me about him but I had no idea. Just wait until I tell my girlfriends about how he kissed my hand! I don't think I will ever wash it again."

Mark still smiling said, "Just one of the many famous people in my life dear." He was now ready to go into depth on the interrogation of Mr. O'Brien when Bunny Meyercord walked into the bar. Seeing Mark, she came right up to him. "Any news on the murder? Any new clues or leads?"

Mark not having time to respond, Bunny started in on the fact that the Nantucket Lightship Basket Committee was going to do their annual pulled pork cook off for charity and would he get with the constable and arrange for a patrolman to help with the parking issue.

"Why now? Not again," Mark thought. Why, at this particular moment, did he have to be bothered with this issue? "Yes Mrs. Meyercord, I will take care of it in due time." He was looking over her shoulder, trying not to encourage any more conversation from her when he saw Mrs. Frechette walking by with her dog Teddy. He quickly tried to look away and shade himself in front of Mrs. Meyercord but it was too late. She spotted him and made a direct bee line into the bar. "Why now? Why me?" he thought.

"Hi Deputy," Mrs. Frechette said, giving Beth a good once over with her eyes. "Deputy, I want to lodge a complaint. There are too many cars parking along the side of the road out front of my house in Madaket. All day long starting in the early morning until after sunset they park there, pull out their beach stuff and don't have a care in the world about my Teddy who starts barking every time a car pulls in to park or departs. It's very annoying, I want you to place no parking signs on the road."

Mark now really flustered said, "Mrs. Frechette, that comes under the Parks and Recreation jurisdiction. Go down on Monday and lodge your complaint with them. I am sure they can handle that for you in a short matter of time. Now you run along Mrs. Frechette, you're not supposed to have a dog in a public restaurant."

"But what about the cars?" she asked.

"Just do what I told you and I am sure it will all be fine. Now have good day."

Finally, Mark said turning to Beth, "I tell you if one more person comes up to me I am going to explode. Doesn't anyone respect a person's privacy anymore? Now where was I when I left off? Oh - I remember we took a short break leaving Mr. O'Brien alone to collect his thoughts when the constable asked me to take the lead. He said that he didn't seem to be getting anywhere. I told him I would be glad to but it might get a little heated, as I wasn't going to be so soft while integrating the suspect. I explained my method and the constable looked mighty impressed at my ideas. He told me I was in the driver's seat and he would just sit back and take notes.

When we went back in the constable and I glanced at each other and I let it rip. I had Mr. O'Brien on the ropes. I was firing off question after question. One after another. He did not even have time to breathe. The constable was looking at me in amazement. Mr. O'Brien was swallowing hard trying to come up with answers. I had him on the ropes. He was mixing up his story, saying one thing then changing it to something else. He started sweating pretty good. When the timing was right, I went in for the kill. He did not stand a chance. I broke him in under ten minutes. He started singing like a canary. He broke down and started confessing. He knew he could not continue his charade. I had him cornered."

Beth all wide eyed said, "Oh Mark you're my hero."

He also explained to Beth that afterwards the constable asked him where he had learned interrogation skills like that. He gently told the chief that well, some people have it, some people don't!

This was news. The gossip wagon started up again. Everywhere you went people were talking about it. Rumors were flying around. At one point someone said, "Well you know the real truth, that guy Germain is loaded and paid Trevor tons of money to take the fall for him." Then there were all sorts of stories circulating about the knife, which was the murder weapon, had been originally discovered off the coast of Southern England on Burgh Island in the early eighteen-hundreds and was at one point in the ownership of a duke who traded it to an Irish boat captain. It was to have a beautiful inlaid green handle and had a curse placed on it. They say it was given to Trevor from his grandfather who told him it had magical powers and never to part with it.

Kim Germain ever so slowly got over the fact that a murder had happened in their basement. The kids, Zachary and Austin, would sit at the lunch counter at Les's Lunch Box and tell anyone who would listen about the story almost daily while running up the Germain house charge.

Rusty, who, finally managed to get the chute lock cut off, laid on his back so he could slide his head inside the coal chute to check for leaks. He was taken back at two things; first there was a piece of two-by-four sitting on top of a carpet mat inside and written on it in pencil was 'Kilroy was here'. Strange, he thought to himself. It must have been meant to be taken as a joke if anyone opened the chute. When Kim heard about that piece of wood and what was written on it, she told Steve, "Uncle Zach always used that saying when he was a kid after he took money out of my change jar. He would leave a note written in the jar." The other puzzling thing to Rusty was that the interior of the chute was spotless. Not a trace of old coal soot and it still smelled of bleach, as if it was recently cleaned in the last year. He had managed to lay on his back and slip his head into the inside looking all the way up to the top of the shaft, spotting nothing but a few cob webs.

Rusty had finished the wine cellar and helped Steve and his friend Bill load up several cases of wine from Hatch's Liquor Store and helped stock the wine racks. They managed to get ninety cases put in there with room for at least another hundred or so.

Zach and Austin loved the new apartment above the garage and asked if they could move all their stuff up there. Kim had to break the news that they only bunked up there when they had house guests and needed more bedroom space.

Kim quickly made new friends on the island. Karen Golav, the owner of Eye of the Needle, and Kim became great lunch buddies. Karen enjoyed her status symbol and the mysterious murder story that kept everyone wanting to meet Kim who was married to one of the premier car dealership owners in the country.

The Dreamland Theater thought it was a fun idea to run the movie 'Pink Panther,' due to the fact that there were some references to Mr. Meyer being a jewel thief in disguise. Rumor had it that some precious stones were found during the investigation into the murder on Mr. Meyer's body. They showed the movies every other Saturday evening starting with 'The Pink Panther', then 'A Shot in the Dark', next was 'Inspector Clouseau', and waiting for a few months, the release of the 'Return of the Pink Panther'. The word from Hollywood was that would be followed by 'The Pink Panther Strikes Again'. Every show was sold out so they added a matinee show time.

People would drive, walk, or bike by the Germain's home and take photos after the story made the papers. At first Mr. Lussier was calling the Police Department complaining about all the onlookers until one day a film crew from a Cape Cod Television Station stopped him for an interview. He was told that it could possibly be broadcasted on many channels through the New England area. Mr. Lussier asked if he might get paid for the interview and began spending time out front, where everyone seemed to gather, getting his photo taken at every opportunity.

Zach and Austin set up a lemonade stand and started profiting from all this. At one point, when Kim and Steve were out of the house, Zach and Austin started giving people a tour of the wine cellar for the small fee of only one dollar. They removed the key from the hook in the kitchen closet to open up the cellar and would show them where the pools of blood had been. That was short lived when Kim returned home one day to find a group of five strangers in their basement. One person, on the way out, asked Kim for her autograph and a photo of them together which she quickly declined.

When Diane arrived at the Phoenix airport a few weeks after Zach had arrived home from his long drive. He picked her up in a brand new 1975 shiny Black Cadillac convertible, loaded with all the bells and whistles. He also surprised her with two first class tickets to Hawaii and a room booked for an ocean front suite at the Royal Hawaiian Hotel in Honolulu.

Constable Kosmo was interviewed along with Deputy Donato several times by the Inquirer and Mirror, Nantucket's local newspaper, as well as the New York Times, Providence Gazette, Boston Globe, and numerous others. In all of the interviews, Kosmo made it a very clear that he could have not cracked the case without the continuous effort of his entire staff and especially the tireless efforts on the part of Deputy Donato.

As island life slowly got back to normal the constable arranged a celebration dinner at Cioppinos which included, Jimmy Jaksic, Beth English, Deputy Donato and himself. A good time was had by all and they agreed that every month they should pick a different restaurant and get together as a group with no shop talk allowed.

As for Marshmallow she was glad that Zach and Austin quit giving tours of the basement, as she did not like all these strange people milling around the property and trying to coax her over to them so they could pick her up. When things got too hectic around the property, she would go upstairs above the garage to the new window ledge that was right in front of the apartments entry and curl up in the warmth of the sun on top of the towel that Kim had placed there for her.

As for Diane and Zach, they kept up their relationship. Going on several first class cruises and he presented her with the largest ruby necklace pendant she had ever set her eyes on and kept asking him if he had robbed a bank to pay for it. On one of her trips back to Nantucket, Diane found a brand new red Jeep Cherokee Limited parked in her driveway with a big bow on top, a note card that read simply "Kilroy was Here".

Emily Dutra and Maureen Maher took a girl's weekend to Cape Cod to try figure out what direction life was going to take them next. Maureen had met and started dating a state policeman after she was stopped on the Milestone Road doing sixty-five miles per hour in a forty-five mile an hour zone. Batting her eyes and using her most innocent expression, "I had no idea officer that I was going so fast," and managed to get away with it, not even receive a warning. Maureen and her new love in life, Chance, can be spotted all over the island loving life in its fullest.

Karen Grant went on with her everyday life. Turning down several interview offers about her life with Chris Meyer. As she was walking towards the entrance of Cioppinos one evening, a rather large handsome man wearing a black fedora hat approached the stairs at the same time she did and stood to the side and said, "After you my fine lady."

"Why thank you my fine sir," she replied, flashing her beautiful smile. As they entered, Karen looked over to the left only to find the bar standing room only. The gentleman whom she had just walked into the restaurant with noticed the look on her face and asked, "Would you like to join me at my table?" The owner, Tracy Root, walked up to the host stand and said, "Mr. Hunter Laroche, I have your favorite table all set for you." Hunter took Karen's elbow ever so gently and said, "We will be a party of two. Myself and this lovely young lady." Tracy said to Hunter, "You know Ms. Grant?"

Hunter looked at her and asked, "Ms. Grant of the Chris Meyer incident?"

"The one and only," she replied.

"Well this is going to be a very interesting evening," Hunter replied as they were led to his requested table number eight. "Better get me two bottles of my red wine. I think this is going to be a long night!"

As for the rest of the story one can imagine what goes on with Island life.

Kim and Steve continued spending their summers on the island. Steve acquiring numerous more dealerships in Ohio, Florida, Arizona and Michigan just to name a few.

Deputy Donato and Beth were engaged. Beth was now the official trainer for all the radio dispatch codes for the Police and Fire departments. Beth had enjoyed the date night scenario so much, she bought Mark a smoking jacket and herself a long vintage cigarette holder and they still go out once a month, find a secluded table in a restaurant and pretend they were spies, making up stories about different people in their line of sight.

Uncle Zach was continuing to travel the world with Diane all first class trips, Paris, South America, Asia, it seemed to go on and on, a never ending journey and never running short on cash.

Simon Gilmore had received several packages from Winship before his tragic accident containing ten of the diamonds in the rough and several bank wire transfers from Winship's accounts. Mr. Gilmore took the stones to Antwerp Diamond Cutters, then to London where Tiffany's was more than happy to purchase all of the flawless cut diamonds from him. No questions asked.

He bought himself a hundred and ten-foot sailing vessel for cash. Again no questions asked. He named it the Ana Sofia and sailed it to the Greek islands every year for two months.

Marshmallow still managed to know ahead of time when Kim was calling on the phone, letting out a very loud meow each time, amazing Steve to no end!

Jim Jaksic applied and got the job working for the Languedoc on a part time basis and was taking full advantage of his employee discount, at least once a week. He had become such a foodie that he is now a featured writer appearing weekly in the Inquirer and Mirror titled, "Dine Around the World Without Leaving Your Kitchen" and in one article he interviewed Julia Child over dinner at the Straight Wharf Restaurant.

Tom Kendrick's, the realtor that sold the Germain's their home, business flourished after a background on the home was featured in an article. People were stopping in his office asking if he had any haunted houses for sale.

The mystery of where the flawless stone found on Mr. Meyer's body came from was never solved and still remains a Nantucket mystery today.

Hopefully coming out soon, "A Deadly Dinner in Dionis" Be careful who you dine with…

A note to the readers
This is a self-published novel and meant
to be a fun read. If you come across a typo just go with the flow.
As you know fog happens. H.L.